FRAN MCNABB

THE WAY HOME
By Fran McNabb

Copyright © 2021 Fran McNabb
Published by: Forget Me Not Romances, an imprint of Winged Publications

This book is a work of fiction. Names, characters, places, and incidents are the product of the author's imagination and are used fictitiously. Any resemblance to actual events, locales, or persons, living or dead, is coincidental.

No part of this book may be copied or distributed without the author's consent.

All rights reserved.

ISBN: 979-8-8689-1088-3

CHAPTER ONE

Independence, Missouri, May 1849

"Haaah," the hoarse voice of the stagecoach driver roared over the commotion in the street. Four horses pulled at their harnesses and jerked the stagecoach into motion.

Abigail Cook yanked her possessions from the path of the horses as dirt hit her already dusty outfit. She closed her eyes against the grey cloud descending on her. As the stagecoach rumbled away, she wiped the grime off her face and looked down the street of Independence, Missouri. Coming straight toward her was a wagon piled high with buffalo pelts. "Noooo." She yanked her two trunks out of the path of the two wild eyed mules, followed by several other oxen-drawn wagons.

Shaking from her first moments in Independence, Abigail dragged her trunks to the side of the road. Loud hammering and banging from what she assumed were blacksmith shops could be heard over the noise of the street. A distant steamship whistle caught her ear, reminding her of the whistles from Boston Harbor near her home, but this was nothing like the city she'd left. Where was the quaint little community Mr. Brown described? Had the stagecoach dropped her off in the wrong town? Covered wagons, horses with single riders, and buggies traveling much too fast along this busy road disturbed more dust and dirt. This chaos certainly wasn't what she expected.

"Watch it, lady." A man with wild hair and a shaggy beard yelled down from his wagon. His mules swerved around her. Proper upbringing made her want to apologize for being in the man's way, but as soon as she looked up, he raced down the dirt road.

Glad the wagon hadn't run over her, she dragged her possessions closer toward the covered sidewalk but stopped short of stepping up. The wooden walkway stood at least a foot above the dirt road and was as chaotic and crowded as the street. Exhausted from her arduous ride, she doubted she could lift the trunk.

"There's only one way to find out." She jerked the first trunk as hard as she could. Instead of landing on the wooden boards, the edge of the trunk caught on the planks and tumbled back onto the road, yanking her down with it. Her knee hit the ground, but she grabbed the post before she landed in the dirt to be run over by horses or wagon wheels. She bit her lip and prayed the tears of frustration and humiliation didn't run down her dust-covered face.

Taking a huge breath, she gripped the post to pull herself up, but before she was able to get her balance, two hands grabbed her from behind. A stifled scream escaped her mouth as she turned to see who held her.

"Ma'am, let me help you. If you roll onto that road, one of these crazy travelers will run over you."

Abigail stared into deep brown eyes almost hidden by a wide-brimmed hat pulled down low on his forehead. Partly covered in a scraggly, several-day beard, his face needed a good scrubbing. She glanced down at his hands that were as dirty as his face. Had he been living in the woods, or was everyone in this town in need of a bath? Whatever the case, at the moment, she needed his help.

"Thank you, sir."

He pulled her up, helped her step up onto the boardwalk, then effortlessly lifted both of her trunks. "I'd be careful if I were you. The wagon train families aren't so bad, but these trappers coming into town with their pack trains will run you over." He tilted his hat in her direction, then stepped back into the crowded road and dodged two wagons as he crossed. Once on the other side, he glanced in her direction, then fell in with a group of people pushing their way down the walkway.

Abigail blinked. Who was the dirty, brown-eyed man? Under the unkempt hair and grime, he might have had some redeeming good looks, but she'd never find out. With throngs of people pushing and rushing through the streets, she'd probably never see her rescuer again.

Not that she was looking for another man. Her priority for the last few months focused on locating a good place to start over away from her ruined life in Boston. As she sat through grueling days in her stagecoach, Independence shone bright as the place to start that life. Now that she stood on its main street, her hopes and dreams dimmed. The town was a jumping off place for wagon trains heading west, but who were these dirty men roaring through the streets with furs? Had she been plopped down in some foreign land filled with dirty people and wild animals?

As unbelievable as her situation, she couldn't stand on this sidewalk all day. The stranger with the gorgeous eyes had helped her out of the chaos of the street and the dirt, but now she had to figure out where to go next.

Four storefronts with shingles hanging from the ceiling gave her a good place to start. She chose the closest one, a mercantile, and dragged her trunks and bag through the threshold. Several people bumped into her as they rushed out of the building. She apologized, held tightly to her trunk straps, then made her way to the counter.

The lady behind a huge, ornate register introduced

herself. "Good afternoon. Welcome to Independence. What can I do for you?"

"I guess my trunks gave away that I've just gotten to town."

"Everyone these days is either just getting to Independence or is leaving. But, I saw you get off the stagecoach. I'm glad you weren't run over by some of those horrible wagons roaring through our roads."

Her sweet smile settled Abigail's nerves for the first time since she'd stuffed some of her belongings into her trunks and hired a driver to take her away from her home.

Abigail introduced herself then asked about the boarding house where she had a reservation.

"Sunny's Boarding House isn't hard to find." The cashier gave her directions then bit a nail on her hand. "I hate to tell you, but I've heard there aren't empty rooms anywhere in town."

"I can see why with all of these people, but I have a room reserved at Sunny's."

"That's good news." She gave Abigail directions. "I hope you'll come back into the general store and visit with me. My name is Beth."

"I certainly will, but right now I need to find the boarding house."

"I'll be at the store until closing. Why don't you leave your trunks and send someone from the boarding house to pick them up?"

Abigail looked down at her heavy trunks, then back up. "That would be wonderful."

Beth helped her drag the trunks to the back of the store.

"Thank you so much for your sweet welcome." Abigail hated leaving the first person in days who had shown her kindness—except for the dirty stranger—but she was exhausted, and the sun would be setting shortly. She didn't want to be walking through a strange town in the dark.

With a fortifying breath, Abigail headed back out into

the crowds on the sidewalk. If she could endure her long journey on the stagecoach, she could fight her way through the madness of Independence to find the safety of the boarding house.

The crowds thinned as she hurried away from the center of town. She turned the corner onto a much quieter street, though she could still hear the hammering. Within a half-block she spotted a dust-covered shingle in a small front yard of a two-story house. She'd found Sunny's Boarding House.

Thank you, God. Thank you.

As soon as she knocked, a tall, middle-aged lady greeted her with a smile. "How can I help you?"

"I'm Abigail Cook."

"I'm Sunny Fairchild. This is my establishment. You are welcome to come in and rest, but if you're looking for accommodations, I'm sorry to say we're completely full, and I don't know any other hotel or house in town with available rooms."

"I understand, but I have reservations. Mr. Brown from the School Board made them for me. I'm the new teacher."

Sunny Fairchild stared at Abigail. "There must be some misunderstanding. That position has been filled, and the new teacher is now occupying the room that was to be yours. Surely Mr. Brown contacted you."

"Of course I was contacted." With shaking hands, Abigail dug in her satchel and pulled out a folded letter. "Here's the confirmation of my job and room reservation."

Sunny took the letter, skimmed over it, then handed it back. "I'm so sorry, but I'm afraid that position was probably filled before you even got this letter. He must've sent you another one. Maybe it didn't reach you."

"This can't be. I traveled all the way from Boston for this job." Abigail's shoulders sagged. Her breath caught in her chest. Her well-laid plans for starting a new life vanished in an instant. *Now what?*

"I don't know what to tell you." Sunny looked behind

her, then back at Abigail. "You can go to the other hotels and boarding houses close by to see if a room is available, but rooms are as scarce as chicken teeth. If you don't find one, I have a small storeroom with a cot in it I keep for emergencies. You can stay here for a couple of days until you decide what you'll do now that you don't have a job."

Abigail's mind spun. "I'm not in any position to decline your generous offer. I'll take the storeroom. I can pay. Surely I won't be here long." The knot in her stomach twisted as tightly as it did when she walked away from her home and the horrible gossips who glared at her as she walked down the sidewalks.

"Independence is growing every day," Sunny Fairchild said. "I'm sure you can find some sort of work even if it's temporary. Of course, most of the jobs for women are in the saloons or shops along the main road."

Abigail swallowed. "Without this teaching position, I'm not sure what I'll do. Are there other towns near here where I might inquire about a position in the schools?"

Sunny grimaced. "I'm sure it's possible. Westport is not far, but the lady who took the position here said she checked there first. Nothing was available. The rest of the towns are nothing more than places to bunk in for trappers or travelers waiting for the next wagon train. We are the only two towns trying to hold onto some sort of civility. You could always travel down to St. Louis to inquire, but I'm told the city is growing so fast people are putting up tents in the streets. And, I don't know that you've heard, but those coming up from there say there's cholera in the city. I wouldn't go there if I were you."

Abigail's hand went to her chest. "Cholera? That's awful."

"We haven't had any here so don't fret your little head."

Abigail stood on the boarding house porch and stared at the lady. No job. No place to stay. Cholera in the area. How could this be? Air escaped her lungs. Would she faint in the entrance of the boarding house?

Sunny looked behind Abigail. "I don't see any bags."

"I left them at the mercantile. Could I pay someone to carry them back for me?"

"Certainly. I'll have my workman John fetch them in the wagon, thenl carry them to your room. Follow me and I'll show you to my storage room."

Thankful to have a place to stay, Abigail smiled and followed Sunny into the lobby.

Two oversized sofas, three high-backed chairs, and several tables filled the room. Three ladies sat on one couch. They nodded and smiled at Abigail but she could feel their stares and their questions as she followed Sunny.

"The storeroom isn't fancy, but I keep it clean."

Abigail followed her through the kitchen.

"I just washed the sheets after one of my kitchen workers dropped a jar of beans on the bed. It was a mess, but I think I got all of it out of the mattress." Sunny opened the door and stepped back.

Abigail's heart sank. Shelves crowded with cans of food, cleaning supplies, and whisky bottles lined three sides of the elongated room. Sacks of potatoes and onions lined the floor and pots and pans hung on every open space on the wall. The cot sat in the middle of the room. A pillow and a thin blanket lay on top.

"I'll make sure my kitchen helpers know you're in here so they won't just walk in on you in the morning. They've just gone home, but I'll find something for you to eat."

Abigail nodded. "Thank you. I appreciate all you're doing for me. Is there a place where I can bathe?"

"We can't draw a bath this time of the day. Possibly tomorrow. A public bathhouse is down the road, but I wouldn't recommend it. The trappers use it when they come in, and I can't imagine a lady going in there alone. I'll have John bring in a basin and a water pitcher after he gets your trunks. You'll find a few clean washcloths on one of the shelves."

When Sunny closed the door, Abigail plopped down on the cot. Fear gripped her chest. How would she survive in this strange town with nothing to her name?

Lord, you've watched over me while I made my way here. Could you please not abandon me yet? Give me a little guidance.

Just as she'd done over and over during her stagecoach ride, she clasped she hands, squeezed her eyes and recited a verse from Proverbs. "Trust in the Lord with all thine heart; and lean not unto thine own understanding." She sat quietly thinking about how her independent nature had gotten her into the predicament she now faced. Maybe had she leaned on the Lord more and not on herself she wouldn't be sitting in a storeroom at the edge of the civilized world with nothing to her name. She finished the verse: "In all thy ways acknowledge him, and he shall direct thy paths."

She looked up. *I promise to try harder and let you lead my way.*

Running her hand across the crisp sheet, she inhaled deeply. "At least I can stretch out."

Within minutes, Sunny brought in a slice of meat and two chunks of homemade bread. "Honey, don't give up. Things will work out for you."

Without tasting anything she ate, Abigail finished her light meal. John had not returned so she headed to the big front porch. She passed through the lobby, happy the two couches sat empty. No way did she feel like talking to the other guests—not tonight. She plopped into one of the big rockers on the porch and let her head rest against the hard back. Listening to the sounds coming from the busy main street a block away brought back the horror of being dropped off in the middle of the chaotic town. Sunny's Boarding House gave her time to decide what her next move would be, but as she stared out in the waning daylight, her mind stayed blank.

As much as she wanted to enjoy a little peace and quiet in the relatively clean air, exhaustion won. Barely able to keep her eyes open, she walked to the storeroom that would be her tiny world until she decided what she would do now that her plans had shattered into a million pieces.

Would she find employment in Independence? What would she do if she couldn't find some way to support herself?

She knew what she would *not* do. Returning to her family home was definitely not an option. Her good name and reputation had disappeared in one horrible afternoon. Now she must find a way to make a life for herself someplace else where no one knew her.

The walls of the storeroom closed in around her.

How do I start over with nothing? Thank you for being by my side, Lord. I know you'll send someone to help.

* * * *

Lucas Fletcher dodged several oxen-pulled wagons driven by Easterners who had no idea how to handle the huge wagons they'd bought to take them to California to find their riches. Lucas shook his head and jumped up onto the sidewalk. Between the emigrants passing through Independence on their way to Oregon and California and the fur traders coming in from the western territories, this town had become unrecognizable.

He entered the quiet of the Sheriff's office. "How're you doing, Victor?"

"If it isn't my long-lost friend. Come in, Lucas." Sheriff Sanchez stood up, then walked around his desk and grabbed Lucas's hand. "By the looks of you, you must've just gotten back into town."

"Yep, and I can't wait to ride out to my ranch. How were things while I was gone?"

"It's been pretty quiet since you left. Had a few saloon fights at the Watering Hole, but that's normal. I was getting worried. You should've been back several days ago. Any problems?"

"No problems on the way up to Quincy. I found the buyer, and we made a nice deal for my cattle. On the way back I ran into a wagon that had run off the trail. I couldn't pass them without helping. Poor guy had no idea what he was doing and his wife and children were terrified. We worked an entire day to get the wagon back on the trail. I hope that guy learns to control his animals before he starts across country."

"I know how you feel. I see these families leave with these wagon trains, and I wonder how many actually make it to California. You look like you could use a cup of coffee."

Lucas turned to the pot and poured a cup. "Thanks, Victor." He took a huge swallow and made a face. "When did you make this? Yesterday?"

Victor laughed. "Not yesterday, but it is from this morning."

Lucas looked around. "I'd love to stay and catch up, but I want to get home this afternoon. I need some Caroline hugs."

"I'm sure you do. I rode out to the ranch two days ago. She and your mother are doing great, but they miss you."

"Not as much as I miss them." Lucas shook Victor's hand. "Thanks for going out to check on my family." He took another gulp of coffee, then turned back around. "You still haven't heard of anyone looking for a job as a governess, have you?"

"No, but I'll spread the word again. New people are flooding in every day, but most of them only stay long enough to get their wagons ready. If I hear of someone, I'll let you know." Victor walked Lucas to the door. "My offer still stands. Caroline can come stay with us during the week to attend school now that we have a new teacher. I'd get her home for the weekends."

Lucas shook his head. "I wouldn't feel comfortable having her here with all of these strangers, but thanks for the offer."

The two old friends shook hands outside the office. Before Lucas got on his horse, he turned to his friend.

"And, Victor, you and Debby need to come out and spend some time at the ranch. We miss our visits."

"I know, but you see what it's like in town these days. After these spring wagon trains move out, we'll show up one day and surprise you."

Lucas left the office grinning. He and Victor were one of the few men raised around the Independence area who still remained. Best friends growing up, they married sisters, fought in the Mexican American War together, and continued to be as close as brothers. Lucas cherished Victor's friendship.

After stopping by the general store to pick up an order he'd dropped off on his way to the sheriff's office, he headed out of town. As he passed the spot where he'd earlier helped the young lady who had fallen, he surveyed the area. Of course, she would not still be there, but that didn't keep him from staring and remembering her sparkling blue-green eyes and gentle smile. Underneath the layers of dust, her tailored clothes and intricately designed leather on her trunks shouted she wasn't the typical female who came to work in the saloons. A few strands of chestnut colored hair escaped the jeweled hair clamp and net of her hat and framed her oval face. She could be joining one of the wagon trains, but why was she traveling alone?

What was a lady like that doing in a place like Independence? With herds of strangers crowding into town, she should have someone with her.

With the image of the beautiful lady in his mind to keep him company, he clicked his tongue for his horse, Charger, to pick up speed. He'd been gone for almost two weeks and couldn't wait to be back on his own land.

He waved to several people he knew as he rode through town with his supply mule in tow, but the masses of new people surprised him. Since gold had been discovered in California, his town had become one of the jumping off spots for the wagon trains. Most of the strangers spent enough time to outfit their wagons then moved on, but more and more of them began to settle near the town. He wasn't sure how he felt about that.

At one time his family had been part of the emigration from the East. They'd come across the Atlanta from the northern English settlement of Ulster, traveled by ship, and started their new life on the land a little west of Independence. For three generations the Fletchers thrived on their ranch. Now as head of the family, he wanted his daughter to have the life he'd had, but change was everywhere he looked. Would his daughter grow up in a world that was totally foreign to the one in which he was raised? He hoped not. Traditions, love of the land, and love of family had made him the man he was today. That's what he wanted for his daughter.

With the noise of the city fading, he headed away from the confusion of the crowded streets.

He couldn't wait to get to his five-thousand acres of peace and quiet and cattle.

CHAPTER TWO

Lucas patted Charger's neck. "We're almost home, boy. You smell it, don't you? You're as eager as I am." He applied pressure to the horse's side. The horse trotted across the flat grasslands, then down a trail through woodlands toward Fletcher Ranch.

Within a few minutes he raced across open fields of his property. The fence line stretched for miles. Even with the waning light, he paid attention to their condition. Thirty men worked on Fletcher Ranch, keeping the cattle grazing safely, replenishing fields of hay, birthing and branding calves, and generally making life for himself and his family comfortable. Nothing was easy living away from town, but the dedicated men who'd been with him over the years kept the ranch going even while he was away.

As he topped the ridge near his home, he stopped. Bronze-colored rays from the setting sun shone on his family's estate. The home with its wide porches running the extent of both the bottom and the second stories stood out amongst the other buildings. Two massive stone chimneys embraced the east and the west side of the house. Six other buildings made up the estate: a huge barn that housed the horses, another barn dedicated to the needs of the cattle, two bunk houses for the workmen, and a newly renovated cabin next to the house.

Lucas stared at the cabin. For the last few years the cabin stood empty. Even after returning from the military, he struggled with the idea of allowing someone else to occupy those rooms where so many of his memories lay. He'd only stepped inside once during the time his ranch hands cleaned and painted the rooms because no matter how much they did to it, the cabin still belonged to his memories of Sarah. Maybe after he found a governess to live there, he could move on.

Maybe Victor could help him find someone to help with the education for his thirteen-year-old daughter. He didn't know how to deal with Caroline's changing needs, and his mother had exhausted her knowledge of math and reading.

"Let's go, Charger. I'm hungry and I know you are, too."

"Welcome home, Mr. Fletcher." One of his younger ranch hands stood by a fence with a hammer in his hand and waved.

Lucas waved back then headed to the house.

Caroline ran out of the house, across the front porch, and down the ten steps. "Father, you're home." She waved her arms and laughed.

Lucas slid off the saddle. "Yes, I am." He grabbed his daughter and gave her a tight hug, then planted a big kiss on the top of her messed up hair. He held her at arm's length. "Have the men made you muck out the stalls?" Her hair, blond and thick like her mother's, was pulled back with a faded ribbon, but most of it fell down around her shoulders. Two black smudges ran along her right cheek. Lucas wiped them away with his thumb.

"You know the men don't make me work. I've been riding Honey Cup all morning."

Lucas pulled her against his body, then handed the reins of the horse to Matthew, the youngest ranch hand who'd run out to help. "Thanks, Matthew. The supplies need to be taken into the house. Mrs. Fletcher will decide what goes to the bunkhouse."

Matthew nodded. "Yes, sir." He took an awkward step with the horse and mule in tow, but not without glancing at Caroline with a shy smile.

"Is there something else you need, Matthew?"

The boy straightened up. "No, sir." He spun around and headed to the back door of the house.

Lucas let out a huge breath. Had that boy just flirted with Caroline? She was still his little girl and certainly didn't need boys looking at her, but when he looked down, Caroline had turned her head and watched Matthew stumble toward the back of the house.

He squeezed his daughter's shoulders and led her up the stairs onto the porch. Yep, he certainly needed someone to help finish his daughter's education and keep her from turning into a tomboy—or worse—into some dreamy eyed girl thinking about any boy that came onto his property. Lucas only thought the last few years of rearing a young girl without a mother was hard—not that he'd been in her life all that time. Guilt swept across his chest every time he thought about being away so long after Sarah had died. Now he worked to regain those years, but since Caroline turned thirteen, he wasn't sure how to deal with her.

Caroline giggled.

Lucas put both hands on his hips. "And what are you laughing at?"

"You. Every time you come home from one of your adventures you look like one of those wild men who live in the mountains."

"Maybe I am secretly one of them." He made a roar like a bear and Caroline laughed.

"Maybe a man from the mountains but never a bear. That sounded pretty weak for a bear."

Lucas pulled her close and kissed her on her head once

again. "Where're your grandmother and my brother?"

"Grandmother is in the garden. Uncle Douglas hasn't come in from the pastures yet." She then jabbered about the fish she'd caught at the stream on her ride.

"Was someone with you?"

"No, I can certainly fish alone."

"I know you can, but I want someone with you. You know things can happen. I heard Mr. Allen had a calf killed by a mountain lion or something even bigger. They never found the animal, and with all the strangers coming into Independence, there's no telling what kind of bad elements might wander out this way. I'd feel better if you wouldn't go off on your own."

She pulled away from Lucas's embrace. "I can handle myself. I always carry my gun. You need to start treating me like an adult."

"You're not an adult. You're thirteen, and you're still my little girl. Now go tell your grandmother I'm home and wash up for dinner. I need to clean up myself."

He headed to the back door so he wouldn't track dirt and dust through the hallway, but not without looking at Caroline once more. How could she be growing so quickly? And how had he become so incompetent when it came to raising a daughter?

Life seemed to stop after Sarah died, but when he looked at Caroline, he realized time had not stopped at all. Throughout his days of darkness and mourning, everything around him still moved on.

He stomped his boots to remove some of the dried dirt, but to no avail. Finally he pulled them off and carried them into the familiar warmth of his family's home and headed toward the comfort of his bedroom.

That evening after a huge meal of beef stew and freshly baked bread, Lucas sat in one of the big rockers that lined the ground floor porch. The warm evening air settled around him like a cloak. He chewed on the end of a weed and rocked while his younger brother Douglas stood at the railing of the porch.

Lucas owed his brother so much. Douglas stepped up to run the ranch while Lucas rushed off to fight in the Mexican-American War. He proudly served his country, but deep in his heart he knew he enlisted to avoid facing life without his wife. Guilt nagged him every time he thought about leaving his family for so long. Now that he was back, Lucas rushed into his duties of running the ranch. He'd hoped Douglas would continue to exert authority, but his brother passed the reins of the ranch back, almost too willingly. Did his younger brother have interests away from the ranch?

Douglas turned to face Lucas. "I'm glad the buyer was receptive to our price for the cattle."

"I was too. We have a few more weeks to get the drive together, but we should be ready even before then."

"I'm also glad you're home to do this. Mason and I did it for the last two years, but I didn't like it one bit. I'd rather be out on my horse with the cattle."

"I understand. I would too, but selling the cattle we raise is part of owning this ranch. If something happens to me, this will be all yours."

Douglas chuckled. "Then don't let anything happen to you. I'm perfectly content to let you run things."

"You know I appreciate all you did while I was gone, don't you?"

Douglas got serious. "I did it because I had to, but running this ranch isn't my life's dream. I've always said I'd like to try something else."

"I understand, but you don't have to ever leave here. There's enough for both of us to do. You can have as much land as you want, build you a house, and raise a family and stay part of this family."

"Just hold your horses, big brother. To raise a family, I have to have a wife, and that's not in the stars right now and might not ever be. I like my life as it is."

"I understand that as well. Now that I'm back I don't ever want to leave Caroline and Mother, even to ride into town."

The door opened and his mother walked out. "It's so nice to see both my boys together." She looked at Lucas. "Every time you ride off alone, I have this horrible fear of you not returning to us."

Mrs. Fletcher sat in the rocker next to him.

"I appreciate that, Mother, but what I did this week was not dangerous at all."

"But couldn't you have sent Mason? He's your foreman and very smart. He could've found a buyer, just as he did while you were gone."

"Mother, it's my job to find buyers for our cattle, not Mason. He and Douglas did their share while I was gone. I wasn't about to ask them to do it again. Anyway, it gave me a chance to see Victor. I told him to bring Debby and the kids out soon. They could probably use some peace and quiet. Every time I go into Independence, I'm amazed at all the strangers." He looked at his mother with her greying hair pulled up in a bun and her smooth skin devoid of wrinkles. She carried the genes of her Spanish mother instead of her Scotch-Irish father. In her late fifties she still had a lot of living left in her, but she was content to live on the ranch.

She leaned against the back of the rocker and looked at him. "You're needed here, not wandering off alone."

He reached over and took her hand. "I hate leaving you and Caroline, but I can't ignore the business of the ranch. Anyway, you had Douglas here to protect you."

"I know, but it won't be long before both of you are off on the cattle drive."

"Again. That's my life and my responsibility. Douglas and I are not sending our cattle off unless we're with them. It's time I get back to doing my job."

Douglas stood up. "One day we'll have a railroad running from here to the railheads, but right now, driving the herds is the only way to get them there." He stretched. "I'm going to check on the horses, then I'm off to bed." He kissed his mother then took the steps two at a time and headed toward the barn.

"Douglas has become quite a man, don't you agree?"

Lucas nodded. "He did a great job while I was gone."

"He was our life saver." She rocked two or three times, then looked at Lucas. "Did Victor try to get you to move to town like he always does?" She looked down at the planks on the porch. "Maybe that wouldn't be such a bad idea now that Caroline is getting older."

"What did you say? You'd want me to leave this ranch and raise my daughter with all those strangers and chaos in town?"

"No, I would never want you to abandon the ranch, but when I look at Caroline and realize she would rather fish and brand cattle than to do the things that young ladies her age should be doing, I'm not sure we're doing all we can for her. She needs so much more."

"I know." Lucas sat back in his rocker." I worry about her growing up without a mother, but I'm still trying to find someone to move out here and help us. I would never allow her to live in town with the chaos that's going on there now." Lucas blew out a big breath. "I reminded Victor again to spread the word about a governess. Maybe we'll luck up and some wonderful lady will answer our plea."

"I wish I knew more about the lessons she needs, but I've taught her all I know."

"And you've done a great job. I don't know what I would've done without your help. Now it's time to ask for help from someone else."

"Lucas, you know if you'd bow your head and ask God to help, you'd probably have more luck than leaving it up to Victor to find someone."

That's not what Lucas wanted to hear. God had not listened to his pleas when his Sarah lay dying. Why would he think God would listen now?

This time Mrs. Fletcher took Lucas's hand. "I guess I need to pray harder—for both of us." She stood up. "But, I'm not giving up on you. God still wants you back in his flock."

* * * *

The next morning Abigail lay under the covers in Sunny's storage room, not wanting to open her eyes. She'd been dreaming of being with her students in her classroom in Boston. She loved her twenty children and would've had some of them again this year if she were still there.

She threw the cover off and sat up. The scent of chalk and book vanished, replaced by four walls of a crowded, stuffy storage room. She squeezed her eyes, holding onto the image of her orderly room and sweet students for a second longer.

But that second wasn't long enough. Pots clanged on the other side of the walls and the smell of frying bacon and baking bread seeped into her room. Her stomach growled.

Tossing the thin blanket off her body she slid her feet into her shoes on the side of the bed and stood up. "Today will be better. Today will be good." She'd recited those words over and over on stagecoach. Some days presented her with the beauty of God's creation as the stage left towns and traveled through magnificent landscapes, but most days were simply monotonous, tiring, and uncomfortable.

She stood in her tiny storeroom next to her cot as if waiting for an affirmation from heaven that today would be a good one.

But, of course, it didn't come.

Thoughts of her grandmother made her smile. *"God may not tap you on the shoulder and tell you what to do, but he'll guide you in the right direction, He simply gives you the means to do a little hunting."*

She closed her eyes remembering the gentle lady. "Thanks, Grandmother. I'll start my hunt today." She opened her eyes and looked at her surroundings. "And standing in the middle of this dark storage room isn't the way to find my answers."

By the time she pulled her hair up and inserted the jeweled hair clamp that her mother slipped into her hand on the morning she'd left home, Abigail threw her shoulders back to start the hunt for her new life.

When she opened the door to the kitchen, two women turned from their work tables and stared at her. She introduced herself then asked for directions to the dining room. As she walked through the double doors, she stopped abruptly. Other boarding house guests filled the long dining table. Everyone stopped talking. One of the ladies smiled. "Good morning. Would you like to join us?"

"Yes, yes, please join the others." Sunny came into the dining area from the front hallway. "This is Abigail Cook. She came in last night. You can introduce yourselves to her as you eat. Abigail, the coffee and hot rolls are on the sideboard. The ladies will bring in breakfast shortly. Help yourself." Sunny scurried into the kitchen and closed the door.

With a nod to those sitting at the table, Abigail moved to the sideboard and poured a cup of coffee. The heavenly aroma tickled her nose. During her travels across the country, she dreamed of having a leisure cup of coffee, but mornings on the trail never allowed for such pleasures. This morning she could savor a good cup, but having a roomful of strangers wasn't how she'd envisioned doing it.

She turned around with a big smile. "I look forward to meeting all of you."

A lady who appeared to be sitting alone patted a chair next to her. "Abigail, I'm Georgia Newman. Please. Come sit with us."

Abigail pulled out the chair and sat down. "Thank you. I've been traveling on a stagecoach from Boston. This home is magical compared to what I've been in."

"We've all come from other parts of the country. Some of us came by steamboat, and some by stagecoach like you." One of the men who sat with a lady raised his cup of coffee. "My name is Louis."

Everyone began introducing themselves. Abigail's mind scrambled trying to remember each and every name, but she knew it would be useless.

Georgia spoke up. "Abigail, why are you in Independence, if you don't mind me asking?"

"I came for a job, but last night I found out the position is no longer available. I haven't had time to look at my other options, but I'm not letting that disappointment be the end. I plan to speak to the man who offered me the position. He might have something else available."

One of the other guests spoke up. "What were you supposed to be doing? My name's Nathan."

"I accepted the position of school teacher, but it seems it has been filled by someone else."

Georgia, the girl next to Abigail, choked into her cup.

"Are you okay?" Abigail asked.

Georgia nodded. "Yes, I'm okay." She put her head down, then looked around at the others at the table. Finally, she turned to Abigail. "I feel as though I should apologize. I'm the new teacher. I have no idea how or why it happened, but Mr. Brown hired me. Please believe me. I had no idea someone else had already been offered the position."

Abigail remembered Sunny said the new teacher now occupied her room here at the boarding house, but she had forgotten that tidbit when she'd joined the group this morning. Abigail stared at her, not knowing how to handle the situation. She wanted to stomp her feet and yell at the girl, but she knew Georgia was not to fault. Mr. Brown should have let her know in a timely manner about the position being taken.

She looked at the others around the table. No one said a word. In fact, no one moved. All eyes were on Abigail.

"Apologies won't be necessary." Abigail found her voice. "I'm sure there was a mix-up through no fault of yours."

"I don't know what to say," Georgia said. "I'm never without words, but I am totally taken aback. I can imagine how you must feel."

Sunny walked back into the dining area, placed a plate of bacon on the table, but straightened up, "Is something wrong? I've never heard this group so quiet."

"We just realized that this young lady has traveled across country for a teaching position that no longer exists." One of the three men sitting together spoke up. "There's got to be something we can do to help her."

"That's awfully kind of you. Thank you." Abigail had a feeling no one could help her at this point. "I'll go speak with Mr. Brown after breakfast. He might be able to connect me with a position elsewhere."

Everyone stared at their plates, then at each other in silence.

Abigail understood. Jobs for women were scarce in this type of town. There wasn't much anyone could do. Remembering her grandmother's words, she knew she had to open her heart to God's will. Only then would she find her solution. "I'd appreciate it if all of you would keep your ears open and let me know if you hear anything that I might be able to do."

Georgia touched her hand. "I'll be glad to go with you to speak with Mr. Brown."

"Thank you, but I would like to speak with him alone." Abigail looked at the scrumptious table of food in front of her, but her appetite had vanished. How could she eat sitting with a group of strangers who pitied her?

After a few bites, she excused herself. She didn't know how to find Mr. Brown's office, but if she could find Independence, Missouri, she could locate a little office in this town.

FRAN MCNABB

CHAPTER THREE

Two days after Abigail arrived in Independence, she sat on a hard bench of a wagon pulled by two mules and driven by John, Sunny's worker. After talking with Mr. Brown about the teaching position he'd already filled, he directed her to Sheriff Sanchez, who told her about a governess position at the Fletcher Ranch. Thrilled her prayers had been answered she held onto her hat and enjoyed the warm breeze.

She talked to her driver, but the man hadn't said two words since she'd climbed into the wagon. That didn't keep her from trying. "This is gorgeous county. I lived in the middle of Boston so I'm not used to seeing so much open space and natural beauty. Of course, crossing the country that's all I saw."

John nodded.

"How far is Mr. Fletcher's ranch?"

"We've been on his ranch for the last thirty minutes."

"What? All this belongs to one man?"

John nodded.

Abigail now looked at the landscape a little differently. The road followed a fence line with acres and acres of green fields. She had no idea one man could own so much.

At the top of the ridge, John surprised her and spoke

again. "That's where you're going."

Abigail blinked at the beautiful scene below her. Fields and fences, big buildings, and cattle— lots of cattle—met her gaze. In the distance several men on horseback rode through one field, several walked near the house, and quite a few gathered in a corral behind one of the barns.

"Oh, my goodness. This is amazing."

"The Fletcher family has lived on this property for three generations. They are a proud family who has always worked hard. They are well respected in this region. If you get the position, you will live on one of the best ranches in the valley."

"I had no idea." She sat quietly and prayed silently for the Lord's help in making a good impression on this family. She needed this position to start over with her ruined life.

John led the mules through a wide gate. An elaborate metal arch with an ornate F in the center stretched across the entrance. Abigail gawked at the house sitting in the middle of an estate that looked more like a small town than a ranch. She'd lived her life amongst Boston's finest architectural structures, but she never expected to find such beauty in the middle of the wilderness. Porches stretching across the upper and lower floors set the house apart from anything she'd seen since she'd climbed into the stagecoach.

She envisioned herself sitting on one of the porches working with the Fletcher daughter.

John pulled up to the front steps, got out, then walked around the buggy to help Abigail down.

A young man ran out from one of the nearby buildings. "I'll take your wagon, sir."

John handed him the reins.

"Is Mr. Fletcher or his mother available?" Abigail straightened her hat and smiled at the young man who nodded, ran up on the porch, and knocked. A young lady with dark hair answered the door, talked with the man, then left.

"You can come up." The young man rushed down the steps and offered his hand to Abigail. "Mrs. Fletcher will be here shortly."

Before Abigail got to the top of the steps, the door opened and an immaculately dressed lady wearing a blue day-dress stepped out onto the porch. "Come in, please. I'm Maria Fletcher, but most of the men and families on the ranch call me Grandmother Fletcher. Welcome to our home."

Abigail stepped near her and offered a hand. "I'm Abigail Cook. Sheriff Sanchez told me about a position open for a governess."

The lady smiled. "Yes, certainly. Come in and I will send for my son. I'm sure you're tired from your trip from town." She looked at John who still stood next to the buggy. "Matthew, would you take the gentleman to the bunkhouse and see to it that he is comfortable while we speak to Miss Cook?"

"Your home is stunning, Grandmother Fletcher." Calling the lady by such a familiar title sent a warm feeling throughout Abigail's body.

Mrs. Fletcher's eyes sparkled as she looked from one side of the porch to the other. "It's been in my family for a long time. We are proud of the work each generation has done to it. My husband is now gone, but my sons have taken over as its guardians."

Mrs. Fletcher led Abigail into the hallway. As she passed through the door that stood at least seven feet tall, Abigail rubbed her hand along the carved wood. "The wood carving is intricate. So beautiful."

"The wood for that door came from the trees found in the valley. My father and his brother felled the trees and carved the wood themselves."

"It's magnificent." Abigail followed Mrs. Fletcher into a sitting room to the right of the hallway. Two long couches faced each other with several large upholstered chairs scattered around the room. Various shaped tables sat near the chairs, all carved as intricately as the door. A large piano sat in the corner of the room.

"Please sit and make yourself comfortable. My son should be here shortly." She smiled and headed out the door.

Abigail sat in one of the single chairs with red velvet upholstery. Worn from years of wear but clean, and with polished wood arms, the chair had seen much love and attention in its long life. She settled back and closed her eyes, but immediately opened them when a girl came in carrying a tray with sweet cakes and a cup of coffee.

"Thank you so much. This looks lovely."

The girl curtsied, turned and left.

Abigail's mouth watered. She sat up and broke a piece of the cake and popped it in her mouth. "Hmmm." She closed her eyes and savored the taste of lemon and raspberry.

A quick knock brought her attention to the door. A tall man wearing work clothes and holding his hat stood at the entrance of the room.

"Miss Cook, I'm Lucas Fletcher. My mother tells me you are inquiring about the governess position."

Abigail stood. "Yes, sir. I'm Abigail Cook. I've just gotten to Independence and found the teaching position I came across country for was no longer available so, yes, I certainly am interested in your position."

Lucas Fletcher looked familiar, but she didn't think she could've possibly met the man.

He stepped closer with squinting eyes and a wrinkled brow. "Do I know you?"

Abigail shook her head, but then stopped. "You're the scraggly. . ." She caught herself before insulting the man. "You're the man who helped me up out of the street two days ago in Independence."

"Yes, of course." He chuckled. "This is quite the coincidence."

"Yes, sir. It is."

"Please, sit and tell me about yourself. Do you have experience working with young girls? My daughter is thirteen."

Abigail sat and lifted her cup of coffee. "I taught students between the ages of eleven and fifteen in Boston. I attended Mount Holyoke Female Seminary in South Hadley, Massachusetts."

"You went to a seminary?"

"In the East, a seminary is synonymous with college. This one is a liberal arts teaching seminary."

"I see."

The man, now clean shaven, though still in need of a bath since he'd been on the ranch working, rubbed his hand across his chin. "My daughter has been schooled by my mother for the last few years, but I would like her to have the opportunity to learn about the new world we are living in. Having someone from the East would certainly help. Do you play a musical instrument?"

"I play the piano."

"Excellent." He nodded toward the piano. "Mother worked with Caroline, but she wasn't interested. You might have more luck with her. Do you have teaching supplies? Books?"

Abigail breathed easier knowing she would be able to give this young lady what she needed. She smiled. "My trunk is filled with everything I need. I'm confident I can help your daughter in whatever direction you'd like me to take her."

The man stared at her with the soft, brown eyes she remembered from the road in Independence. Finally he nodded.

"You seem to have the qualifications to do a good job with my daughter. You'll live on the ranch. If you need time away, we can talk about that as the time comes up." He told her what her salary would be, then he ambled to the window and looked out. "I do expect you to do one more thing for my daughter."

Abigail sat up straight and hoped she'd be able to help the man with his wishes.

"My daughter has lived on this ranch away from town all of her life. We have a school in town, but I didn't want her there especially since so many people are traveling through on their way out West." He stopped talking and turned around to Abigail. "Caroline needs to learn how to be a lady. She's a beautiful child, but she'd rather hang out in the barn with the men than to sit with my mother and sew."

Abigail stood up. "Mr. Fletcher, I would love to work with your daughter in more feminine endeavors. Not all young ladies like to sew or paint or even play the piano, but I'll introduce her to as much as I can to help her be an accomplished lady."

Mr. Fletcher let out a huge breath. "As I said, she's a beautiful girl, but she has no interest in working with her attributes."

Abigail had no idea what to expect from this young girl, but she was determined to help. "I look forward to meeting Caroline and beginning our work."

"I do have to ask you if you think you're equipped to live and work in this part of the world. We have a good life on the ranch, but we don't have the modern conveniences that you had in Boston. Do you think you are capable of living without the museums and theaters and dress shops you've grown accustomed to? I would hate for Caroline to get used to having you here, and then for you to leave."

Abigail swallowed. Could she live in what her friends and family called the Wild West?

"I can assure you I will learn to live without the niceties of my old life. I didn't expect to be thrown into a riotous town like Independence, but your ranch seems to be a quieter and safer place to live. I can deal with whatever challenges this area of the world offers."

Mr. Fletcher seemed to relax. "If you think you'd like to work here—and can survive here—I'll have my mother escort you to your quarters."

Irritation nipped at her chest. She straightened her shoulders. "Mr. Fletcher, I survived years away from my family while I was getting my education, then several weeks on a stagecoach. I can certainly survive living on a ranch."

Before answering her, the man looked directly into her eyes. A tiny lift of his lip told her he was amused. Abigail swallowed a retort to let him know she did not appreciate being ridiculed.

"I hope so because I do need a governess." He cleared his throat. "If your driver needs to stay the night, he can stay in the bunkhouse with the other hands. Your cabin is well equipped, but if you need anything, please don't hesitate to speak up. My family or the ranch hands will try our best to accommodate you." He turned to go, still holding his hat in his hand.

As he got to the door, he turned. "We eat at seven. I'll see to it that Caroline is prepared to meet you. Right now you need to rest, I'm sure." He nodded. "Thank you for coming."

Lucas Fletcher left Abigail standing alone in the sitting room. The weight of the world slid from her shoulders. She raised her gaze to heaven. "Thank you, Lord. Thank you for giving me direction. I won't let you down." She listened to Mr. Fletcher's heavy footsteps in the hallway. When she heard the front door close, she looked up to heaven once again. "Of course, I might need a little more direction dealing with my new boss who thinks I'm some sort of weak city girl who can't live without the modern accommodations in town."

She crossed her arms in front of her body. *Maybe at one time I was weak for not standing up to the gossips in Boston, but I survived that stagecoach ride. I can deal with this man.*

Mrs. Fletcher came back into the room and escorted her to a small cabin on the side of the big house. Abigail opened the door and inhaled a huge cleansing breath. After sleeping in rode-side stations or sitting up in the stagecoach, and then staying in the storage room of the boarding house, she wasn't sure what to expect, but the clean interior of the cabin put her mind at ease. Fresh white-washed walls and a small bed covered by a hand-stitched quilt assured her that her stay here would be pleasant. The rest of the room contained a desk and a wooden chair, a small table with a basin and a pitcher, and an upholstered chair. Her trunks and a bag sat on the side of the door. She couldn't wait to pull out her supplies to start organizing lessons for her new student.

She pulled out her grandmother's gold pocket watch, flipped it open, and realized she had two and a half hours to relax before dinner. Wasting no time, she loosened the buttons on her bodice and lay across the bed. "Ooh, this is wonderful," she said out loud as her body stretched across the mattress. Within minutes, she floated into the best sleep she'd had since she left her home.

A knock on the door startled her. Abigail's eyes flew open. For a moment, she had no idea where she was, but with the next knock, she jumped out of bed, fastened her bodice and opened the door.

A young man stood on the stoop. His gaze lowered to the floor. "Ma'am, Mrs. Fletcher wanted to remind you about dinner in thirty minutes."

"Oh, my. Certainly. Thank you for coming to tell me. I'll be there."

The dimming light of the western sky told her she'd slept the entire afternoon. Frantically, she darted back into the cabin to make herself presentable.

Within thirty minutes, Abigail stood inside the cabin door, inhaled a huge breath, and looked down at the dress she'd pulled from her trunk. She smoothed several large wrinkles but decided her new family would have to understand. "I can't believe I slept that long," she mumbled as she closed the door behind her and headed toward the big house, not knowing what to expect from her new employers.

Having rushed to get ready, she hadn't had time to worry, but now that she headed to the big house, her stomach twisted. She prayed she would fit in with the Fletcher family and that Caroline would welcome her as her new teacher.

Before climbing the steps to the expansive front porch, Abigail took in the beautiful workmanship in the railings, the shutters and the massive door. Mrs. Fletcher had told her the family had built the home and had added to it over three generations. Abigail could envision the Fletcher men laboring on their family estate.

Before she reached the top of the steps, the door opened and Lucas Fletcher greeted her with a nod. "I'm glad you could join us, Miss Cook. Please, come in."

Mr. Fletcher had cleaned up from the time she'd seen him earlier in the day. He wore black trousers, gleaming black boots, and a light blue shirt that emphasized his broad shoulders. His dark hair, clean and shining, was neatly combed back away from his face. From her two earlier encounters with the man, she knew he worked hard on the ranch, but as he stood in the doorway, he looked as refined as any businessman from Boston.

Abigail blinked. Was this the same scraggly man who had helped her avoid landing in the street just two days before? Tall and well-built, he towered above her and seemed to take up the entire doorway. Realizing she still stood on the first step gawking at the gentleman, she cleared her throat as she walked to the top of the stairs. "I look forward to meeting the rest of your family."

As she walked past her new employer, she inhaled the clean scent of soap.

"The dining room is to your left." He closed the door behind them, stepped next to her and gently placed a hand on her arm to escort her into the large dining room. Grandmother Fletcher and a beautiful girl sat at one end of the massive wood table. Just as everything else she'd seen in this home, the heavy table was intricately carved.

"Come and join us, Miss Cook." Mrs. Fletcher greeted her with a gorgeous smile. "This is my granddaughter, Caroline."

The girl, with wavy blond hair cascading to her shoulders, eyed Abigail. Eventually she nodded a greeting, but didn't speak.

Behind Abigail, she heard Mr. Fletcher let out what sounded like an exasperated sigh.

"Caroline, I'm so glad to meet you. I can't wait until you and I can begin our lessons. I've brought some exciting books and supplies I know you'll enjoy."

Caroline looked from her father to her grandmother, then back at Abigail. Was she going to dash from the table, or worse, cry?

"Come have a seat, Miss Cook." Grandmother Fletcher nodded to a chair near her. "You and Caroline can talk after dinner, or if you'd like she can be available in the morning after breakfast."

Abigail smiled in Caroline's direction. "We can wait until the morning unless you have questions tonight."

"I want to wait until tomorrow." Caroline's low voice was barely audible.

Abigail nodded.

Lucas Fletcher stepped around Abigail and pulled out her chair.

Though he didn't touch her, she felt his presence, sending a streak of warmth zipping through her body. Hoping she hadn't blushed, she sat. "Thank you."

Another man stomped into the room, immediately went behind his mother, and planted a kiss on the top of her head. "Mother, sorry, I'm late, but I was afraid Major was having some stomach issues."

"Is he okay?" Lucas looked at his brother and took a sip of water.

Douglas nodded. "He looked fine when I left him. I'll check again after dinner." The man looked at Abigail. "And you must be the new governess. I'm Douglas, the younger, better looking brother."

Abigail laughed. "I'm Abigail Cook. I'm thrilled to be at your ranch." Douglas was almost as tall as his brother. With slightly lighter hair and hazel eyes, he was just as handsome.

"Take a seat, Douglas, and let's say grace." Mrs. Fletcher waited for her son to sit, then bowed her head, and began a beautiful grace, asking for blessings of the food and thanksgiving for Abigail being at their ranch.

Abigail thought it strange that Mr. Fletcher or his brother didn't ask the blessing, but she bowed her head and listened to Mrs. Fletcher's words. When grace concluded, Abigail added her own silent prayer asking for strength to be a good governess to Caroline without being distracted by the two handsome but confusing gentlemen sitting at the table.

Several servants, Spanish in appearance, brought in platters of beef, bowls of vegetables and several baskets of bread. Abigail's stomach growled. Except for the light snack when she arrived at the ranch, she had not eaten since the early morning before leaving Independence.

Mrs. Fletcher smiled at the ladies. "Miss Cook, I'd like you to meet Bonita, the best cook and baker in the valley, and her daughter Carmella. Bonita's family has lived on our ranch for over thirty years, and they are like family to all of us."

"It's so good to meet both of you." Abigail smiled at each lady.

Neither lady said anything, but each nodded in Abigail's direction.

Lucas picked up the platter of meat, served a huge portion on his plate, then passed it to Douglas. Abigail waited until the platter reached her, then she, too, took a nice portion. When her plate was piled high with food, she picked up her fork and tasted. "Hmmm." The approval slipped out before she realized she'd made a sound.

"Glad you like our meal." Lucas took a huge bite. After swallowing, he looked directly at Abigail. "Bonita and Carmella make the best meals around here. You'll get to know them and appreciate their talents in the kitchen."

"This meal is wonderful." She remembered her manners and slowed down.

"Tell us how you came to be in Independence." Mrs. Fletcher smiled in her direction. "Did I remember you saying your home is in Boston? That's quite a long travel for a young lady. Was someone traveling with you?"

"It certainly is a long way, but I traveled alone. I found the stagecoach to be quite safe."

"Why would you choose to cross the country?" Lucas took a second piece of bread. "I hear Boston is a bustling, progressive city with opportunities abounding."

Abigail knew eventually she'd be asked such a question. She was ready with an answer. "I needed a fresh start, and Independence seemed to be the place where dreams could come true. When I received word that I had the job of the new teacher, I wasted no time in planning my trip. Unfortunately, the job had already been given to someone else when I arrived."

Lucas looked up from his plate. Mrs. Fletcher picked up her glass of water but did not look her way. Caroline and Douglas actually looked at Abigail with interest.

Abigail knew they wanted more of an explanation as to why she left leave Boston, but she wasn't ready to blurt out her entire, humiliating story.

Lucas nodded. "I'm sorry the teaching position in town didn't work out for you, but we were glad you found out about our position here. Yes, Independence is certainly the place to start fresh. It seems thousands are flocking in from the East, mostly to head out to California." He speared her with his gaze. "You don't have plans to continue onto California in search for gold, do you?"

Abigail laughed. "Heavens no, Mr. Fletcher. I wouldn't

know the first thing about mining for gold. I did listen to travelers along the route talk about how they were going to get rich, then return to their home in style. I'm not sure I believe that will happen, but, again, I know nothing about the gold rush except for what I've read in the newspapers back home."

Mr. Fletcher concentrated on his food, but spoke before he took a bite. "You saw how chaotic Independence was when you passed through it. I don't advise any young woman to go alone there or the other cities around here."

Abigail wasn't sure if he had just chastised her for traveling alone, or if he was genuinely showing his concern. She chose to think he cared about her safety but didn't respond.

When the meal was over, Mr. Fletcher stood. "I'll have to tell Bonita and Carmella how wonderful this meal was." He looked at Abigail. "We usually sit awhile on the porch before retiring. If you'd like to join us, we'd love to have you."

Again, Abigail's new boss spoke the right words, but his tone did not sound sincere.

"I should go back to my cabin. I didn't get a lot done this afternoon. I was more exhausted than I thought and slept most of my time there. I'd like to organize my belongings and get lessons ready for Caroline." Abigail looked in the girl's direction, but Caroline lowered her gaze and didn't respond. In fact, she had not said much during the meal. Between Mr. Fletcher's serious nature and Caroline's obvious reluctance to have a governess, Abigail's earlier excitement about being on the ranch vanished.

Douglas stood up. "I'm passing on the porch sitting, too. I want to check on Major." He gave his mother a quick kiss, then turned to Abigail. "It was nice to meet you, Miss Cook. I hope you can beat some academics into this wild girl here."

Caroline laughed for the first time since dinner had started. "Uncle Douglas, I'm not wild."

"Close to it." Douglas laughed as he walked out into the hallway.

Grandmother Fletcher stood. "Breakfast is served at six so my boys can get out on the ranch with the hands. If you're not up that early, I'll have Bonita save you a plate."

"Thank you. I'm an early riser so I should have no trouble being here on time. I don't want to cause Bonita more work than she already has. Thank you for a wonderful meal." She stood. "One more thing, I'd like to write a note to my family to let them know I have arrived safely. Is there a way to post a letter?"

Mr. Fletcher pushed his chair back. "After you have the letter written, give it to me, and I will see to it that one of my men takes it to town. I don't guarantee how long it will take to get the letter to Boston, but the sooner we get it to town, the faster it will get there."

"Thank you so much. I know they are worried about me." Abigail excused herself and headed to the door, wondering if her family even thought about her since she'd left. Were they relieved that she was not in the city? She knew her mother and grandmother thought about her and still loved her, but her father was another story. Would he ever forgive her for what he considered bringing disgrace on the family?

She inhaled the warm evening air and shook her head. She'd done nothing wrong and would never understand her father.

As she walked across the front porch, she glanced at the big rockers. She wished she'd feel comfortable enough to sit with the family and enjoy the pleasant evening and the feeling of being part of a family. She sighed. There would be time to do that later. Right now she was a stranger here. It would take work to become part of the Fletcher household.

* * * *

Lucas watched Abigail leave the dining room.

"You were not very friendly to our guest, Lucas." Mrs.

Fletcher pushed her chair under the table. "That poor girl traveled all the way from the East—maybe not to be here on our ranch—but here in Missouri to teach."

"I wasn't unfriendly. I made sure she knows how much we appreciate her being here." He looked at Caroline. "Of course, our Miss Caroline certainly could have offered more of a welcome."

"I don't want a governess. I like having Grandmother as my teacher."

"Your grandmother is not a teacher. She is an intelligent lady, but teaching is not her profession. You need more than she or I can offer you right now. Miss Cook seems to be that lady."

"I'll bet she doesn't even know how to ride a horse."

Lucas chuckled. "That might be true since she's from a big city, but that would be something you could teach her. She needs to know about horses if she's to survive in our part of the world." He straightened up. "I think I'll skip the porch. I have to work on the books for the ranch so I'll see you ladies tomorrow." He took two giant steps to his mother and kissed her on the cheek. "I'll try to be a little friendlier to our new employee."

"You do that. She's a beautiful girl and seems to be very sweet."

"But I wonder why she left Boston." Caroline rolled her eyes and smiled. "I wonder what kind of secret she has. Do you think she'll ever tell us?"

Lucas frowned. He, too, wanted to know why Miss Cook left her life in the East, but he wasn't going to admit it. "Why Miss Cook left Boston is her business, not ours. If she feels comfortable enough to tell us, then that will be wonderful. If she doesn't, it will give that beautiful head of yours something to contemplate."

"Father, you know you want to know."

"Maybe, but I have enough good upbringing not to ask. So do you."

"Your father is right." Mrs. Fletcher picked up her glass of water and took a sip. "If he or you make Miss Cook uncomfortable, I'll get the broom after you."

Caroline laughed. "Grandmother, you're funny. You couldn't catch me with the broom, and if you caught Daddy, he'd just take the broom from you."

Mrs. Fletcher's face softened. "That may be, but she is our guest and our newest employee. We will certainly give her space and her privacy."

"You're right, Mother. She has answered our request for a governess. We have no right to question her motives." Lucas kissed Caroline, said his goodnights, then walked down the hallway and up the stairs to his bedroom. Immediately, he closed the door behind him but didn't go to his desk where his books lay waiting. Instead, he stood by the door and thought about the beautiful lady who'd come into his family's life. Before falling in love with his wife Sarah, Lucas knew Miss Cook's beauty and intelligence would have attracted him but not anymore. Having loved Sarah, he couldn't imagine looking at another female, especially one who probably had a secret, and one who probably couldn't get up on a horse or cook a simple meal.

Thinking about the city lady trying to get up on a horse, he chuckled, but then got serious. What was a woman like that doing in Independence? He needed a governess for Caroline, but would this lady be the right person for the job? Would she catch the next stagecoach back when she found out how hard life could be living away from town? Was she a strong enough person to fit into this lifestyle?

His mother told him to ask God for someone to help with his daughter. Now that Miss Cook was here, maybe he ought to ask Him what he was supposed to do with the beautiful lady living in his and Sarah's cabin. As much as he needed a governess, he wasn't expecting someone young. Why couldn't God have sent an older, stern woman to be Caroline's governess? He laughed. His mother probably prayed for a beautiful governess to catch her son's eye. She wasn't subtle about wanting him to move on.

Lucas pushed away from the door. Three years had gone by, but he was not ready to look at another woman, no matter how beautiful she was. He still carried Sarah's memory in his heart, and he wasn't ready to push it aside for someone who left her hometown for who-knows-what reason. Nope, Caroline needed a teacher, and Miss Cook had answered the call, but it didn't mean he had to socialize with her.

CHAPTER FOUR

As hard as Abigail tried, she couldn't get to breakfast for six o'clock. At six-twenty, she rushed from her cabin and up the front steps of the big house. When she got to the door, she stopped. Yesterday evening Mr. Fletcher opened the front door for her when she arrived for dinner, but now no one was around. Did the Fletcher family expect her to knock or to simply enter as the family did?

Not feeling comfortable about walking into the home unannounced, she knocked. Shortly, one of the servants answered the door. Grandmother Fletcher and her two sons still sat at the table talking, but they had finished eating.

Mrs. Fletcher looked up. "Good morning, Miss Cook. Please have a seat. Bonita will bring in some breakfast."

"I'm so sorry to get here late. I unpacked last night, but my belongings are in disarray. Finding what I'll need this morning for Caroline's first lesson presented a problem, but I did it. I'm excited for our first lesson."

"Your timing is fine." Mrs. Fletcher, dressed in a green dress with a large, lighter green collar, smiled in Abigail's direction.

Mr. Fletcher nodded but said nothing.

"Good morning, Miss Cook." Douglas smiled at her,

making her feel welcome.

Bonita walked through the door carrying a platter of ham and eggs and a bowl of potatoes. Carmella followed behind her with hot bread and butter.

"Oh, my, this looks wonderful. Thank you, ladies."

"Coffee is on the sideboard." Mrs. Fletcher nodded toward the table.

Abigail poured herself a cup, then sat. "I was wondering where I might wash my clothes."

"After breakfast I'll have Carmella go to the cabin and get the clothes. She or one of the other workers will wash and press them for you." Mrs. Fletcher placed her cup on the table.

"That won't be necessary. I don't want to cause anyone extra work."

"You won't." Lucas Fletcher's voice was stern. "You are to devote your time to working with Caroline, not washing clothes."

His harsh tone and serious expression made Abigail sit up. "Certainly, I understand."

Lucas pushed his chair back and stood up. "I will see everyone this evening for dinner. Miss Cook, if you need anything, please tell one of the workers or my mother." He bent down and kissed his mother. "You ready, Douglas?"

Douglas stood up, took one last swallow of his coffee, then nodded to the two ladies and followed his brother out the door.

Abigail didn't know either of the Fletcher men, but Douglas seemed to be much more approachable. She wasn't sure how to take Lucas Fletcher. He needed her to help Caroline, but his demeanor wasn't what she expected from a new employer.

"Please excuse my older son's manner. He has a lot on his mind running this ranch and seeing that Caroline gets what she needs." Mrs. Fletcher placed her used napkin on the table and stood. "Caroline rarely eats breakfast with the family. If you'll bring her back to the dining room midmorning, I'll ask Bonita to have something ready. She's usually a big eater, but recently she has chosen to sleep in. Her father is not happy with the idea, but I explained she is no longer a child."

"I'll see to it that she gets her nutrition during the day." Abigail scooped a big helping on her plate, then laughed. "No one has to worry about me eating."

Mrs. Fletcher laughed with her. "Enjoy your breakfast. I will wake Caroline shortly and send her to your cabin."

After Mrs. Fletcher left the dining room, Abigail enjoyed her breakfast, but even more so, loved the fact that her life was now back on track. Since February when she'd made the decision not to marry Mr. Baker, her life and mind had been in turmoil. Her family was one of the prominent families in Boston. The wedding had been the talk of society for months. Pre-wedding parties had been attended by some of the most well-known politicians and businessmen and women in the city. Her father had spared no expense to make his daughter's marriage a memorable occasion.

At twenty-nine, she'd accepted the proposal from William Baker, III, not so much as a love match, but as a way to keep her family's standing in the community. She'd convinced herself she was too old to think about marrying for love. Accepting Mr. Baker's proposal would heal the rift with her father but still allow her to teach the children she so loved.

Reality set in at dinner one night when Mr. Baker declared his future wife would never work outside the home. She would stay home to raise his three sons. The next morning she cancelled the wedding, and her life spiraled out of control.

Abigail pushed her eggs and ham on her plate with her fork. A shudder ran down her back. She'd learn to suppress the memories of the weeks following the cancellation. Her time on the stagecoach kept her mind occupied, but now sitting in the solitude of the Fletcher dining room, she couldn't push the memories away. Horror and shame of those weeks weighed on her shoulders.

Here at the Fletcher Ranch, she had a position, a home, and a purpose. She wanted to make this work and prayed she could live up to the family's expectations even though her boss didn't seem too thrilled she was here.

After breakfast Abigail pulled out books and supplies and set up a corner of her cabin as a classroom. She'd been told she could use any room in the big house, but she wanted Caroline to feel as though she was in a school setting during their lessons. She also found her journal tucked away in her trunk. She'd worked hard to keep an account of her travels, but as the trip stretched on, her energy and enthusiasm diminished. Now on the ranch, she could start working on her entries once again. She placed it on her side table of her bed and hoped she could devote time to it tonight.

By eight o'clock, with her supplies laid out and knowing what her first lessons would be, Abigail answered the knock on the door. "Good morning, Caroline. I'm excited to start our lessons. Come in."

Caroline had her hair pulled back with a long, limp ribbon. Just as Mr. Fletcher said, his daughter was beautiful, but she obviously wasn't concerned about the way she looked. This morning she wore a plain day dress that was too tight across the bodice. Abigail didn't mention that fact. She stepped aside to let the girl inside.

"I'd rather have lessons on the front porch so I can see what the hands are doing."

"On some days we might do that, but we need to have a quiet space so we both can concentrate. This morning we will do some exercises to determine where you are in your academics."

"I know all I need to know. Grandmother taught me my letters and some arithmetic."

"That's wonderful, but there is so much more for you to

study. Please, come in and we'll start."

Caroline looked around the cabin. "This looks different."

"I assumed someone else lived here before I was hired."

"Not really. No one lived in here." Her gaze slowly moved from Abigail's trunk to the bedside table. "This was my father's and my mother's cabin. They lived in the big house with the rest of us, but sometimes they stayed out here alone. On those days I stayed with Grandmother and Grandfather and wasn't allowed to come over here."

Abigail sucked in air, not knowing what to say. She, too, looked around the room, this time seeing the furnishings in a different light. She knew Caroline's mother was no longer in the picture, but no one had said what happened. If she and Mr. Fletcher used this as their special place, she could see why the man might not want her in here.

"Would you tell me what happened to your mother?"

The girl looked down at the floor, then up at the quilt at the foot of the bed. "Mother died in a horse accident. I was ten, but I remember it like it was yesterday."

"I'm so sorry. That's hard for a young girl to handle."

Caroline frowned and looked at Abigail. "I lived through it and survived without her. Grandmother and Father see to it that I have everything I need. Grandfather died two years ago, but Grandmother is like my mother now."

"You are lucky to have such a loving family."

"I don't want to talk about Mother." Caroline's voice was harsh.

"Certainly." Abigail took a huge breath. "Let's get started on our lessons."

For the next two hours Abigail worked with Caroline to see how much Mrs. Fletcher had taught her. Surprisingly, the girl had learned quite a lot. She knew her letters, had a nice handwriting, and knew some arithmetic. Making mental notes about how to approach her future lessons, Abigail moved on to something more enjoyable for the girl. She opened a beautiful textbook that showed an updated account of what the United States looked like and of different countries in the world.

Caroline sat up straight and turned the pages. She asked question after question about other countries, then wanted to know about the big cities in the East.

"I know you have some beautiful buildings in Independence and right here on the ranch, but in some of the big cities in the East, massive buildings line the streets. I recently went to a fabulous performance at one of the newer opera houses. So much is happening in the East, and I'm sure one day the same types of experiences will be open for this area of the country. Missouri will be as modern as our eastern cities."

Page after page sparked Caroline's interest. She asked questions about everything, and Abigail felt good about being able to answer her.

By ten o'clock Abigail leaned back in her chair. "Did you eat breakfast this morning?"

"I drank some milk."

"Milk is excellent, but you need more than that. You're a growing girl and you want to be healthy. Eating right will help your skin and hair shine and your eyes sparkle."

"I don't care about that."

"You will when the young men start to look at you and you have to compete with other girls your age."

The girl's brows came together. "Maybe I won't want them to look at me if I have to be fake and not who I am."

"That's a good point, but being healthy and naturally beautiful isn't being fake." Abigail stood up. "Let's go see what Bonita has for us in the kitchen. You need a break, I'm sure."

"Maybe she still has dessert from last night."

Abigail smiled, wanted to tell her she should eat healthy, but decided the morning had gone too well to get on the girl's bad side. "You're right. Dessert was great last night. I could use a bowl as well."

Caroline laughed and skipped toward the house.

By mid-afternoon Abigail put away the books, pleased that Caroline had been cooperative though not enthusiastic about anything except the book of geography—and the dessert from last night's dinner.

Abigail walked with Caroline out onto the porch of her cabin. She reminded her new student about the work she expected her to do before class tomorrow, then watched as the girl ran into the house. Abigail sat in one of the smaller rockers and relaxed, hoping she could make an impression on her.

From the corner of her eye, she spotted a rider coming through the field behind the closest corral. Within minutes she recognized Lucas Fletcher. Like the first time she'd met him in the streets of Independence, he had his hat pulled low on his forehead against the afternoon sun. Something besides the man's good looks piqued Abigail's interest, something deeper.

She'd love to sit and talk with him, but she had a feeling that would never happen. Did he have a rule about getting too friendly with the hired help? Being raised with a household of servants, she understood that concept. She didn't agree with it, but she followed her father's rules, at least as a young girl.

Lucas stopped to talk with several men outside the barn. Whatever was said made all of them laugh. She yearned for that type of rapport with him. Had he already picked out another female to be his wife and mother to Caroline? That would explain his not getting too friendly with her. That was definitely okay with Abigail. She was not in the market for another man. One humiliation in a lifetime was enough. Still, she wished her boss would converse with her.

She watched as he rode near the barn. He made an impressive showing, sitting tall and straight in the saddle. Even though she couldn't see his eyes, she knew how deep his brown eyes were. Still remembering them on that first day in Independence, she smiled.

Inhaling deeply, she pulled her gaze away from him. The man might be handsome, but teaching his daughter should be her main concern, not gawking at her boss.

She'd picked up her journal on the way out the door so she opened it and immediately began to write. *My first day with Caroline was productive. I learned quite a lot from her about the ranch, but I also found her to be sensitive beneath the tom-boy exterior she presented.*

Curious to see where Lucas was going, she looked up. He'd stopped outside the barn. What was he thinking?

She shook her head and focused on her journal.

Ranch life will be different for me. Even though I get the impression my boss thinks I'm too weak to live here, I know I can do this. From what I've seen, the people here are devoted to the land and will do whatever it takes to survive away from the niceties of the city. Like them, and with the help of God, I can too.

* * * *

After speaking to one of his hands, Lucas nudged Charger toward a side gate, then headed toward the barn. Abigail sat on her porch talking with Caroline, but then Caroline darted down the steps toward the house. Lucas stopped and propped his elbow on the horn of his saddle and waited.

Charger threw his head back. "Just a minute, boy. Let's see how long it takes my daughter to run out the back door to the barn."

He glanced at Miss Cook. Would she be able to interest Caroline in more feminine pastimes? Riding was necessary for every young girl to learn, but Caroline spent too much time on her horse. He worried about her riding off alone. One day he'd have to put a stop to it, or at least have one of the men ride with her for her safety.

The back door flew open and Caroline darted out

wearing her usual riding attire, trousers and a work shirt. He chuckled and shook his head. "That didn't take long."

He had a few minutes to spare before meeting with his foreman, so he turned Charger toward the barn, but not before looking at the cabin once more. Miss Cook still sat in her rocker and appeared to be writing. What did she think of her new assignment and her new living arrangements? And, more importantly, how did he feel about another woman living in his and Sarah's cabin? Would she keep it straightened and as clean as Sarah did? He smiled remembering how Sarah had told the help she was quite capable of taking care of her space and would not let them come in except to do heavy cleaning about once a month. His mother never understood why her daughter-in-law didn't want to use the servants, but he understood. The cabin was their private space, a place to enjoy each other without the rest of family gathered around. When they chose to spend time there, everyone knew not to bother them.

Lucas pulled his gaze away from the cabin and stared into the western sky. Sarah's memories faded with each year passing. Sometimes he'd reach into his pocket and pull out her picture, hoping to keep her smile vivid in his mind. His memories were all he had left of her. His love for her had never died so why were her memories fading?

Charger tugged at his reins. "Okay, boy. We'll go. I'm not accomplishing anything sitting here."

With one last look at the woman on the porch, he headed toward the barn, hoping to catch Caroline before she rode off alone.

* * * *

For the next two weeks, Abigail worked hard with Caroline. The girl showed sparks of brilliance. Her interest centered around buildings and geography and literature, but not so much with numbers or science. Abigail had not approached music lessons, but planned to in the coming week.

As she prepared for her next day's lessons, a knock interrupted her. No one but Caroline or one of the servants ever knocked on her door, so she was surprised to find Mrs. Fletcher on the small porch. "Grandmother Fletcher, this is a surprise. Please come in."

"Thank you." The matriarch of the family stepped into Abigail's small room.

"I was working on my lessons for the week. Please forgive the papers and books spread on the bed."

"That is not a problem. Our Caroline should be your primary concern so I'm thrilled to see you working on her lessons."

"I don't have any refreshments to offer you, but I can get you a cup of water." Abigail stood a few feet away from her guest and wished she could be more hospitable.

"I don't need a thing. In fact, I came to invite you to attend church with us tomorrow morning. We can't get into town often, but we try to attend services when the weather seems agreeable for our ride in."

"I would love to attend. Is the church in Independence?"

"Yes. It's one of the older buildings on the outskirts of town. As you know, it takes about an hour or more to ride into town so we need to leave early. Could you be ready by seven? Bonita usually joins us. She brings along food so we don't have to waste time eating breakfast before we leave."

"That sounds lovely. Thank you for thinking of me."

After Mrs. Fletcher left, Abigail finished her lessons for the week, then concentrated on what she'd wear for her first trip into town since she'd left Sunny's Boarding House.

Saturday night's dinner outdid anything that Abigail had eaten since she'd been at the Fletcher Ranch. Bonita served chicken cooked down in a spicy sauce, three different vegetables, hot bread and pudding for dessert.

"That was spectacular." Abigail leaned back in her chair. "I'm not sure I've eaten that much since I left Boston."

Lucas lifted his wine glass. "As usual, Bonita and

Carmella outdid themselves. I'm glad you enjoyed it."

"I agree. We are so lucky to have those two ladies." Douglas took a last sip of water and placed his crystal water glass on the table.

"Are you two men riding into town with us tomorrow?" Abigail surprised herself with a tingle of excitement.

"I am," said Douglas. "We don't get into town enough. What about you, brother?"

"I have some business with Victor so I'm going."

Abigail wasn't sure how to take his comment, but since Mrs. Fletcher and Caroline both looked at him then down at their plates, Abigail didn't question either. Would he attend church service with them? No one said anything else. Awkward silence ensued.

"Shall we sit on the porch for a spell?" Mrs. Fletcher stood up.

"I would love to do that after this wonderful meal." Abigail also stood up. She glanced in the direction of the two Fletcher men.

Finally Lucas stood up. "Ladies, I'll see you bright and early tomorrow morning."

"Son, can't you spare a few minutes to be cordial tonight?"

He looked at his mother, twisted his lip, then nodded. "For a few moments."

Mrs. Fletcher looked at Douglas.

"I'm coming. The porch will give my body time to let this dinner go down. I'm stuffed." He pushed his chair back and stretched.

"Good. Come along, Caroline." His mother smiled big and headed out the dining room door followed by Caroline and Douglas, leaving Lucas and Abigail alone. She looked down at the table but her gaze moved to Lucas, who stood next to his chair.

He still held his glass. The delicate stem looked much too fragile in his large hand, but he raised it to his lips and took a sip, never looking at Abigail.

Abigail fidgeted. Not sure why she felt awkward being in the room alone with her boss, she straightened her shoulders. "I'll see you on the porch."

Scrambling into the hallway, she stopped for a moment to catch her breath. What was wrong with her? She was an educated twenty-nine year old woman who had been on her own at school for years. Tonight she acted as if she'd never been around a man.

Maybe she hadn't been around anyone like Lucas Fletcher. He was bigger-than-life when he walked into a room, got a person's attention without saying anything, and was built like the Greek gods she'd studied in her mythology classes.

Grow up, Abigail. The man has no interest in you at all, and you definitely don't need to be looking at a man. Not now.

Stepping out onto the porch, she immediately felt better. Mrs. Fletcher and Caroline each sat in rockers. Douglas stood by the railing. Caroline smiled, then kept talking to her grandmother.

"She's telling me about the lesson you're working on, the one about buildings in Boston and in New York." With a big smile on her face, Mrs. Fletcher rocked.

"I'm glad you enjoyed your studies today."

"I really loved looking at the theater in Boston—and the museum. Both of those are great."

Douglas turned with his back to the railing. "I might have to stop in and listen to your lessons. I'd love to learn about the East. One day I plan to travel away from this area of the world."

The door opened and Lucas walked out. Caroline looked up and got quiet.

"Don't stop talking because of me." He pulled out a chair and sat. "What were you discussing?"

"I was telling Grandmother about the buildings in the

East Miss Cook showed me. I'd love to see them one day."

Lucas looked directly into Abigail's eye, then smiled.

Surprised, Abigail smiled back. Was that the first time she'd seen him smile?

"The East has some wonderful offerings." Lucas walked to the rocker on the other side of his mother, then sat. "I'm glad Miss Cook is able to introduce them to you."

Caroline leaned forward. "Did you go that far when you and Uncle Vic traveled with the troops?"

"Not to Boston, but we went to Washington at the beginning of the war, and then I returned afterwards."

"The Mexican-American War?" Abigail's interest was piqued. "You were involved in that?"

"Both Sheriff Sanchez and I fought in it."

"Both of them were officers. We are very proud of both of them." His mother's eyes sparkled.

"Victor and I were fortunate enough to stay in the same squadrons for the entire campaign." He looked out over the front of the yard. "Unfortunately, we were away from our families for over two years."

"That must've been hard." Abigail watched her boss get serious, swallow, then answered.

"It was. Caroline was only ten. Mother and Dad had to take care of her while I was gone."

"Douglas helped, too. He taught me how to fish."

"That I did, young lady, and I must say she's better at it than I am."

Caroline beamed.

Mrs. Fletcher stopped rocking. "You helped to gain our independence from Mexico. The time you were gone was worth it."

Lucas nodded.

Abigail was going through the time-line of the war and assumed Lucas's wife had not been dead long before he'd joined the service. So many questions spun around her head, but she dared not ask. It was none of her business. Caroline had told her a little about the lady's death. Maybe one day she'd feel comfortable enough with the family to ask more, but tonight was not the night. "Which battles did you fight in, if you don't mind my asking?"

"I was an officer under Colonel Kearney and then under General Winfield Scott."

"Then you must've been part of the march into Mexico City."

"I was. From there the battles diminished and in February last year the treaty was signed." He chuckled. "Had Mexico known that gold had just been discovered in California I'm sure they would've never signed that part of the treaty."

"I had no idea that timeline of those two events was so close together."

Lucas stood up. "They were. All that gold would've gone to the Mexican government had word about the gold traveled a little faster than it did." He bent down and kissed his daughter. "Don't stay up late. We have a big day tomorrow."

"I won't, Father. I'm excited about going into town."

Lucas tilted his head as if in doubt about having a pleasant Sunday in Independence, but he didn't say anything. Instead, he kissed his mother as well and nodded to Abigail. "I will see you ladies early tomorrow morning."

"I'll call it a night also. Thank you for a lovely evening." Douglas bowed from the waist and swirled his arms through the air.

Caroline laughed at her uncle's antics.

After the two men left the porch, Abigail stood up as well. "I should get to my cabin and prepare for tomorrow. Thank you for a wonderful meal."

She walked calmly as she could, but excitement bubbled in her chest. She had not left the Fletcher Ranch since she'd arrived several weeks ago. Tomorrow she'd venture into town with the family, attend church services, and enjoy a potluck lunch afterwards. The outing would be simple, nothing like Sundays in Boston where she sat with her family in a grand church, strolled through parks, or took buggy rides along the harbor, but being able to leave the ranch and see other people thrilled her.

As she stepped up onto the porch, she turned. Mrs. Fletcher and Caroline still sat in their rockers so she waved to them before stepping into her living area. As soon as she closed the door, she spun around and laughed. "Yes, yes, yes! Tomorrow I'm going to town!"

Before picking out what she'd wear, she spotted her journal lying on the bedside table. She'd written several posts since being on the ranch, but tonight she eagerly lifted the book and grabbed her pen and ink bottle. *"Tomorrow I'll meet some of the people who live in Independence. I wonder if I'll see Beth from the mercantile who greeted me with such a sweet smile or any of those who were at Sunny's Boarding House. I'll wear my lavender dress tomorrow. It's special but not too fancy."* She read over the entry, then put the journal on the bedside table.

Before blowing out her lantern and crawling into bed, she picked up her journal and her pen and wrote. *"I wonder if Lucas will join the family at church."*

CHAPTER FIVE

Sunday morning in Independence presented a much quieter picture than the other days of the week. Lucas guided the buggy down the main street, wishing the town would stay this peaceful every day. As a boy, he loved riding here with his father or one of the ranch hands. Even though the town was tiny, he saw it as magical. Even with only a few stores, he loved going into the buildings where necessary goods and luscious treats amazed him.

Today as he headed toward the sheriff's office, he shook his head. Store fronts lined the entire main area of town, and even on Sunday morning, strangers walked the sidewalks and mule-drawn wagons headed out of town. The discovery of gold in California had given businesses a much-needed boost even here in Independence at the expense of a peaceful existence for its citizens. He didn't understand why his friend Victor or anyone else would want to live amongst the noise and crowds, but then everyone didn't have the opportunity to live on a ranch like his.

His thoughts went to Miss Cook. Did she miss the big city with all its amenities? He demanded himself to look straight ahead and not turn to see how she responded to being in town. Did she approve of the activities or did she think their little town was sorely inadequate? And, the big question, would she stay on the ranch for him to find out? He still felt she would not be able to cope with the lonely life on the ranch during the cold winter months. Would she soon be on one of stagecoaches to the East?

He sighed. Caroline was already getting attached to the lady. If Miss Cook left, his daughter would be devastated. He gripped the reins tightly. Had he made a mistake by bringing the governess into his family?

With a thousand emotions clogging his thoughts, Lucas pulled his buggy in front of the sheriff's office. Douglas and Lucas got out, and Douglas headed inside the sheriff's office. Lucas walked to the side door. "Ladies, go inside and tell Sheriff Sanchez hello. After you freshen up, I'll walk you to the church. It seems you have a few more minutes before the service begins."

Abigail sat on the seat behind the driver. She stood up, straightened her shoulders and smiled in his direction. Caroline jumped out of the buggy alone and ran into the office. Lucas offered his hand to help his mother. Abigail stepped to the edge of the buggy and looked down at the ground. Lucas knew she could hold onto the side and jump out, but wearing church clothes, the motion would be awkward. He swallowed and stuck out his hand to help her.

Abigail smiled and extended hers. He grabbed it and inhaled. Her small hand nearly disappeared in his big one. For a split second she looked directly into his eyes, but then immediately looked away. When he thought she was balanced on the edge, he placed both hands on her waist and lowered her to the ground. The same motion he'd used for his mother now made him jittery.

"Thank you." She smiled, then brushed her skirt to smooth the wrinkles.

He nodded, turned quickly, then stepped up on the walkway. Behind him, he heard Abigail pull in a big breath as she followed the Fletcher family.

Inside, Victor stood talking with Caroline and Mrs. Fletcher. As he and Abigail stepped in, Victor turned and stuck out his hand to Abigail. "It's so nice to see all of you. My family just walked to the church. It will be a wonderful surprise when you walk in."

"I can't wait to see Aunt Betty and the boys." Caroline gave her uncle another hug, then followed her grandmother to the back room of the office.

"How are you, Miss Cook? Is this man being a decent boss? If he's not, let me know because I know how to whip him into shape."

Lucas chuckled. "That'll be the day."

"The Fletcher family has been more than I could have imagined. Everything is wonderful." Abigail looked toward the back hall. "If you'll excuse me, gentleman, I'll follow the ladies to the back."

Both men stared at Abigail as she disappeared down the hallway.

"She seems to fit right into your family, Lucas. Looks like things are working out well, right?"

"I guess."

"What do you mean, 'I guess'? Is she teaching Caroline what you want her to learn?"

Lucas nodded.

"Then, what's the problem?"

Lucas squirmed. "No problem. I'm scared she won't be able to handle living away from town and will leave."

"I don't know about that. She traveled by herself on those dad-blasted stagecoaches. She's got to be a pretty tough lady."

"Maybe. That, too, makes me wonder why she left her comfortable home and traveled all the way here."

Victor returned to his desk but didn't sit down. "One day she might tell you why she left."

Lucas shrugged. "Maybe you're right, but right now we're doing fine."

"I'm not so sure about that. You act like you did when Margaret Spenser kissed you on the playground."

Lucas shook his head. "Really? Is that where your mind is going?"

"Just saying what I see in front of me. Where's my confident friend and tough military officer?"

"He's standing in front of you. Now, what's the big issue you needed to talk with me about?"

"Change the subject. Right." Victory stepped back around his desk and sat down. "Make yourself comfortable. I want to tell you what I'm hearing in your part of the world."

* * * *

Abigail walked with the Fletcher family and Sheriff Sanchez along the sidewalk toward the church near where Sunny's Boarding House stood. Would she recognize anyone else at the service? Would Sunny or Beth be there?

When they got to the church grounds, Caroline waved to a group of girls. "There's Emma. I'll see you after the service."

"You make sure you go sit with your grandmother."

"I will." When Caroline reached the girls, they all hugged.

"She has a lot of friends in town, doesn't she?" Abigail watched Caroline giggle and laugh with the group.

"She does." Lucas watched his daughter for a few minutes, then turned to Abigail. "I wish we could get into town more. I know she gets lonely at the ranch."

"From what I've seen, she's pretty well-adjusted for a girl her age, but it's true, girls need friends to talk with."

Lucas turned. "I know you're not one of her young friends, but having you on the ranch might help."

"I hope she feels that way." Just as with all the other conversations she'd had with her boss, she detected more to his words than what he said. Was he not happy with her lessons? Was she not living up to what he had imagined?

This was not the time or the place to ask if he had

problems with her performance, so she simply smiled and turned her attention to his mother.

Grandmother Fletcher, who stood under her blue, ruffled parasol, talked with several women. "Ladies, I'd like to introduce Miss Abigail Cook, Caroline's new governess. She's joined us all the way from Boston."

One of the ladies stuck out her gloved hand. "It's so nice to have you in the area. We heard talk you had come in for the teaching job in Independence, but it had been taken."

Abigail shook the lady's hand. Amazed that the woman had heard about her filled position, she simply smiled. "Yes, that was disappointing, but being on the Fletcher Ranch has been a blessing."

"My name is Mrs. Walton and this is Mrs. Stafford. I'm sure we'll see you after the service."

Abigail shook the other lady's hand. "It's nice to meet both of you."

"We'd better get inside. Pastor Smith will be using us as the subject of his sermon if we walk in late." Mrs. Fletcher called to Caroline and started toward the church door.

Abigail followed, but realized Lucas had not. She turned. "Are you coming?"

"No, I have some things to do."

She couldn't imagine what he had to do in town on a Sunday morning, but, like other subjects, that was none of her business. "Then I will see you after the service."

"I'll be here. I wouldn't miss the social afterwards. I'm not sure how so much food materializes, but tables will be loaded with enough food to feed everyone in the valley. Enjoy the service." He tipped his hat and walked away.

Abigail headed inside a small, white-washed church with a tall steeple. Wooden benches lined both sides of the building. She found Mrs. Fletcher and Caroline and squeezed in by them. As she looked around, she saw Bonita sitting with a group of ladies across the aisle. Behind them Abigail recognized Beth from the mercantile. She made a mental note to find her after the service.

A young man, slender, and quite handsome with thick brown hair, stepped to the pulpit. He smiled at his congregation, then asked everyone to rise and turn their hymnals to the first song. As the first notes of the piano floated through the church, tears flooded Abigail's eyes. The music reminded her of being in church with her mother and father in Boston. Would she ever be able to experience those moments again with her parents, and how would they act if that opportunity arose?

She squeezed her eyes remembering the past few years. She and her father had always been close until she chose to go away to finish her education. He ranted and raved and swore his daughter would not go to another city alone. When she left against his wishes, her mother hugged her, but her father simply nodded. For the next few years, she studied hard hoping he'd be proud of her accomplishments. After receiving her teaching certificate, she lived under his roof, but their relationship suffered. He didn't want his daughter working, always saying the women in the Cook family didn't need to labor outside the home. Only when she'd agreed to marry Mr. Baker did he become the father he once was.

Abigail concentrated on the hymn, but the horrible argument she and her father had when she broke off the engagement filled her head. She could see nothing but her father's face and hear his nasty words. She looked down at the hymnal, then up to heaven. *Please, God, forgive me for causing my parents such pain and disappointment.*

The song ended, pulling her back to her presence in church. Pastor Smith began the service by introducing several new members of the congregation who had settled in Independence and two families who would leave on wagon trains in the following week.

"Is there anyone else new?"

Mrs. Fletcher stood. "Our new governess, Miss Abigail Cook, has joined us today. She's from Boston."

Everyone clapped. Pastor Smith nodded and smiled at her.

Embarrassed to have been singled out in the service, Abigail nodded and hoped the rest of the service would go smoothly.

Pastor Smith spoke about forgiveness. Once again Abigail thought about her father. Had he ever forgiven her for not marrying? How did he expect her to give up years of education and settle for being a stay-at-home wife in a loveless marriage? That's not what she wanted out of life. She loved children and sharing what she'd learned. Breaking off her engagement with her fiancé had been best. She and Mr. Baker would've been unhappy. If only he had understood and not retaliated. She shook her head and listened to Pastor Smith's words about forgiveness. Would she ever be able to forgive Mr. Baker for what he had done?

After the service, Abigail followed Mrs. Fletcher out the door. Pastor Smith grabbed her hand and personally welcomed her to the community and to his church. "I certainly hope I get to see you in church often, Miss Cook."

"Thank you, Pastor Smith. I'll be here whenever the Fletcher family can travel into town."

"I know you'll enjoy the social. Our ladies do a wonderful job with the food."

She said her goodbyes and looked around for the Fletchers. Douglas talked with two young ladies away from his family. She smiled. He was quite the eligible bachelor. Another beautiful lady stood next to Victor and the rest of the Fletcher family. Assuming she was Victor's wife Abigail headed toward the group but stopped when she felt a tap on the shoulder.

"Abigail Cook, I remember you from my store. I knew it was you when Mrs. Fletcher introduced you during service."

Abigail turned to find Beth from the mercantile. She grabbed Beth's hand. "Yes, I saw you in church and wanted to talk with you. I want to thank you for being so sweet the day I arrived in Independence. Your smile made me feel so welcome. It's exactly what I needed."

"Good. I could tell you were not in the best of states. I'm glad everything worked out for you. I hope you can get to town again so we can visit."

Abigail doubted she'd ever have that opportunity, but she told her she would, then walked toward the Fletchers.

"And you must be Miss Cook." The lady talking with Mrs. Fletcher stepped next to her and hugged her. "I'm Betty Sanchez, Victor's wife. Welcome to Independence. Victor has talked a lot about you."

"Thank you. I've only been here a few weeks, but the Fletchers have made me feel at home, and Caroline is such a bright student. I love working with her."

Caroline and the Sanchez boys ran toward a group of other teens. "They miss their cousins." Betty took Abigail's hand. "Let's go see what kind of food we have today."

Three long tables covered with baskets and bowls of food stood under several large oak trees. As the ladies pulled away the linens covering the food, the aroma made Abigail's stomach growl. She followed her group and filled her plate with fried chicken, beef slices, beans, and sliced tomatoes.

"I hope I don't have too much food. I want to save space for a piece or two of those beautiful cakes." Abigail realized that Lucas had joined them. He threw a blanket on the ground away from the crowd, then went back to fill his plate. Finally, after talking with several people, he and Victor came to their group and sat.

Pastor Smith got everyone's attention. "Please bow your heads and let's bless this food." Afterwards, he headed to their group.

"Lucas, I missed you in church once again. You know we always have a seat for you."

"I'm aware, Pastor. I had some business to attend to."

"Certainly." Pastor smiled at everyone but took a little

longer to pull his gaze away from Abigail.

Feeling her face blush, she smiled, then concentrated on her food.

When the pastor stopped at another blanket of parishioners, Mrs. Fletcher grinned. "Our Pastor Smith has his eye on our new governess."

Abigail's face burned even redder. "Mrs. Fletcher, what a thing to say. He is simply being friendly and welcoming as all pastors should be."

"You could've fooled me." Mrs. Fletcher took a big bite and smiled.

Abigail wanted to vanish into the ground. She wasn't one to get embarrassed easily, but being singled out by the pastor had done just that. She glanced in her boss's direction. He took a huge bite of bread, then watched with a frown as Pastor Smith walked from one group to another.

Betty and Mrs. Fletcher chattered about everything from the newest fabric the general store had gotten in to the jars of foods that were flying off the shelves.

"With all these new people in town, it's so hard to find anything at the store. They get things in and within minutes the shelves are empty."

"My late husband would be appalled at all of this activity in Independence." Mrs. Fletcher stared into her tin cup of water. Finally, she smiled. "He adored the quiet life on the ranch and hated coming into town even when the population was small. I doubt he would ever come to town now."

Lucas looked at his mother. "Dad was set in his ways, but he knew life as we know it on the ranch would one day have to change. He was always interested in the conversations of people from other areas of the world. In his heart he wanted to see the world beyond Independence."

Mrs. Fletcher eyed her son. "I agree, but he chose to stay on the ranch and work to keep it going. He was so dedicated."

"I'm sure he would've loved talking with Miss Cook about Boston." Lucas looked over at Abigail and smiled.

"And I wish I had had the opportunity to do just that. Mr. Fletcher must've been an interesting man."

Abigail listened to bits and pieces of their conversation about Mr. Fletcher but had little to contribute. She finished her meal in silence.

Finally, Lucas took his last bite and stood. "Would any of you ladies like a dessert? I'm heading in that direction."

"Would you mind if I walked with you? There are so many choices, I wouldn't know what to tell you to bring back." Abigail didn't wait for his answer. She got on her knees to push herself up.

"Certainly." He reached for her hand and helped her up. "The ladies around here are the best cooks along the Missouri River. You'll have quite a decision to make."

Still holding her hand, he took a step, then dropped it and stepped away from her.

Was he embarrassed to have held her hand? Should she have pulled hers away first? Being near this man unnerved her.

As they perused the selections of desserts, Pastor Smith walked up to them. "Miss Cook, you will love trying these desserts."

"They all look so wonderful. I had to come choose for myself." She picked up a thick piece of chocolate cake. "I haven't had this since I left Boston."

"I'd love to hear about your life in Boston sometimes. If you're ever in town and have some time, please stop by the church office."

Abigail smiled, knowing she'd never be in town alone, but she admitted she was flattered that such a handsome man wanted to talk with her.

Pastor Smith turned to Lucas. "I meant it when I said we always have a space for you in the church. I hope you'll join us one day."

"Thank you." Lucas nodded. "Have a good day, Pastor." He turned and walked away.

"I hope I haven't offended him." Pastor Smith let out a sigh. "I know a lot of widows and widowers have a hard time returning to God when they've lost their spouses. I feel sure he will come around."

Abigail watched Lucas walk to their blanket, carrying several desserts for himself and his mother. "I hope he does. He is such a good family man. I don't know a lot about him or his situation, but I can usually tell when a person has a good heart."

A young lady stepped up to her and the pastor. "Pastor Smith, can we drag you away for a moment. We need an opinion from someone with your knowledge."

"Certainly." He nodded to Abigail. "Again, we welcome you to our congregation." He followed the young woman who held onto his arm tightly.

Abigail made her way toward the blanket and was about to greet the two ladies whom she had been introduced before the service, but as their conversation floated her way, she stopped. Her hand flew to her mouth. They were talking about her.

"Disgraceful." Mrs. Walton had her hand on Mrs. Stafford's elbow and spoke near her ear, but the words were clear to Abigail. "How could a young single woman travel all that way alone? I wonder what happened to make to make such a journey without a companion."

"Some horrible scandal must have happened for her to do what she did. I'm surprised Mr. Fletcher would allow a woman like that to be alone with his daughter."

Abigail blinked, turned quickly and headed away from the two ladies. Heat inched up her neck. What did those two ladies know about her? She squeezed her eyes and fought back tears.

She wanted to be anywhere but here. How could she face this town again now that she knew what some of the people thought of her? Had anyone in the Fletcher family heard this gossip? Did they think bad of her for traveling alone?

Since she had no place to escape, she took a couple of minutes to calm herself, then headed toward the family. Her pleasant day shattered into a million pieces, but she had to hold her head up high. Having gotten control of her emotions, Abigail sat near Grandmother Fletcher. Lucas was not with her.

Betty came back from the dessert table carrying two small plates of pudding. "I brought some extra for Victor. He loves it, but I'd like to give you a scoop to taste."

Abigail offered her plate with chocolate cake still on it. "Thank you." Her throat muscles clinched. Would she be able to swallow?

"You're quite welcome." Betty sat down and picked up her pudding, then after taking a couple of bites, placed a hand on Abigail's arm. "Our pastor is quite eligible bachelor. I think he'd like to get to know you better."

Again, Abigail felt her face flush. "He's simply being a welcoming pastor."

Both Betty and Mrs. Fletcher raised their eyebrows. "We don't think so." Mrs. Fletcher spoke but she wasn't smiling. "He is certainly a nice looking man and a wonderful person. He'd make any woman a fabulous husband, but there are other single men around our town and our ranches. Don't jump at the first man who is taken by you."

"Grandmother Fletcher, I don't know what to say. He's a very nice man, and yes, he's quite handsome, but I can assure you I am not looking for a husband."

"Every single woman is looking for a husband." Betty laughed. After finishing her pudding, she gathered her dirty dishes and stood. "It's so wonderful to have met you, Miss Cook. Please, get Grandmother Fletcher to town sometimes to visit. I'd love to show you around and would love the company."

Abigail watched as Betty hugged Mrs. Fletcher and put her head on her shoulders. When she stood, Abigail was shocked to see tears in Betty's eyes. She bit her lip, then turned away.

Mrs. Fletcher watched Betty walk toward Victor. "She misses her sister so much."

"Did her sister leave Missouri?"

Grandmother Fletcher turned to Abigail. "You don't know, do you? Her sister was Sarah, my Lucas's wife. He and Victor had been friends since school. They married sisters."

Abigail blinked, letting the information sink in. She reached out and took Mrs. Fletcher's hand. "I am so sorry. I had no idea. I know it must be hard on Mr. Fletcher and you to see Betty. Did she and Sarah look alike?"

"Oh, yes, Betty was two years older, but if you didn't know, you'd think they were twins." She looked up in the direction where Lucas had walked. "It's very hard on him to be near Betty."

"My heart goes out to him and to Caroline." Abigail looked at her boss in a new light. She knew he had been widowed, but now that she'd seen Betty, her heart ached for him.

The Fletcher family said goodbyes to everyone. After Lucas shook Victor's hand, he turned to Betty and put his arms around her shoulders and pulled her close. For a long moment, he buried his head in her hair, then quickly stepped away, turned and headed back to the buggy without saying a word to anyone.

Mrs. Fletcher, still sitting on the blanket, swiped her hand across her eyes. "Would you give an old lady a hand getting up?" Mrs. Fletcher lifted a hand to Abigail.

"Certainly."

"My legs aren't as strong as they used to be."

"Grandmother Fletcher, you're in wonderful shape. I can't believe all you do. Sitting on the ground is hard for any of us so don't apologize for not being able to hop right up."

"You're sweet." Mrs. Fletcher touched Abigail's arm. "I'm so glad you were able to join us today. I hope we can get back to town soon. I'd love for you to get to know the town's people. You'd like them."

Abigail smiled though she wanted to blurt out about the two women who were talking about her. She didn't, of course, so she walked quietly next to Mrs. Fletcher toward the buggy.

Being in town with the Fletchers had given Abigail an opportunity to learn a lot more about the Fletcher family and their association with the people of Independence. The Fletchers were a well-respected family, and she was so grateful to be part of them. If only she had not heard the harsh words of gossip, her day would've been perfect.

She closed her eyes and clenched her hands. How many of the women in town had talked about her situation? Most of these women were satisfied to be wives and mothers and not to work outside the home. She wished she could be like them, but she wasn't or at least she wasn't when this new path of her life had started. Were her feelings still the same? Did she still feel the need to be so independent? She'd gotten her education. She'd refused to marry someone she didn't love. She'd survived everything that had been thrown at her. Now would God show her how to find happiness and maybe settle down with a family one day? Is that what she wanted?

She looked at Lucas Fletcher sitting in the front of the buggy handling the reins. The more she learned about her boss, the more she understood why he acted as he did. He still loved his wife deeply. She raised her face to the heavens. Would she ever find a man who would love her the same way Lucas loved Sarah?

The sun inched its way toward the horizon as they neared the ranch. Even though darkness had not set in, everyone disappeared into his or her own world. She returned to her cabin and dressed for bed. Events of the day swirled around her head. She picked up her journal and her pen and ink. Maybe writing down her feelings would help her understand all that had taken place today.

I met some friendly people at church today, as well as the in-laws of my boss. His wife's sister is beautiful and the affection they showed to each other was heartfelt. Now I have an idea of what Caroline's mother looked like.

She lowered her pen. Sarah must've been gorgeous. Immediately, feelings of self-doubt swept over her. She'd never felt beautiful, didn't have the desire to keep up with fashion trends, and never felt comfortable around the young men in Boston. Sarah Fletcher must have been the total opposite. No wonder Lucas was stand-offish with her. In his presence she called him Mr. Fletcher, but in her mind she thought about him as Lucas. She wondered how he'd feel if she slipped and called him by his first name.

Under the covers she stared at the ceiling as the words of the two ladies in town came back to her. All the way home in the buggy, their remarks plagued her and now in the quiet of her room, their words resounded over and over. Embarrassed and hurt, she squeezed her eyes and demanded her brain to think about something else, but the words remained. Would she feel the same way had she been in their shoes? She hoped not especially about someone she didn't know. Her own father showed the same resentment to her choices in life.

Once more she sat up and picked up her pen.

Grandmother always told me to be my own self as long as it didn't go against God's teachings.

She stopped writing, closed her eyes, and prayed she'd find her place in this world.

CHAPTER SIX

The next morning, Lucas rode along the fence line several miles from the house. Normally his ranch hands did the job of checking fences, but after talking with Victor on Sunday he wanted make sure the back acreage and his cattle were okay. Victor told him about rustlers coming up from across the river stealing cattle from the outlying ranches. So far, Lucas had seen no signs his property or cattle had been involved. He would talk with his foreman to make sure all of his hands kept an open eye for anything suspicious.

"What's this world coming to?" He mumbled as he got off Charger and tightened a fence wire. Strangers constantly passed through his property heading to Independence to make their way to the California gold rush. Most of them respected his private property, but some damaged his fences and never put them back. Now with cattle rustlers in the area no rancher could let down his guard.

As he got on Charger, he saw a rider coming his way in the distance. Immediately he checked his rifle and gun to make sure they were loaded and within reach, but as he watched, he realized the man was Juan, one of his ranch hands. He eased Charger in the man's direction.

Juan stopped his horse alongside of Lucas. "Señor

Fletcher, Mr. Mason asked me to find you. The men found a cow dead in the west pasture."

"Dead? Was it shot?"

"No. It looks like an animal attack."

"I heard there was a family of lynx not far from here." Lucas shook his head. "Add wild animals to the rustlers and emigrants."

"Si, but we heard a mountain lion has been seen around here."

"A mountain lion? I thought we'd seen the last of them. We'll have to be on high alert until things calm down. I have this last fence line to check. If you'll finish for me, I'll ride out to the west pasture." He tipped his hat. "Thanks for riding out."

"Si, señor."

Lucas turned Charger toward the pasture and hurried off. He cherished his cattle. They had kept his family fed and affluent for the last several generations. He and Douglas would do everything in their power to keep rustlers and wild animals from harming them and crazy Forty-Niners from messing with his fences as they crossed his land.

By the time he reached the western pasture, his foreman already had his men butchering the young cow. The kill appeared to be very recent and the cool night air had kept the meat from spoiling. Nothing was wasted on the ranch. The area where the animal attacked the cow was cut away and not used, but the other meat was salvaged. Even the hide was stripped. One of his men was a master tanner and would make the hide into something useful for the men.

Lucas examined the portion of the cow that had been attacked. The downward strokes of the claw marks made it clear it had been a big cat attack. He shook his head. "We need to find this animal. We don't have enough men to watch every cow on the ranch, much less the horses and our families." Lucas looked around the range. "This cat will definitely be back. We'll get some men out here immediately to find him."

With more instructions to his foreman, Lucas headed back to the house. He'd been out on the fence line since early this morning. He had other details to take care of before he ate a light lunch.

Thinking about dining with his family made him remember yesterday's social after the church service. Caroline and his mother were thrilled to see some of her friends, but how did Abigail feel? What did she think about the people she met at the service and about Pastor Smith, who seemed to give her a lot of attention? He should be happy for her to make friends in town and possibly have a suitor, but he wasn't sure he was. He pushed thoughts of the pastor away and thought about Betty. Being near her tore at his heart, but today, even though he had to fight tears from his eyes, he did better. Maybe he was learning to accept life without Sarah.

He squeezed his legs against Charger's side. "Let's go, boy."

The wind cleared his mind as he rode, except for thoughts of Abigail. He smiled remembering how she enjoyed the food at the social. Each time they'd eaten together, Abigail openly showed her love of a good meal. Sarah had been a tiny lady and a dainty eater. Abigail wasn't much bigger than Sarah, but she loved to eat. He enjoyed watching her at dinner. In fact, if he was serious, he'd admit there was a lot he liked about the lady from Boston. She was smart, interesting to talk with, and he couldn't deny she was beautiful.

Admitting that fact sent a wave of guilt through his body. Could he ever look at another woman without feeling he was turning his back on Sarah?

* * * *

"Miss Cook, would you like to ride with me today after we finish our lessons?" Caroline looked up from her book with sparkling eyes and raised eyebrows.

"Thank you for asking, but I'm not very good with horses."

"Did you have horses in Boston?"

"Our family did have a carriage with several beautiful horses, but they stayed at the stables and were taken care of by the men there. I never had any contact with them. I did get on a horse once when our family took an outing away from the city. We visited a relative who lived on a farm and he put me on a horse." She giggled remembering how awkward she must've looked.

"Did you ride?"

"Not really. My cousin led me around a corral. I did enjoy the ride, and I didn't fall off, but that was my only experience. So, I should probably decline your offer."

Caroline stood up. Her eyes shone with excitement.

"I could teach you. We could practice here at the house and then when you learn, we can ride. Our ranch is beautiful. I go to a stream on the other side of the hill behind the house. It's my favorite place in the whole world."

"You ride alone?"

Caroline shrugged. "I do. Father doesn't like me to, but I'm not taking someone just to watch me. If you were with me, he would approve."

"But isn't it dangerous alone? What about wild animals? Aren't you afraid?"

"I've never had a problem. I saw a mountain cat one day, but he was in a tree and he didn't do anything. My horse didn't like him, but no one was hurt." Caroline sat back down and picked up a pen to practice her handwriting. "Will you think about letting me teach you to ride? We have lots of old horses that are very gentle."

Abigail laughed. "If you promise to put me on a really old, slow horse, maybe we can have a lesson or two."

Caroline clapped. "Today. Let's start today as soon as we finish our lessons."

By four o'clock, Abigail walked out of her cabin

wearing a simple, full cotton skirt she hoped would allow her to sit on a horse. Caroline would be in boy's trousers, but Abigail didn't own anything like that. She looked down at the skirt she had on. Maybe she could make it into a riding skirt if she ever learned to ride a horse.

She closed the door and stood for a moment. "What am I doing?" But as soon as the words came out, she knew she should learn anything to help her cope with life on a ranch. "I can do this. I can do this." She grimaced as she headed toward the barn and walked through the two huge doors. Caroline stood inside one of the stalls. "You're here?"

Caroline worked on a strap hanging from a saddle that sat on a huge speckled white horse. "I am. I wanted to start getting the horse ready for you."

Abigail blinked. "Is that the horse you want me on?"

"Yes, her name is Sugar. She's old and very, very gentle."

"But she's so big. How will I ever get up on her?"

Caroline looked from Abigail to the horse and scratched her head. "I guess you'll just step in the stirrup like I do and swing your leg over. That's the only way I know how."

Abigail bit her bottom lip. "Oh, dear, I don't know. Maybe this isn't such a good idea."

"No, Miss Cook, you promised. You have to learn so we can ride together. Please, try. I'll help you."

Abigail inched her way toward the horse.

"Here, pat her on the head. She'll love you for that."

Abigail reached up and touched the horse's forehead, but when the horse lifted its head, she jumped back.

Caroline laughed. "She's not going to hurt you. She told you she liked you rubbing her head."

Wringing her hands together, Abigail stepped next to the horse again and touched its side.

"See, she likes you. Let me show you how to get the saddle ready. I already have it on her, but I want to show you what straps you should check." Caroline pointed out each strap, what its purpose was, and how tight it should be pulled. "If you don't put the saddle on correctly, you and the saddle could wind up on the ground." She giggled.

"You're a good teacher, but again, how am I going to get up there?"

Caroline looked around and found a bucket in one of the stalls. She turned it upside down by Sugar. "Now, hold the saddle horn, put your left foot in the stirrup, then swing your right leg over the horse." With no effort or strain, Caroline showed her how to do it. "See, it's simple." She jumped down. "You try it."

Determined she could do this, Abigail swallowed. She raised her skirt slightly, placed her left foot in the stirrup, then swung her right leg halfway up the horse. She slid back down to the floor. On the second try, she managed to swing a little higher, but her leg didn't go over. "This isn't going to work."

"What are you ladies doing?" Lucas stepped into the barn.

Abigail snapped her head around.

"I'm teaching Miss Cook how to ride, but we have to get her on the horse first."

Lucas laughed.

His deep chuckle sent warmth through Abigail's body. Had she heard him laugh since she'd been on the ranch?

He took several long steps toward Abigail and Caroline. "Maybe I can give you a hand. The first time up is always the hardest. Eventually, you'll be able to swing up on your own, and you'll wonder how you ever had trouble doing it."

"You think so? I'm not so sure."

Lucas looked at Abigail, then looked at Sugar. "Would you allow me to lift you?"

Abigail swallowed. "Lift me?"

"Just to give you a little push to get your leg over the horse."

Thinking about having Lucas's big hand on her body,

Abigail big her lip, then nodded. "Tell me what to do."

Lucas hesitated. "Get back up on the bucket and put your left foot in the stirrup. I'll help you balance. When you're ready, I'll give you a lift and you swing your right leg over the horse."

Abigail nodded. "You make it sound so easy."

Again, a chuckle escaped from her boss. "It's not hard. I promise." His words were soft, almost a whisper.

She lifted her skirt slightly and placed her foot on the bucket. Before she could tell him she was ready, his hands clasped her waist.

"Now, lift and throw your leg over."

How can I think or act or do anything with your hands on me?

Caroline stepped near them. "Miss Cook, you can do this."

"Yes, of course." She found her voice, blew out a breath, and lifted her right leg. Even with Lucas lifting her, her leg only made it halfway up the horse. Instead of landing on the saddle, she fell back into his arms. He pulled her away from the horse and off the bucket and held her close to his hard body.

"You're okay. Get your breath and let's try it again."

Get my breath? Saddle a horse? How can I do anything being this close to you? She shook her head. "Mr. Fletcher, this is hopeless. I'm a city girl. I can't ride."

"You're not in the city anymore. If you're to live on my ranch, you have to know how to ride. It isn't a fun pastime. It's a necessity." Still holding her close, he turned her.

Abigail was inches away from him. His warm breath touched her cheek.

"You never know when riding will mean the difference between life and death." He let her go.

She stumbled backwards against the horse but caught herself before she slid to the floor. "You're right, of course, but I'm not sure I have the dexterity to do this."

"I guarantee you can do this. Now, let's try again."

With a silent prayer to make her body cooperate, she nodded. "I'm ready, or at least I think I am."

Again, Lucas chuckled. He placed both of his hands on her waist. Whenever you're ready, I have you. You won't fall."

This time Abigail forced her body to move. She swung her leg almost over the horse, and with Lucas's help, she ended up in the saddle with her head lying against the horse's mane.

"There. See. You did it." Lucas stepped close to Sugar and patted her. "Good girl." He looked up at Abigail. "You have to sit up straight in the saddle, Miss Cook."

Abigail inhaled, straightened up, then looked down to make sure the skirt hadn't exposed too much of her leg. "It's so high up here."

"It is, but when you're out on the ranch, you'll be able to see beautiful things from your vantage point." He bent and placed his hands on her bare ankle. "Let's get you in the stirrup."

How could she think? No man had ever touched her foot or ankle. A chill ran down her spine, but, of course, her boss had no idea how she felt. He gripped her ankle and slid her foot in the stirrup, then walked around the horse and did the same with her right foot.

"Are you okay?"

Abigail looked at Lucas. "I think so."

Lucas reached across her and grabbed the reins and placed them in her hand. "You have to hold onto these because what you do with the reins and with your legs will tell the horse what to do." He looked at Caroline. "Miss Cook is all yours. Let's see what kind of a teacher you are." He stepped away from Sugar, then headed toward the barn door.

Caroline started explaining how to use her legs to give the horse instructions. Abigail listened but was all too conscious of the man walking away from her. Why was she reacting like this? Never had a man affected her in this way. Of course, she didn't have much experience with men. Even her fiancé had never sent her nerves in a flutter as Lucas Fletcher did.

She turned and listened to Caroline. Could she remember all her student told her?

"Let's start by walking around slow." Caroline looked up and smiled big.

Her enthusiasm prompted Abigail to hold on tighter and figure out how to ride this horse. From her perch high above the ground, she concentrated on sitting up straight and not leaning from one side of the saddle to the other. The ground was a long way down.

"I can do this. I can do this." Once more she repeated the statement that kept her going throughout her ordeal crossing the country, but as her body slid from one side of the saddle to the next, she wasn't so sure she could.

CHAPTER SEVEN

Lucas walked toward the big house, hoping to have some quiet time to work on the ranch books and to figure out what else he could do to protect his family and animals from the lion or whatever attacked his cow. Several men from Independence teamed with him a year ago to push the lions back into the mountains and to eliminate the ones that refused to give up their territory. Now, he wasn't so sure they had been successful.

Before stepping onto the porch, he caught a glance of Caroline leading Sugar and Miss Cook into the corral area. He stopped and took in the image of his daughter's governess struggling to sit on top of Sugar. He smiled. Riding was second-nature to him. His dad had plopped him on top of a saddleless horse when he could barely walk, but he imagined it would be difficult for someone who had never been around such a big animal.

Thinking about helping her into the saddle made him pause. Lifting her body up, then placing her foot into the stirrup brought back feelings he hadn't had in a long time—feelings of wanting to protect a woman and to hold her in his arms.

He shook his head. Thoughts like that did nothing but cause a man trouble. Look what it did with Sarah. So much for protecting someone you loved. He could, however, protect Caroline by not getting too close to her governess. If Miss Cook decided to leave Missouri, his daughter would be his primary concern. He didn't want Caroline to suffer the loss of someone else in her life.

He stomped up the last step and pulled his gaze away from Abigail on Sugar. Earlier he'd left the barn abruptly to free his mind. He could pull himself away from her now.

"Good afternoon, son. How was your day?" His mother shuffled across the terrazzo tiled entryway, heading to the kitchen.

"The day was good. I wanted to find that lion that killed the cow yesterday, but he's smarter than we thought. He didn't show himself to my men. I have several out there this afternoon. They'll stay out tonight. Maybe he'll get careless."

His mother waited for him at the kitchen door. When he reached her, he put his arm around her thin shoulders and gave her a quick hug.

"I hate to see a beautiful animal killed, but I understand you have to do what's necessary." Mrs. Fletcher let out a huge sigh.

"I've told the men to first try pushing him away from the ranch, but I'm not so sure it will work. We'll do everything we can to keep him alive, I promise."

She smiled. "Thank you." She looked around the room. "Where is Caroline? Her lessons are bound to be over. I hope she's not riding out alone."

"No, not today. I'm happy to report she's teaching Miss Cook how to ride. Caroline has her up on Sugar right now."

His mother clapped her hands. "Oh, that's wonderful. I'll have to go on the porch to watch. Caroline needs someone to ride with her. I'll feel so much better if she doesn't ride alone."

Lucas nodded. "I agree, especially with all these people traveling through Independence and now this lion." He didn't mention cattle rustlers Victor warned him about. "I'm heading to my office to do some work before dinner."

"And I'll be on the porch to see what kind of teacher my granddaughter is. I hope you and Douglas won't be late for dinner."

"We'll be there early."

Lucas headed toward his office, but instead of sitting behind the huge mahogany desk that had been in his family for three generations, he stepped toward the window. He pushed aside the heavy dark green curtain and looked toward the corral. An unexpected wave of disappointment hit him. Caroline and Miss Cook had moved across the corral and were in an area he could not see. With a sigh, he closed the curtain and sat in his desk chair. He glanced at his leather-covered ledger. Usually he couldn't wait to work on the numbers for the ranch, but this afternoon, he pulled the ledger closer and simply rubbed his finger across the embossed cover.

Where was his business sense and drive? Why was he feeling as if something wasn't right in his life? Working the ranch, keeping everything organized, and making sure his family was healthy, safe and happy kept him busy from daylight to well into the night. As long as he stayed busy and worked hard, he could fall into bed at night satisfied that he'd done his best to keep the ranch running and exhausted enough he'd go into a deep sleep without staring into the dark thinking about Sarah.

Losing Sarah had taken away his joy with the ranch. Going off to war with Victor gave him something to keep his mind busy. Even when the war ended, he couldn't force himself to return to a home without the woman he loved. He worked with the troops longer than necessary until news that his father had died reached him. Now, as long as he worked hard every minute of every day, he was able to keep himself from tumbling into the deep black hole he'd crawled in for so long. His plan worked. He'd survived Sarah's death, a war, and now he struggled to make up for lost time with his daughter.

Things had been going great. Why had the discontent begun to creep back into his life? He refused to believe Miss Cook's appearance at the ranch was the reason, but why was he feeling so misplaced and confused?

Before opening the ledger, he got up and looked out the window once more. Caroline and Miss Cook were still not in sight. He turned to his desk. Fletcher Ranch needed his full attention. Watching a lady from the East try to stay up on a horse didn't take priority, but he couldn't deny she had caught his attention from the first moment he'd helped her out of the street in Independence.

Could he pretend she hadn't? What difference would it make if she had? He felt sure she'd return to her easy city life when the harshness of living on a ranch sunk in.

Neither he nor his daughter needed to get too attached to the lady.

* * * *

Riding back into the safety of the barn was a welcomed relief for Abigail. Matthew met them at the door and led Abigail near Sugar's stall. He held out his hands and helped her slide off of Sugar.

"That was fantastic, Miss Cook." Caroline stood away. "You're learning fast."

"I'm not so sure. With Matthew's help I did manage to get down, but I don't think I could've gotten down alone." She looked at the young man. "I'm thankful you were in the barn." She laughed and stepped away from Sugar. "That's a long way up there."

"Yes, ma'am, horses are tall creatures, but knowing how to ride is necessary."

"Of course. Mr. Fletcher said the same thing. I will try hard to master the art of riding."

Matthew looked at Caroline and laughed. "I've never heard anyone call riding an art."

"To me it is. It's not something all people can do, and it certainly takes talent."

He shrugged. "Yes, ma'am, I know you will be able to do this." The boy smiled at Abigail, then with a furtive gaze, glanced at Caroline.

Caroline giggled and put her head down.

Abigail looked from Caroline to Matthew. Was the boy flirting with Caroline, and was Caroline enjoying his attention? She made a mental note to talk about boys and men in her next session with Caroline. Lucas had mentioned helping Caroline with feminine endeavors, though she wasn't sure he'd include the topic of boys.

Giving Caroline advice about the male gender made her roll her eyes. What did she know about men and boys? She'd fumbled through her engagement with William Baker, the only man with whom she had ever spent a lot of time. That relationship turned into a disaster. Earlier she'd almost lost her breath when Lucas helped her up into the saddle. She had no experience to share with Caroline. Maybe she'd talk with Grandmother Fletcher and get some suggestions.

"Miss Cook, do you have time to help me take off a saddle? It's a good way to learn. If you don't, Matthew can help me." Caroline stood near Matthew and bit her lip.

Abigail knew Caroline wanted Matthew to help her, but she also knew she should not leave the girl alone with him. "I would like to see how to unsaddle a horse, but Matthew would be more of a help than I will be." She looked at Matthew, who looked as if he was swallowing a smile. "Can you stay to help?"

"Yes, ma'am, I'd be glad to help Caroline—and you." Now he let the smile fill his face.

Caroline had the reins in her hand, but she handed it to Matthew. He led the horse to her stall with Caroline close behind. Abigail followed.

For the next ten minutes, Matthew and Caroline together unsaddled Sugar. Abigail stood back just far enough to give them space, but close enough to hear and see what they were doing. Several times, Caroline remembered her teacher still there and explained the correct way to do something, but she never stepped too far away from Matthew.

Even though she was just thirteen Caroline seemed to enjoy Matthew's attention. Thinking about own life at Caroline's age, she remembered wanting nothing more than to explore any book she could get her hands on. One of her teachers encouraged her to borrow as many of her books as she wanted. She then introduced her to several other adults with private libraries in their homes. Abigail remembered thinking she was the luckiest girl in Boston.

At seventeen Abigail realized her few female acquaintances from school were all involved with young men and all had been introduced at elaborate coming-out balls. She didn't want any part of that life. By eighteen, she had already applied to the seminary and had been accepted. Her father was appalled. Her mother cried, afraid their daughter would never marry. The family would be the talk of the town and be pitied because they would have a spinster as a daughter and would never have grandchildren.

Abigail never understood their dismay. She didn't want a family, at least not back then. After leaving school with her teaching certificate, she considered becoming more social and possibly letting a gentleman court her, but she never seemed to have the time or the interest. Her goal was to have a fulltime teaching position. As a young girl before college, she didn't know one male acquaintance she'd want to marry, and circumstances had not changed after she returned home. Agreeing to marry Mr. Baker was done more to please her family than to bring happiness into her life.

Watching Caroline interact with Matthew opened her eyes. The girl fluttered her eyes and asked the boy how to do things with the saddle. Abigail hid a smile trying to form. The girl knew more about saddles than that boy would ever know, but she knew how to make Matthew feel good about himself. Maybe she needed to get some advice from Caroline when it came to men.

* * * *

That evening, Abigail hurried into the dining room after everyone had been seated. "I'm so sorry I took so long to get ready for dinner. Riding took a toll on me."

"But you did so great." Caroline looked at her father. "Before we quit the lesson, she handled Sugar all by herself."

Lucas looked directly at Abigail. "You rode out of the corral?"

"Oh, heavens, no." Having Lucas look into her eyes confused her as much as sitting on Sugar. "I'm lucky I stayed upright riding in circles with Caroline walking alongside of me."

Caroline sat up straight in her chair. "But you didn't fall off or anything."

Abigail hadn't seen Caroline this excited since she'd come to the ranch. "You're so right. I actually stayed in the saddle. You're a very good teacher."

Bonita and Carmella carried in dishes from the kitchen. Caroline looked from her father to her grandmother. "I want to say grace tonight, but where is Uncle Douglas?"

Lucas answered as he sat lifted his glass. "He had to go to town. He's staying the night."

Caroline shrugged, then lowered her head. "Thank you, God, for this food we're about to eat. Thank you for Miss Bonita and Miss Carmella because they are such good cooks."

Abigail smiled.

"And thank you for letting Miss Cook try to learn to ride. We're going to have fun together. Amen."

Caroline's words warmed Abigail's heart. "Your prayer was so thoughtful. Thank you for including me. Now, I hope I can live up to your expectations."

"You will. I can tell you will be riding alone in no time."

Caroline's eyes sparkled.

"I'm not so sure about that, but I promise to do my best."

Caroline jabbered about what she wanted to show Abigail, but Lucas said nothing. Before Carmella brought in the last dishes, Abigail glanced at him. He didn't seem amused listening to Caroline. Had she misunderstood him? Didn't he want her to work with Caroline in other areas besides books? She made a mental note to question him once more about his expectations when it came to his daughter.

Carmella placed a basket of bread on the table, and Abigail didn't hesitate to put some of everything on her plate. "This looks wonderful." She savored each and every bite, but made herself eat slowly. She might not be in civilized Boston, but she was still a lady. She placed her fork down and took a sip of water. As she put the glass down, she felt Lucas look in her direction.

Their gazes connected, but he quickly looked down at his plate and cleared his throat. "Miss Cook, I promised my daughter I'd ride with her to the stream tomorrow. We'd be honored if you'd join us. It would be good practice for you, and you'd get to see the ranch. Tomorrow is Saturday. I assume your day won't involve lessons with Caroline, but I don't want to intrude if you have other plans."

Abigail put down her fork. "I would love to see more of your ranch, but I'm not sure I'm ready to ride beyond the corral."

"We would both be with you. Unless you get experience on a horse, you'll never get your confidence."

Abigail grimaced and looked at Caroline.

"Please, Miss Cook, it will be so much fun to have you with us."

In spite of the fear that nipped at her heart, she nodded. "I'll go, but I can't promise I won't hold you two up."

"We will be in no hurry." Lucas picked up his fork and speared a huge piece of meat. Again there was no smile.

Abigail couldn't tell if his expression showed delight or hesitation. Did he feel obligated to ask his daughter's governess to ride with them, or did he really want to spend time with her?

And two big questions: Would she be able to stay upright on her horse, and how would she feel about being with her boss all day?

* * * *

Lucas told her he had some business to take care of in the early morning but asked her to be ready about ten. After breakfast the next day, she walked out of the big house and headed to her cabin. Lucas came out one of the barns followed by his foreman. They stood and talked by one of the corrals. Since he had not seen her on the porch, she sat in one of her big rockers as he talked with Mason. Lucas wore work clothes and stood with his legs apart and hands on his hips. Her breath hitched. She'd never encountered anyone like Lucas before she'd left her home. His good looks and refined manners contrasted with his ruggedness and hard-working lifestyle.

Until coming to the Fletcher Ranch, Abigail had no idea what it took to run a ranch, but now, little by little, she understood more about the hard work involved. Lucas usually began his day before she went to breakfast and, from what he'd say at dinner, he sometimes worked well into the night. Compared to living in Boston, life away from a city demanded hard work and dedication.

The two men laughed, then Lucas turned and headed around the barn. Thinking about life away from the city, she rocked a few more minutes. Everything was so different here. Would she ever fit in? If not, where would she go? Her father didn't want her back with the family. His ranting about the rumors Mr. Baker spread still hurt. Maybe she should have stayed to fight for her reputation, or maybe she should've been more understanding of what her father wanted for his family. Why was life so confusing? All the ladies she knew in Boston seemed to slide into their lives effortlessly. Why couldn't she?

With a long sigh, she walked into her cabin, wondering what she'd wear on her outing. Going on a ride with Lucas and Caroline made her jittery, but for the umpteenth time since leaving Boston, she whispered, "I can do this."

Several hours later, Abigail stepped through the doors of the empty barn wearing the same cotton skirt she'd worn the day before when she had her first lesson with Caroline.

She walked directly to Sugar's stall. "Hi, Miss Sugar, remember me? You let me ride you yesterday." Feeling brave, Abigail rubbed Sugar's head. "Please, let me get on your back today and stay upright." She rubbed her hand down Sugar's neck, looked toward the door to make sure no one had come in. "Lucas will be with us. I'd really hate to fall out of my saddle and have to be picked up. I'd be humiliated."

Just thinking about riding with her boss made her want to return to her cabin. "I'm sorry, Sugar. I can't do this." She stepped back and turned, but before she escaped, the barn door opened. Caroline and her dad stepped in. Letting out a huge sigh, she plastered a smile on her face. Caroline rushed toward her. With a nod in her direction, Lucas headed to Charger's stall.

"Miss Cook, you're here." Caroline rushed over. She wore the slacks she usually rode in.

Abigail looked down at her skirt and wished she had something else more appropriate to wear.

"Did Sugar remember you?"

"Yes, she let me pet her."

"That's a good start." Caroline unlatched the stall and stepped in by Sugar. "Come on out and let's get your saddle on."

Lucas grabbed a bridle and stepped into Charger's stall. Charger stomped his front hoof and nudged Lucas's hand. He rubbed the horse's neck. "You eager to take a ride, boy?"

Lucas laughed and put his arm around the horse's neck. "It's going to be a great day for a ride."

Standing while Caroline and Lucas worked with the horses, Abigail felt useless. She turned to Caroline. "Can I help with Sugar's saddle?"

"I was just going to ask you to do it. You have to learn."

"I do." She walked into the stall and hoped Sugar wouldn't step on her feet.

"Here, I'll help." Caroline positioned the bridle, then let Abigail fasten the strap around Sugar's neck. "You did it. Father, look. Miss Cook put the bridle on right."

Abigail glanced across the barn. Lucas had already thrown the saddle onto Charger, but he looked up and smiled. "That's a good start."

Abigail had hoped for more, but his compliment, as small as it was, would have to do.

Caroline slipped the saddle off its railing and tossed it over Sugar, then explained to Abigail which strap had to be fastened first.

Feeling inadequate but determined to do right, Abigail stretched her arm under Sugar's belly and pulled the strap. After fastening the first one, she worked on the others. Caroline left her alone as she headed to Honey Cup's stall.

With Charger walking close behind, Lucas walked up to Sugar's stall. "Do you mind if I check those straps?"

"Please." Abigail stepped back.

He tugged on each strap, all the time talking to Sugar. When he finished, he turned to Abigail. "You and Caroline did a good job. I didn't doubt my daughter's ability to show you what to do. I simply wanted to double check. A loose strap can scare anyone. I'd like for your first ride to be pleasant." He looked down at the dirt floor, then up at Sugar.

"I appreciate your checking. Thank you."

"Father, I'm ready." Caroline led Honey Cup to Sugar's stall.

Her dad let out a big breath and nodded. "That was fast."

He walked to Honey Cup and checked her straps.

"Father, I can put my saddle on correctly. I do it almost every day."

"I realize that, but I also know there is usually someone in the barn with you to check, or at least there should be." He patted her hair and smiled. "Let's get going."

As they walked their horses out of the barn, Carmella met them with a pouch.

"Thank you, Carmella. I'm sure whatever you packed for us will be perfect." He fit the pouch behind Charger's saddle, then effortlessly got up on the horse. Caroline did the same as they talked to one another.

Abigail eyed the tall horse. How would she ever get up?

Lucas turned. "I'm sorry. I forgot you might need some help." He turned Charger and when he was next to Sugar, jumped down. "Let me give you a hand."

"Thank you. She's so tall."

Lucas chuckled. "That she is."

Abigail placed her left foot into the stirrup and her hand on the saddle horn, but as she lifted her right leg over Sugar, she failed.

Before her foot reached the ground, Lucas placed both his hands on her waist and lifted. "Try now."

Determined, Abigail threw her leg up and over the saddle, but, like before, ended up leaning forward with her head on Sugar's mane.

"You okay?" Lucas stood by Sugar.

Hoping she'd stay upright, Abigail nodded.

"Now sit upright or Sugar won't know what to do."

She nodded, blew out a big breath, and sat up.

"That's it. Remember what my daughter told you yesterday. Use your legs to give the horse demands. You're in change. You need to let her know it."

"I'm sure Sugar is smarter than that. I'm sure she knows I have no idea what I'm doing."

Lucas ran a hand down Sugar's neck, then headed to

Charger. "Let's go, ladies."

Both Lucas and Caroline headed out the barn door. Abigail squeezed her legs and gave her command. Sugar followed the other two horses.

"Look at me. I'm doing it. Thank you, girl." She whispered and looked up to heaven. *And thank you, God.*

CHAPTER EIGHT

Lucas kept his eyes on the trail leading out across the ranch and into the valley, but he knew exactly where Abigail was at all times. Except for his mother and Caroline he didn't want to be responsible for the safety and happiness of another woman. He'd spent the better part of his adult life watching over Sarah and loved every minute. When she died, he knew he never wanted to live for another person. His daughter and mother were different. He'd give his life to protect them any day, but that was a different kind of love. He wasn't ready to open his heart to anyone else.

Lucas glanced at his daughter with her hair pulled back with her usual faded ribbon, but it didn't distract from her beautiful sun-touched skin. His heart swelled knowing she was his and Sarah's. Each day she looked more like her mother with the way she walked, her laughter, her eyes, and, of course, her hair. She would be as beautiful as Sarah one day.

He chuckled. Caroline might look like her mother, but she had not gotten the feminine side of Sarah. Sarah loved to sew and embroider. She loved beautiful dresses and having her hair adorned with ribbons and sassy hats. Caroline didn't like any of those things. She wanted to be outdoors with the men and the horses. She learned to shoot a gun when other little girls were still playing with dolls. He shook his head. She had a lot of him in her. He loved that she could out-ride and out-shoot most of his hired help, but he knew she would soon have to act like a lady or she would never find a husband.

That thought made him sit up straighter in the saddle. He frowned. He didn't want another male looking at his daughter, but he was a realist. She wouldn't stay his little girl forever. He shook his head. He needed to pay attention to the trail, but he had a hard time pulling his attention from the two females on his side.

Caroline, who rode between him and Abigail, pointed out the different trees, fence lines that marked specific fields, and the names of the men working on the fences. He couldn't hear what Abigail said, but her voice floated toward him and swirled around his head. He didn't want to be that conscious of his daughter's governess, but he wasn't sure what to do about it.

"Father, can we stop to rest. Miss Cook needs a break."

Lucas looked from Caroline to Abigail, who gave him a crooked smile. "Certainly. That oak tree will give us some shade." He headed in the direction of an open field where two large trees sat at the bottom of a slope. When he got there, he jumped off Charger, looped his reins on a low bush, and walked over to the governess. "May I help you down?"

Abigail bit her lip and nodded. "Yes, please."

Lucas held up both hands close to her body.

Abigail looked at the ground and grimaced.

"You can do it, Miss Cook, just like you did yesterday." Caroline ran next to her father.

Lucas swallowed hard as Abigail slid into his hands. When she got her foot on the ground, she pulled her left foot out of the stirrup and fell into Lucas's body. He held her around her slim waist until she got her balance.

"Thank you. I wouldn't have been able to do that without your help." She turned and faced him.

With the governess inches from his face, he felt her warm breath on his skin. Quickly, he backed up. "You'll be able to do that alone in no time." He looked around and rubbed a hand across his chin. "Caroline, take Sugar and your horse and tie them by Charger. I'll get us a drink." He had to get away from the lady.

He walked to Charger and took the time alone as he faced his horse to catch his breath. Being near Abigail made him jittery, uncertain of his movement. He needed a few minutes to settle his nerves. Finally, he pulled out a canteen and turned, expecting a sweet smile. Instead, she had walked near Caroline and talked quietly with her.

Relieved, Lucas found a log near one of the trees and sat down. Caroline and Abigail walked over and sat.

"This is a beautiful area. Are we still on your land?" Abigail straightened her skirt over her shoes.

"Yes, we won't leave my property anytime today. The stream isn't far from here. It's a small branch flowing from the Missouri River. It's been a major source of water for the Fletcher cattle since the beginning of the ranch when my great-great grandfather bought the land. We cherish the stream and keep it cleared. Where we'll go today is narrow and closest to the house." He handed her the canteen.

Abigail took it and drank. "Thank you. I didn't realize how thirsty I was. I can't wait to see the stream."

"As soon as you feel strong enough to ride, we'll head out." He stood up and headed to Charger. Tending to his horse was easier than talking to a strange, beautiful lady.

She definitely was beautiful, though he had the impression she didn't see herself that way, but was she a stranger? Abigail had been at his ranch for several weeks. She should not be considered a stranger, except for the fact that he had been avoiding her. He glanced at her and Caroline conversing easily and a tiny bit of envy slid across his chest. He turned back to Charger. "You doing okay, boy?" He rubbed the horse's nose. "I'm not so sure I am."

"Father, we're ready to get back on the horses. Miss Cook is eager to see the stream."

"Are you sure you're ready to get back up. We haven't been here but a few minutes."

Abigail walked to Sugar and rubbed her neck. "I'm okay. I just needed to stretch my legs a bit. As Caroline said, I really am excited to see the stream."

He nodded, not sure how he would feel about having the lady in his family's special place. Sarah had fallen in love with the stream the first time he'd brought her out. He and Sarah would slip away from the house and come to the stream alone, lying in the shade of the trees or sitting with their feet in the cold water. At the stream and in their cabin they'd share their innermost thoughts, something he had never done before and knew he could never do again with anyone else.

Now, he was bringing someone else to their stream to enjoy its beauty. Why had he encouraged Abigail to come?

* * * *

Determined to master the art of riding, Abigail put her foot into the stirrup, grabbed the saddle horn, and pulled herself up as high as she could. Her leg almost made it over the saddle. Before she slumped back to the ground, Lucas grabbed her waist and lifted her just enough to get her leg over.

Delighted that she'd almost made it up alone, she smiled down at her boss. "Thank you. I almost had it."

"And you will. Don't quit trying." He headed back to Charger.

Abigail sat up straight in the saddle and tilted her head. She hadn't expected the man to do cartwheels because she'd almost made it into the saddle, but he could've acted a little excited. She wanted to get to know the man as she had the rest of his family, but by his tone when he talked with her, she wasn't so sure it would ever happen.

"Ladies, let's go or we won't have time to enjoy the

stream." He nudged Charger past her without looking her way.

So why did you invite me to come if you can't be civil to me? Abigail frowned, wishing she could escape to her little cabin. All of a sudden spending the day at the stream didn't seem as appealing.

"Come on, Miss Cook. You're going to love the stream." Caroline rode past her.

"Okay, Sugar, let's go."

As they left the two trees, they headed into a valley lined with low trees and bushes along the trail and tall, magnificent trees behind them. Abigail spotted wild flowers in reds, pinks, and yellows. Wishing she could stop and pick some, she decided she and Caroline would ride out one day—after she could ride better, of course—just to spend the day picking flowers.

The ground suddenly leveled off and Abigail found herself in the middle of a fenced grass-covered area. Hundreds of head of cattle roamed the field.

"Are those long-horn cattle?"

Lucas turned in his seat. "They are. We have about a thousand head this year. We'll drive them up to Illinois at the end of the month."

Abigail slowed Sugar and stared at the cattle. She'd seen them at a distance as she came to the ranch, but this was as close as she'd gotten. "I'm amazed. They're so big and their horns are gigantic."

Lucas laughed. "That they are."

They rode into another level area shaded from the noonday sun by tall trees in a circular pattern. She took in the beauty around her, then realized that Caroline and Lucas had stopped. A gentle stream flowed near them.

"This is lovely. I've never seen anything this beautiful." Sitting on top of Sugar, Abigail could see beyond her riding companions to the stream flowing from what she assumed to be the north, but what did she know? She had no idea in what direction they had ridden.

"Miss Cook, this is my favorite spot in the entire world." Caroline slid off her horse easily. "Come on. Sugar will love grazing on this grass."

Abigail nudged Sugar near to Caroline. Lucas had already gotten off Charger and let him graze freely.

"I can help you get off, Miss Cook." Caroline stood close to Sugar and lifted her arms to Abigail.

"Thank you, Caroline, but I need to learn to do this myself." With a huge intake of air, she slid over Sugar's saddle and held on until her feet hit the ground. Thrilled that she'd gotten off alone, she turned to Caroline.

"You did it. I told you riding wasn't hard."

"It wasn't easy, but I'm getting better." Involuntarily, she looked toward Lucas, who had turned toward them.

He nodded. "Let the horses graze. I have a lunch for us to share." He untied the pouch from Charger's back. "I'm sure Carmella packed some great food." He pulled out a small blanket and spread it near the stream.

"Let's go see what Miss Carmella packed." Caroline took Abigail's hand and led her to the blanket.

Feeling like a child having to be shown every move, Abigail followed. Finally, she pulled her hand back. "This is just lovely."

Caroline had already plopped down on the blanket near her father, who unpacked food wrapped in cloth or packed in tin containers.

Abigail knelt down near her boss. "I'll be glad to help."

Lucas looked up. "I'll let you serve." He stood and backed away from the blanket.

Did the man think so little of her he didn't want to be near her? Hiding her hurt feelings, Abigail concentrated on the food. She spread out freshly made tortillas and rice, along with sliced tomatoes and a container of beans.

Caroline immediately grabbed a tortilla, piled vegetables and rice on it, but before she took a bite, she looked at her father. "We should say a blessing. Grandmother would want us to even though we're away from the house."

Lucas nodded and stepped close to his daughter. Caroline lowered her head and said a fast blessing for the food and for the beautiful day.

As soon as Caroline finished, Lucas grabbed a tortilla, piled it high, then took a big bite.

Abigail had the feeling it was not her boss's option to say the blessing and remembered at each meal someone else always said it. Was Lucas not a Christian? He didn't attend Sunday services with the family. Did something happen to tarnish his faith or had he always been stand-offish when it came to God? She remembered Pastor Smith saying some spouses had a hard time with their faith when they lost a partner. Was that his reason? So many questions. After being with the family for over three weeks, Abigail felt at home, but there was so much she didn't understand. Would she ever feel comfortable enough to ask the personal questions that needed answers?

After the meal, Caroline pulled off her shoes and rolled up her trouser legs. When she stepped into the stream, she jumped back. "Ouch, it's freezing." She looked at her father and laughed.

"You say that every time." Lucas laughed along with his daughter.

"It's okay. I can handle it." She bent over to search the bottom.

He looked at Abigail. "That stream originates in the Missouri river, but it cools as it descends the ridge. It'll be a little warmer by the middle of summer."

"It might be cold, but it's gorgeous. I'll settle for simply looking at it."

"Good choice."

Abigail helped Lucas pack the left-over food then sat back down on the blanket. With her skirt securely tucked close to her legs, she pulled them up and rested her elbows on them. Lucas leaned back with one elbow on the blanket and watched his daughter. Awkward silence surrounded them.

Abigail looked his way. "Caroline is so beautiful. She doesn't know it yet, but one day she'll be aware of her beauty."

Lucas finally looked at Abigail. "I hope you can help her in that respect. I want her to love the ranch and the animals, but, as I told you when I hired you, she needs help with her feminine attributes. Mother has worked with her, but Caroline shows no interest."

"Mr. Fletcher, your daughter is at an awkward age. Some girls at her age are still playing child's games. Others are already looking at the boys and trying to be older than they are. Caroline will come around."

"I hope so." He chuckled. "I'd love to keep her as my little girl, but I know she has to grow up."

"And she will." Abigail looked at her boss, but he turned his head away. She let out a big breath. Would her boss ever feel comfortable around her? She started to get up.

"Miss Cook, uh, would you mind if I call you Abigail?"

Shocked at his words, Abigail nodded and relaxed. "That would be nice."

"My first name is Lucas. You can use that if you'd like? I know I'm your boss, but if we are to live in the same household, we should be on more familiar terms."

"That would be perfect, Lucas." Abigail wanted to tell him she already used his first name in her thoughts. She held back since Lucas seemed embarrassed and stared at Caroline wading through the water. Remembering how uncomfortable she felt calling her former fiancé by his first name, she waited to feel the same way today. It didn't happen. In fact, she was thrilled he wanted her closer to his family.

"Caroline seems happier now than she's been in a long

time. I attribute that to you." He looked at her. "Thank you for whatever it is you're doing."

His gaze burned into hers. Her heart slammed against her chest. She sat up straighter and looked toward Caroline. This man was her boss and father to her student, not some admiring bachelor. She cleared her throat and waited for her heart to stop pounding. "She simply enjoys another female being on the ranch. Girls need to talk to other girls. I might not be a young girl, but I still remember what it was like to be her age."

"If you don't mind my asking, how old are you?"

Abigail squirmed before answering. Her single status at such a late age embarrassed her family. She hoped Lucas wouldn't be put off. "I'm twenty-nine. I chose to continue my education to be a teacher rather than to marry." She bit her tongue, aggravated at herself for always feeling a need to explain her situation.

"So you've never been married?"

Lucas stared at her.

Abigail looked down at the blanket then back up at Lucas. "No, I've never married to the chagrin of my parents, but I did come close last year."

Lucas didn't say anything. She knew he waited for an answer. "At Christmas I accepted a proposal from a widower who needed a mother for his three boys. Since I had humiliated my parents by staying a spinster, I thought everyone would benefit from the arrangement." She looked down once more. "I wanted to go through with the marriage, but in the end, I backed out. I know it's unrealistic, but I want to love the man I marry. I didn't want a marriage like I witnessed in my own home."

Lucas stretched out his long legs. "I'm sorry your parents didn't have a good marriage. What I've witnessed in my family has been good marriages. My mother and father truly loved each other, and from what I remember about my grandparents, they did as well." He looked out over the stream and stopped talking.

Was he about to tell her what kind of marriage he had with Sarah? She wanted him to open up but dared not ask.

Finally, he looked back at her and smiled. "I find it admirable you stuck to your beliefs, both to get an education and not to marry someone to keep your family happy. Yes, I find that admirable."

Relieved that he didn't condemn her as her father did, Abigail laughed softly, but Lucas must've heard.

Lucas frowned. "Don't you agree your actions were admirable?"

"I do, but my family certainly didn't. Had they believed I'd made the right decision to cancel my marriage to Mr. Baker, I wouldn't have had to leave Boston. They were devastated. My father did everything but physically throw me out of the house."

Abigail stopped talking, not sure how much to tell Lucas. Would someone with such strong family connections understand? She wasn't sure she understood all that took place, especially what Mr. Baker did to save his name, her father's actions to Mr. Baker's rumors, and the reaction of the community. She looked at Lucas and decided she'd told him enough. Maybe one day she'd be ready to fully explain.

"I felt I needed a change. That's why I answered the ad in the newspaper for a teaching position in Independence." She shook her head. "How was I to know the man who hired me didn't want to wait for me to cross the country?"

"I'm sorry your family didn't understand your desire to help young students. They lost their daughter and our little town lost a wonderful teacher by not waiting for you, but I have to say my family got the better of the deal."

Amazed that Lucas understood her and did not look down on her for not marrying young, she looked at him in a totally different way. Maybe he wasn't such a stern, serious ranch owner. Maybe there was a warm side of the man, but then she'd thought Mr. Baker had a warm and understanding side as well. She couldn't have been more wrong. She wanted to ask about Sarah, but she knew she'd be pushing her luck.

Lucas stood up and held out his hand. "Let's go join my daughter by the stream."

Abigail looked at his hand and smiled. "I would like that."

Now that they had broken the ice and they'd had a short, but real conversation, would he return to being the solemn father and businessman? She hoped not. She'd seen a different side of him and rather liked it.

She took his hand. The rough, callused skin rubbed against her soft flesh. Her heart flopped once again, but this time she ignored the silly reaction and enjoyed the remainder of the day.

That evening before going to bed, Abigail took out her journal.

Today was wonderful. I thoroughly enjoyed the beauty of the valley. I'd love to have the time to paint its beauty, but that's not my purpose at Fletcher Ranch. My job is to help with Caroline's education. Watching her and her father together was both heartwarming and sad, reminding me that the decisions I've made in the past year have separated me from my own family. After today's ride and having a real conversation with Lucas, I know I've made the right decision in coming here, but I have to find a way to reconcile with my parents.

She closed the journal, but opened it once more before putting it away.

Lucas Fletcher has a soft side of him that I truly admire. I'd like to get to know more about him.

With a big smile, she shut the journal and put it on her bedside stand. She pulled the covers up to her neck. She did want to get to know Lucas better, but he was her boss and was definitely a man. She'd learned her lesson. Men couldn't be trusted.

Thinking about her father and Mr. Baker, Abigail stared at the ceiling. Was Lucas like the other men in her life who had disappointed her?

CHAPTER NINE

On Sunday afternoon Abigail walked to the big house where she found Grandmother Fletcher stitching a beautiful piece of delicate blue fabric.

"You seem to be in a good mood." Grandmother Fletcher looked up from her sewing.

Abigail stepped up onto the porch. "I am. The ride yesterday was just what I needed. It gave me the confidence to know I can ride a horse, and I saw some of your gorgeous ranch land. I can't imagine any one family owning such a large amount."

Grandmother Fletcher smiled. "We're proud of our land and how it's been so good for our family. Come sit by me and enjoy this beautiful warm afternoon.

Abigail sat. "That fabric is beautiful. Did you buy it in town?"

"Lucas saw it and bought it for me to make Abigail a party dress. In the past, we always had a big celebration at the ranch after our men come home from the cattle drives. My late husband started the tradition to celebrate my birthday, but now it's more to give the ranch hands and families around the area a reason to celebrate. Summers are beautiful and a perfect time of the year to have a party."

"A party on the ranch sounds like a wonderful idea. I'm so glad I'll be here to enjoy it."

"I, too, am glad you will be able to celebrate with us." Mrs. Fletcher looked down at the fabric, then back up to Abigail. "We haven't had a get-together since Sarah's death. Lucas came to me several weeks ago and suggested we have one this year. He thought it would be good for Caroline, and I agreed with him. It will be good for all of us. I loved the gatherings. I'm thrilled he is feeling good enough to celebrate life again." She lifted the fabric and smiled. "He saw this fabric and knew the color would look good on Caroline."

"He has quite the eye for fabric. It certainly will make a gorgeous dress, and she'll look exceptional in it. Tell me about the party. Who will be invited?"

Grandmother put down the fabric and stretched. "I know you don't see them from here, but there are several families living not too many miles away." She pointed over the cabin. "There are those in town who also will come out. Some come only for the day. Some stay for the night. As I said, we haven't planned anything like this for almost four years so I'm not sure how many will be able to come this year."

Abigail's grasped her hands in front of her chest. "It sounds exciting. Where do you put the people who stay?"

"The men camp outside and the ladies stay in the house. We have several unused bedrooms, and Caroline gives up hers. It used to be that she stayed with the children in the parlor, but since she's older, I'm sure she won't be happy doing that."

"Caroline is welcome to stay in the cabin with me if she feels comfortable."

Grandmother smiled. "Thank you for the offer. She would love to do that."

"This is exciting. Would you allow me to help with the preparations? When will it be?"

"The cattle drives have already started. Ours will begin next week. The men can be gone for three weeks up to a month, depending on what weather conditions they have and trouble they encounter along the way. Usually we can plan it for the first week in July. I know this is early to get started, but without Sarah doing the planning, we'll need all that time. Lucas has already checked with Victor to make sure he and his family will set aside the week. Since he's the sheriff, he has to get someone to cover for him in town. Lucas has also told others about it, but a final date hasn't been determined." She looked down at the fabric. "I will need every bit of the time to finish this dress. I used to sew pretty fast, but I'm a lot slower now."

Caroline and Matthew walked out from the barn together. Mrs. Fletcher looked at them.

Abigail watched the two of them laugh and run toward one of the corrals. "Caroline has found a friend in Matthew."

"Yes, but I'm not so sure her father approves of her having a boy as a friend and possibly an admirer. She's only thirteen. She and Matthew have been like brother and sister for so long, I can't imagine seeing them change."

"Caroline is a sensible girl. She'll tread cautiously. It's time for her to take notice of boys. In fact, I've seen them exchanges glances. I'm sure she will be thrilled if he asks her to dance at the party. He seems to be a fine young man." Abigail thought for a moment. "Has the boy had any classroom training? Does he know how to read and write?"

"Sarah worked with him for a while when he was younger, but after she died he started hanging around with the men more often and lost interest in books."

"I'll have to speak with Lucas about letting Matthew sit in on some of our lessons."

"That's a wonderful idea, but don't be offended if he refuses. Men who work on ranches don't always put a lot of value on book learning."

"It won't hurt to try. Now, about the party, will there be

music?"

"We definitely will have music. Several men play instruments and they put on quite the show. You'll love it."

"Do I need to include a lesson about music and dancing?"

"Maybe for Matthew, but Caroline probably knows how. As a young girl, she loved music and would sit with her mother at the piano and try to play. Sometimes she'd dance around the piano with Lucas. She hasn't shown any interest in the piano since Sarah died, and neither has Lucas."

Abigail smiled. "Lucas plays?"

"He did at one time. My mother made all of us learn a little, and I passed on what I knew to Lucas. He enjoyed playing, but as a kid, he thought the guys on the ranch would make fun of him."

"Aaah, that's normal."

"Lucas said you played. We would love for you to help Caroline again."

"I can certainly do that. Maybe I can help Matthew with his dancing before the party. I'm not so sure he'll go for it, but I can try."

Mrs. Fletcher nodded, then watched Caroline and Matthew climb onto the corral fence. "Matthew is certainly a good boy. He's been living here with us since he was six. His father and mother died in a house fire. Matthew didn't have any other family so Sarah and Lucas took him in. He used to stay in the house with us, but now he chooses to stay with the men in the bunkhouse. He's growing up."

"It's a strange age for young people to go through, but I'm sure you, Lucas, and Sarah have given him a good set of morals to live by."

"I hope so." With a big sigh, Mrs. Fletcher picked up the fabric and examined her stitching.

Abigail rested her head against the rocker back. Mrs. Fletcher had given her more insight into Lucas. She'd seen a little glimpse of his soft side at the stream. Having taken a young boy into his home proved he was certainly not the harsh man from her first impressions, though since she'd been at the ranch she hadn't seen any closeness between the Lucas and Matthew.

A buggy coming down the long entrance to the house caught her attention. "Are you expecting company?"

Mrs. Fletcher looked up. "No. I have no idea who that could be." She put down her sewing and stood by the porch railing.

Abigail did the same. As the buggy got closer, Abigail looked at Mrs. Fletcher. "The man looks like Pastor Smith."

"My eyes aren't so good anymore. I can't make out the driver, but I'd best go tell Bonita to have some refreshments for whoever it is." Mrs. Fletcher placed the fabric on a table next to her rocker and walked into the house.

Abigail stood by the railing at the top of the steps as the one-seat buggy driven by Pastor Smith pulled in front of the steps. One of the hands ran out of the barn to take care of the horse.

"Good day, Miss Cook." Pastor Smith got out and brushed the dust from his trousers and suit coat. "I hope the Fletcher family is home."

"Yes, everyone is here this afternoon. Mrs. Fletcher just went inside, and Lucas and Caroline are in the barn." Abigail called out to the hand to tell Lucas the pastor was here. She had almost used his first name in front of the pastor, but caught herself. "Please, come up and have a seat. Mrs. Fletcher will be out shortly.

Pastor Smith turned to the young man who had come for his buggy. "I won't be long. You can take the horse for a drink if you'll bring her back."

The man nodded and led the horse toward a trough near the house.

Abigail's chest tightened. Why was the pastor here unannounced? Did he visit his congregation regularly? As he passed her to step onto the porch, Abigail detected the scent of musk. Was that something he always wore, or was he trying to impress the Fletcher family or her? Flattered that a man of the cloth might pay attention to her, but feeling silly to think he would, she shook her head. "Have a seat. I hear Mrs. Fletcher coming down the hall now."

He sat in one of the rockers. Abigail left the one closest to him empty for Mrs. Fletcher and sat in another one.

The door opened and Mrs. Fletcher stepped out. "Why, Pastor Smith, this is a wonderful surprise. I hope there isn't a problem for you to be out this far from town,"

He stood up, took her hand graciously, then sat back down after she sat. "No problem at all. I didn't have any pressing obligations today. Quite a few of our congregation were busy planting their crops so we didn't have the potluck. The McDonalds invited me for lunch after services today. Since I was already away from town, I wanted to drop in to see your family. It's been a couple of weeks since I've seen you in church."

"Yes, I know. I would love to attend every Sunday, but we don't always have an entire day to devote. This ranch takes our men working seven days a week to keep it running properly."

"I'm sure it does."

Abigail caught a glimpse of Lucas coming out of the barn wiping his hands. He headed to the porch.

"Here comes Lucas now. I'm glad he was close to the house. I'm sure he would feel awful had he not gotten to see you."

Abigail didn't think that was a correct statement, but she kept her feelings inside.

Lucas took the front steps two at a time but stopped at the top. "Pastor Smith, this is a surprise."

"Yes, I was at the McDonald's today, and your ranch wasn't that much out of the way." Pastor Smith rocked a little too fast and looked away from Lucas.

Was the pastor nervous?

Bonita and Carmella came out of the house. One carried a tray of sliced cake, the other a tray with cups for tea. They placed them on a table in front of the rockers.

"Thank you, ladies." Mrs. Fletcher bent over and poured tea into three cups, asked what the pastor what he wanted in his, then served him.

He sipped his tea, then put it down and took a slice of cake. "This is just lovely. I wish I was hungrier, but Mrs. McDonald had a wonderful spread. I certainly didn't disappoint her."

"I for one love my afternoon tea." Mrs. Fletcher fixed her cup then leaned back in her chair. "Lucas, would you like a cup?"

Lucas, still standing against the porch post, shook his head. "Is there any news from town other than the wagon trains passing through?"

"The wagon trains have almost come to a stop. If they don't leave the area before late spring, there's too much danger crossing some of the passes." Pastor Smith told them about the arrival of a new baby girl and the upcoming marriage of two of the other parishioners.

"My, our little town is growing by leaps and bounds." Mrs. Fletcher smiled.

"Is the new school teacher doing a good job?" Abigail put her cup down.

"As far as I know she is. The children seem to like her, and I haven't heard any complaints by the mothers."

"That's good." Abigail smiled. "It seems things always work out for the best."

"That's right. I did hear you were supposed to be the new teacher."

"Yes, but I'm happy to be here with the Fletchers. They've made me quite welcome."

Pastor Smith nodded and talked about a few more of the parishioners and about a short rail being built between Independence and Wayne City. "They're also starting construction of the two-story brick station to go along with it. As you said, our town is growing fast and becoming quite modern."

He put his cup down and looked from Lucas to Abigail. "I, I was wondering if Miss Cook might want to take a ride with me just around the ranch. I'd love to hear about her life back in the East."

Abigail stopped rocking. She looked from Mrs. Fletcher to Lucas then to the pastor.

Mrs. Fletcher put her cup down. "That sounds like a splendid idea if Miss Cook wants to go."

Abigail's mind spun. Did she want to go with the pastor? What was his motive? Was he being a good pastor and ambassador for Independence or was he thinking about courting her? "A ride on this beautiful afternoon would be lovely. I have lessons to work on this afternoon, but I can certainly spare a few minutes for a nice ride." She stood up, not sure how to act in front of the Fletcher family and the man who obviously came here today to be with her. Is that what she wanted?

He stood up and took her arm. "We won't be long. I'd like to get back to town before it gets dark." When he led her past Lucas, he nodded. Lucas nodded back, but did not smile or speak.

Abigail's chest tightened. Did Lucas disapprove of this man taking her for a ride? He certainly shouldn't care since only yesterday at the stream they had had their first real conversation. She couldn't imagine him not wanting her to have a social life—not that she expected a social life here or in Boston.

When they got to the bottom of the steps, Abigail stepped away. The ranch hand led the horse and buggy back to them, and she allowed the pastor to help her up into the seat. Before they pulled off, she glanced up to the porch. Lucas had disappeared into the house. She let out a loud breath.

Pastor Smith flicked the reins and the horse eased away from the house.

"It was much too pretty of a day to go back to the rectory after lunch. When I realized how close I was to the Fletcher Ranch, I had to come see how you were doing here."

"I'm doing quite well, thank you. Caroline is an excellent student. She makes all my work worthwhile."

"That's wonderful. I worked with students while I was at seminary, and I can attest to the fact that some of them can make the life of a teacher very difficult."

Abigail fidgeted. "I've heard horror stories of some incidents with students, but I am fortunate. I've never had really bad students."

Pastor Smith looked straight ahead. "I'm glad you decided to come for a ride with me. I'd like to get to know you better. Tell me about living in Boston."

Glad to have something to talk about, Abigail relaxed and told him about her family home, her father's profession, and the theaters and parks available for Boston's citizens, keeping the conversation away from anything personal. Even though pastors counseled parishioners about their personal problems, she didn't feel comfortable opening up about her former fiancé or her father's anger. As she spoke about events and interesting spots around Boston, she realized she felt more comfortable opening up to Lucas at the stream yesterday than to this man of the cloth.

"This land is lovely, but I'm sure you miss those exciting places in Boston."

Abigail chuckled. "I never was much of a socialite. I did enjoy the theater and concerts in the park, but I never got involved with the seasonal balls. I was more concerned with my studies, and then after I got my first teaching position, I spent my time preparing for my students."

Pastor Smith looked at her. She realized he had beautiful green eyes set against his black hair. He wasn't a big man—nothing like Lucas—but he seemed healthy for someone who probably stayed inside a lot.

"That's quite admirable for a young lady to admit. I like that, but everyone needs some sort of leisure time."

"I enjoy the piano and still play on occasion. I hope I can get Caroline interested in it as well." Not sure what else to add, she changed the conversation. "And where do you call home?"

He flicked the reins and started with his life's story, living in Missouri and attending seminary in the state. "I truly love this part of the world, and believe me, there is so much that can be done here with so many travelers passing through. I could stay busy twenty-four hours a day if I chose to."

They talked a little longer until Abigail suggested they return to the house. "I know you must get back to town, and I have lessons to work with before dinner with the Fletchers."

He obliged by turning the wagon.

By the time the Fletcher house was in sight, Pastor Smith slowed the horse. "Miss Cook, may I call you by Abigail?"

"I guess that would be okay." She bit her lip, not sure she felt it was. After several weeks living on the ranch, she and Lucas had just gone on first-name basis. She had only seen the pastor one other time. "But, not in front of the church congregation," she added. "I'm not sure they would approve."

"Certainly. You can call me Alfred, if you'd like."

She smiled. This man was her pastor, and at the moment she had no intentions of calling him by his first name, at least not now.

By the time he pulled the buggy to the front of the house, the sun had started its descent. He helped her out of the buggy and up the front steps. Immediately, she stepped away from him on the porch.

"I enjoyed the ride. Thank you for the afternoon."

"Will I see you in church next Sunday?"

"I have no way of knowing. I depend on the Fletchers, and they can never plan too much ahead of time."

"I understand, but I would love to see your smiling face in one of the pews next Sunday." He reached for her hand.

Abigail shook, but before she pulled it back, Pastor Smith lifted it to his lips.

Had anyone ever done that before? Abigail blushed, but was flattered. "Again, thank you for a lovely afternoon. Have a safe trip back into town."

Pastor Smith nodded, looked as if he wanted to say more, but left without another word. She clutched her hands in front of her body. Had the pastor come to Fletcher Ranch because she was here? The idea of having a man seek her out was foreign. Maybe it would be nice to have a gentleman caller, but then she thought about Lucas. He'd attempted to be friendly at the stream and even though he was her boss, she enjoyed his attention a great deal.

She shook her head and headed to the cabin to look over her lessons for tomorrow. It was silly of her to even think either of the men looked at her as anything other than a governess or a member of a congregation. And that was fine with her. She had run away from an intolerable situation in Boston and certainly didn't need a reason to leave here as well.

Once up on her porch, she stopped. Where would she go if ladies like the two at church spread rumors about her? She certainly didn't want to go any farther west than Independence. When she'd answered the ad for a teacher, her only thought was to get away from the horrible gossip and start a new life without judgment. Now that she was here there was no turning back. She didn't know if she would ever be invited back into her home.

Was she to be here forever, never to see her parents again? Maybe she'd made her decision to leave Boston too hastily. Had she been a coward not to fight for her reputation, or had she shown strength and independence? Whichever was correct, she was in Missouri and would have to remain for a while. The weeks since she'd been on the ranch had flown by and soon summer would be gone and winter would be here, making travel difficult. Next spring, she'd have to consider where her choices would lead her, but this afternoon she had lesson plans to complete.

Sunday night dinners were small meals. Abigail was the first to enter the dining area. Mrs. Fletcher came in shortly afterwards.

"You and I will be eating alone tonight." She carried two small bowls of meat and vegetables and bread.

"Please, let me help you." Abigail took one of the bowls. "I forgot Carmella and Bonita leave early on Sundays. I should've come over earlier."

"Heavens no. Carmella had this laid out already." She placed her bowls on the table then took a seat. "How was your ride with Pastor Smith this afternoon?"

"It was quite enjoyable. He's a good conversationalist and was curious about living in Boston."

"He is quite the eligible bachelor. I'm sure there are several young ladies in town who would love to be taken on a buggy ride with our pastor."

"Mrs. Fletcher, I'm not looking to find a man. At twenty-nine, I'm quite satisfied with my life."

"Oh, dear, listen to yourself. Just as Betty said at the church social, all young ladies are looking for a husband."

Abigail opened her mouth to answer her, but the words didn't come. Would she be satisfied with her life if she realized she had to live alone forever?

After she and Mrs. Fletcher ate their light meal, she excused herself and headed straight to her cabin. She had a lot to think about.

At bedtime she pulled out her journal and wrote one simple sentence. *This afternoon I went on a buggy ride with Pastor Smith.*

She stared at the entry, then closed the book. She had no idea what to say about her ride. She'd been flattered to be sought out by the pastor but had no idea what she'd say if he asked her again.

She opened the journal again and read the entry she'd written about her horseback ride yesterday with Caroline and Lucas. She'd had no trouble putting down her feelings about that ride.

Is this what it felt like for a young lady to get the attention of a man? Her social life had been almost non-existent at her own choosing. How did she know what she was supposed to feel or do?

* * * *

Lucas let Charger ease along a trail behind the house. In no hurry to get home, he examined fence lines and watched for signs of anything that could harm his cattle. Whatever had killed his cow seemed to disappear, at least he hoped it had. His men had already covered this trail today, but he needed to have some time alone away from the house.

Having Pastor Smith come to the house yesterday to take Abigail on a buggy ride had confused him. He should be happy that Caroline's governess might have the beginning of a social life here in Independence so she would choose to stay on Fletcher Ranch. For someone from a big city, she'd have to really love the simple life away from town to choose to stay in her position. Livestock and land were the center of life on a ranch, not parties, theater, and big dinners. He had already talked with his mother about having a party as they used to do to celebrate the end of the cattle drives. He'd done it for Caroline, but in the back of his mind, he wanted to have a party that Abigail might enjoy, but after Pastor Smith's visit this afternoon things had changed.

"What do you think, Charger?" He rubbed the horse's neck. "Is it possible she liked having the Pastor's attention?"

Lucas had let his guard down at the stream yesterday and asked if they could use their first names. That had been a big step for him. Now he wished he hadn't done it. It was better if she looked at him as only her boss and nothing more, but is that what he really wanted?

He shook his head. "What am I doing, boy? I'm a thirty-year-old widower. What am I doing even thinking about another woman?" He chuckled. "A widower talking to his horse." This time he laughed out loud. "Let's head back. We don't want to miss supper."

He rode toward the house retracing the fence lines he'd just ridden past. All of it looked in good repair.

Suddenly, Charger tossed his head and neighed.

"What's up, boy?"

Charger stomped his hooves.

"Whoa." Lucas pulled back the rein, then yanked his rifle out of its sheath. With eyes and ears alert, he examined the area he'd just passed through. Nothing seemed out of kilter, but as he looked closer he saw several broken branches on a bush and a small patch of stomped down grass. He held the rifle tighter, eyeing the brush on the side of the trail and up in the branches of the trees. Nothing.

Then he looked down. Fresh tracks from what could be a mountain lion crossed the trail.

Again Charger threw his head back. The horse smelled the animal even though he couldn't see him.

Lucas aimed the rifle where the brush had been beaten down then up into the tree limbs, but the lion didn't show himself. If he was still near, he was waiting for the right time to attack. Sweat ran down Lucas's back. With his body rigid, he moved nothing but his eyes as he searched the dark brush. *Where are you?*

Finally, Charger relaxed. Lucas lowered the rifle. The lion was gone.

Lucas slid off the horse and examined the tracks. They were fresh. The animal had crossed the trail in the few minutes since Lucas had passed earlier. He stood up and once more stared into the brush. Was the animal staring back at him? Would he attack as Lucas got back on Charger or was he gone?

"Let's go, boy. It'll be dark soon." With one last glance into the dark brush, he jumped back on the horse but kept the rifle in his hand. The responsibility of running Fletcher Ranch weighed heavily on his shoulders, and having a mountain lion disrupting its tranquility needled him. Something had to be done to keep his men, the cattle, and his family safe.

As he got back to the house, he headed toward the barn.

Douglas was working on a saddle strap. "Hey, brother. Good ride today?"

"It was until a cat crossed my path."

Douglas stepped toward the railing of the stall. "That mountain lion? Where? Did you see it?"

"It wasn't far from here, right before the end of the line on the front acreage. I didn't see him, but he'd crossed the trail from the time I passed until I got back. Charger knew he was there, but I couldn't get a shot. He never showed himself."

"I'll get some men together, and we'll patrol the area tonight."

"Are you sure you want to go? I don't mind doing it."

"Nope, I haven't slept well lately." Douglas pulled his hat off and ran his hand through his hair. "Maybe being out in the night air will relax me."

"Your choice, but don't let the men travel in groups fewer than three. I don't want anyone out there alone. I also want a couple to be on guard around the house."

"We'll handle it. You have enough on your mind with the cattle drive next week. I'll let you know if we run across anything. Get some sleep tonight."

"Thanks, Douglas. I really do appreciate it."

Lucas watched his brother leave the barn. Every day he expected Douglas to tell him he was leaving the ranch in search of something else to do. Since Lucas had returned from the war, he could tell Douglas wasn't content. His brother had kept the ranch running while Lucas had been away. Maybe it was time for Douglas to find out what he wanted to do in life.

Lucas took off the saddle and led Charger into his stall. "You're a good horse. I would've never known that cat was around had you not alerted me." Charger went to his feeder. Lucas grabbed the brush and started brushing the horse down. "Your life is pretty simple, isn't it? Mine used to be."

After he finished Charger's grooming, Lucas talked with Douglas and Mason about their night ahead, then went into the house through the back door. No one was in the kitchen so he helped himself to leftovers and headed up to his room without seeing anyone. He wasn't in any mood to talk about how he was feeling. His mother showed concern when he'd left the house earlier after telling her not to expect him a dinner. More confused than ever, he certainly didn't want to explain himself to anyone else.

He had a lot on his mind. The lion on his property, a cattle drive in a few days, an upcoming party he wasn't sure he wanted to have, and now a pastor who might be coming around his family more often.

Yep, Charger, you don't know how good you have it.

CHAPTER TEN

Monday morning didn't go well. Caroline came to class late. Immediately Abigail knew she had her mind on something other than her studies. Nothing Abigail said or did seemed to get the girl's interest.

Finally, Abigail closed her math book. "We should go for a ride and look at the flora around the ranch."

"Flora?" Caroline wrinkled her nose. "What's that?"

Abigail smiled. "Flora is vegetation. Plants and flowers and trees."

"I want to go for a ride, but I already know about the plants and stuff that grow out here. Why would I want to study them?"

"Because there's a lot we can learn about this area by what grows here." She shrugged. "If you don't want to go for a ride, we can certainly finish our math lesson."

Caroline stood up. "No, I didn't mean I don't want to go. I can learn about the plants and trees. Can I go change clothes?"

"Sure. Come back here when you're dressed and make sure your grandmother or someone in the kitchen knows where we'll be." She watched her student run from the cabin toward the house. She then dug into one of her trunks and pulled out an old edition of beautifully illustrated examples of plants and trees. Most were from the eastern states, but some varieties were out here as well. She also grabbed a sketch pad and several pens and hoped Caroline would like to draw what she found.

After packing her book and supplies in a leather satchel, she looked down at her clothes and shook her head. Her skirt would have to do.

Caroline knocked on the door. Abigail opened it to find Caroline with a beautiful smile instead of the frown she'd worn all morning.

"Now, that's the sweet smile I like to see." Abigail grabbed her satchel and followed Caroline to the barn.

As they passed one of the corrals Matthew raised his head and waved at them. He'd been working with a young horse, but he left the corral and met them. "Are you two going for a ride this time of day?"

Caroline stopped. "Yes, we're going to study the flora."

Matthew opened his mouth but didn't ask. "He tipped his hat. Have a good ride and be careful." He turned to go.

"Matthew, would you like to go with us?" Abigail blurted out the question before

considering how Lucas would respond to taking the boy away from his chores.

Matthew looked from Abigail to Caroline with longing in his eyes. "I'd like to, but I have chores to do."

"We understand. Maybe the next time we go out on a fieldtrip, we can arrange to have you go with us." Disappointed that Matthew would not join them, Abigail decided she'd plan ahead the next time. The young man needed an education as well.

Caroline frowned as Matthew headed back toward the corral. "Do you think Father would allow Matthew to go along with us one day?"

"I have no idea, but I'll certainly talk with him. The way I understand it, he's been part of the family for quite a while. I'm sure Mr. Fletcher wants everyone associated with the ranch to be as knowledgeable as possible."

Caroline walked straight to Honey Cup's saddle, hoisted it, and walked toward the horse's stall. "I'm not so sure Father would understand why he'd need to know about flora and stuff, but you can ask." She swung the saddle over the railing, then went into the stall by Honey Cup.

Abigail looked at Sugar's saddle, hoping she could lift it as Caroline did. With all her strength focused on the saddle, she lifted it and headed toward Sugar's stall.

"You did it, Miss Cook. You're getting stronger."

Huffing, but determined to carry the saddle by herself, Abigail made it to the railing and swung it over. "Whew. That's heavy."

"But you did it."

By the time Abigail got the saddle on Sugar's back, a trickle of perspiration ran down her back, but she ignored that and used a bucket to step up into the saddle without any help. *Yes, I did it!* She held back a shout of joy as she followed Caroline out the barn.

As they passed the corral, Matthew lifted his hand. Abigail waved back, wishing the boy could be going with them. He smiled but his eyes told another story. He wanted to join them.

Abigail asked Caroline to direct them to an area where the vegetation grew thicker than on the well-used trails, but not too far from the house. Within a few minutes they got off the horses.

"This is perfect." Abigail pulled her book and sketch pads from the saddlebag while Caroline tethered the horses.

"Father told me when we ride not to get too far off the trails. He heard there might be a mountain lion near here."

"A mountain lion?" Abigail held her book near her chest and surveyed the area. "Do you think we're safe here?"

Caroline shrugged. "I guess. The horses don't seem to be worried."

"Do the horses sense when a wild animal is near?"

Caroline laughed. "Of course they do. They'll stomp and snort and try to run."

"Then we'll stay near the horses. They'll be our canary."

"What? A canary?"

"Yes, a caged canary is used in the mines back east to let the miners know if there is dangerous carbon monoxide and other gases in the air. As long as the bird is singing and is alive, the miners know they are safe."

"But the bird dies if the air is tainted?"

"I'm afraid so. Sometimes they'll grab the cage and carry it out with the men and the bird revives in the fresh air. It's a sad commentary on life in the mines, but the little birds have saved lives of many miners."

"That's horrible. Why don't they just fix the gas problem?"

"Maybe one day somebody will discover a solution, but right now relying on the bird is the best method available." Abigail looked around. "If you think we're safe here, let's look at the flora."

"Right. Flora." Caroline's chest heaved, followed by a loud sigh.

"It's not that bad. I'm sure you'll find something you like today."

Abigail recognized several low bushes and started the lesson about the difference in the vegetation in Missouri and those that were found farther east. She pointed to the nearest tree. "That tree is an oak tree." She flipped pages in her book and showed her a picture. "And that one over there is a red cedar. Let's sit down and sketch these."

Caroline plopped down on a log. "I don't draw good."

"Don't draw well, not good. Remember we talked about adverbs and adjectives. But, it doesn't matter how well you draw, it's always fun to sketch." Pulling out two pads and two pencils, she gave one to Caroline and kept one for herself.

For the next thirty minutes, they both sketched the plants around them and looked up the correct names in Abigail's book. Abigail loved watching Caroline get interested in sketching. A noise in the branches overhead caught Abigail's attention. She looked up and closed the sketch book. Both horses pulled at their reins and neighed. Honey Cup lifted her front legs and pulled at her tether. Caroline looked up as well.

Fear clenched Abigail's chest. "We have to go." Abigail stood up and grabbed her belongings, stuffed them in the satchel and yanked Caroline up. "Hurry."

Abigail made sure Caroline was up on her horse before she attempted to get on herself, but without a bucket to stand on, it was impossible. She pulled a reluctant Sugar to the log where they had sat. Trying to keep Sugar from running off, she used the log to hop into the saddle. With one last look into the brush, Abigail hurried after Caroline toward the trail. Her breath came in short gulps and sweat trickled down her back. Had a mountain lion come close to them? Had they been in danger?

Caroline put Honey Cup into a gallop. Abigail gritted her teeth to keep up. She gripped the reins as tightly as she could and hoped she wouldn't fall out of the saddle. The short distance to the ranch house was the longest Abigail had ever been on. By the time the house and the corrals came into sight, her body ached from being tense.

Matthew met them outside the corral. "Why are you riding so fast? You're not racing, are you?"

Caroline jumped off Honey Cup. "The horses got spooked. It was probably a snake or something little, but Miss Cook was afraid it was that mountain lion. We came back as fast as we could."

Wide-eyed, Matthew looked from Caroline to Abigail. "Where were you?"

As Caroline explained to Matthew where they were and what happened, Abigail led Sugar into the barn and started the process of removing the saddle. Deep in thought about what could've happened today, she didn't realize she'd removed the saddle and had carried it across the aisle and threw it over the railing. Any other time she'd be ecstatic to have accomplished the feat alone, but not today. Her spur-of-the-moment decision to take Caroline out for a field trip put both of them in possible danger.

What would Lucas say? Would she lose her job? Where would she go if it came to that? With shaking hands she brushed down Sugar, who panted horribly. She probably put the old horse in danger of dying from over exhaustion.

Bad decision. Bad decision.

"I'm so sorry, Sugar. Please don't die on me."

Caroline and Matthew came into the barn. Matthew helped her finish Sugar's grooming. When he left, Abigail turned to Caroline. "I have to tell your father what happened."

"But, Miss Cook, he won't ever allow us to leave again if you do. It was probably something little like a rabbit that spooked the horses."

"Possibly, but your father has to know. He might need to have men check out the area to see if they can determine what it was. Why don't you take the rest of the afternoon off?" She handed Caroline her sketchpad. "Take this to your room and work on the sketches you did. If you can remember other bushes and plants around the area, draw them as well, and we'll see if we can come up with a name for them tomorrow."

"But, Miss Cook. . ."

"Caroline, don't argue. Please do as I say. I have a lot on my mind."

Abigail sought the refuge of the cabin and sat on the side of her bed. How would Lucas react when he was told? She squeezed her eyes tightly. Would she have a job tomorrow?

* * * *

"We have to talk." Lucas stomped into the dining room at the dinner hour, stopped just inside the door, and crossed his arms.

Abigail sat alone at the table awaiting Lucas's arrival trying to figure out how to tell him about the outing today and praying he wouldn't fire her. His looks told her he already knew.

"What's this I hear? You took my daughter away from the house alone without telling anyone?"

"We told Matthew, and Caroline told Bonita. No one else was around. Caroline said she rides alone all the time. I assumed it was okay, but I understand why you're upset if she told you something spooked the horses. I'm upset as well."

Lucas pulled out a chair but instead of sitting, he stood behind it with his hands on the back. "Matthew told me, not Caroline. Didn't you know there could be a mountain lion in the area?" His voice echoed throughout the room. "I realize I didn't talk to you personally about it—and maybe what happened today is partly my fault—but you're a teacher and your student's wellbeing in is your hands."

Abigail swallowed. "Yes, sir, I'm aware of that. The field trip was only a short ways from the house. I truly thought it would be safe. I didn't know anything about a dangerous animal in the area." She held her head high and looked directly at him. She would not cower, knowing it was not entirely her fault.

"Father, please don't yell at Miss Cook." Caroline ran into the room and up to her father. "Nothing happened. We're okay. You know how skittish Sugar is. She probably heard a squirrel or rabbit."

"Or smelled a lion." Lucas shook his head. "You and Miss Cook are not allowed to ride out again, not until this lion is caught. It's already killed one of the cattle. I can't have you out there without one of the ranch hands or me."

Caroline spun around and sat. "That's not fair."

"I didn't say it was fair. It's dangerous. I'm not allowing my daughter to be put in harm's way." He glared at Miss Cook. "I have enough on my mind with this cattle drive coming up. I can't worry whether you two will be in danger here at the ranch while I'm gone."

Mrs. Fletcher stepped into the room. "I have to agree with my son. Until the men get rid of the danger, I don't want either of you away from the house alone."

"I'm not a baby." Caroline's eyes filled with tears.

"But you're not an adult or a man. Did you even have a gun with you today?"

Caroline looked at the table.

"That's what I figured." Lucas sat. "Let's eat before I get any more upset." He looked at Abigail. "You and I will talk later."

* * * *

The next day Abigail stored her teaching supplies after Caroline left the cabin. Throughout the day, she waited for Lucas to knock on the door to reprimand her or fire her for taking his daughter away from the house yesterday. The knock never came.

She finished her lessons for the following day, then walked out on the porch. As she sat, she saw Lucas walking in her direction. He still had on his work clothes and wore his hat pulled low just as he had on that first day he'd saved her from humiliation in the street of Independence. She couldn't see his expression, but his determined steps told her everything she needed to know. She braced herself for whatever the man was about to tell her.

"Good afternoon, Mr. Fletcher." She didn't think he wanted to be called by his first name today.

He stopped and nodded. "It is a good afternoon, better than yesterday."

Abigail squirmed.

"May I come up?"

"Certainly." She felt like a little girl about to be

reprimanded by her father for failing to do something he'd asked. She clasped her hands on her lap and faced her boss. "I've been waiting for you to come all day. I'm sure you have lots to say about yesterday."

"I do." He leaned against the porch rail and removed his hat. His black hair fell onto his forehead, but he immediately pushed it back. "First, I want to apologize for yelling in the dining room. I'm usually much more in control of my emotions, but when it comes to my daughter, I'm a little overprotective. When I heard what happened, I was enraged and blamed you."

"I would've done the same had I been in your shoes. I blamed myself as well. I should have checked with you first before taking Caroline away from the cabin. I didn't think there would be danger since we planned to stay close to the ranch house. Obviously I was wrong."

"I'm pleased you're trying to keep Caroline engaged in her studies. She's not the best student, I'm sure." A hint of a smile creased his face. "I have to take some of the blame myself for what happened yesterday because I didn't talk with you personally about the danger. I guess I assumed you knew. The threat has been the topic of conversation with all of my workers and even my mother, but then last night after dinner when I calmed down a little, I realized you probably didn't have the opportunity to hear those conversations."

"Caroline mentioned a possible mountain lion to me only after we had ridden out, but I didn't think it would be so close to the house."

"Caroline should have known the roaming habits of the animals around here. I realize now you are not from here and didn't understand the risk. I'm sure there are not a lot of dangers like that in Boston."

"We have dangers, but not wild cats and other animals unless one leaves the streets of the city." She hoped for another smile from him. It didn't come.

"Until we catch this animal, I want you and Caroline to

stay near the house. If you must leave, make sure I know and one of the ranch hands goes along."

His eyes filled with worry.

"I understand."

"Do you, Miss Cook? Living out here away from town is a wonderful existence. I wouldn't want to live anywhere else in the world, but it comes with risks." He held his hat tightly and looked down. "I'm not sure you know what happened to my wife, but Sarah died while on an innocent horse ride. I was with her, but I couldn't do anything to save her. A snake spooked her horse. It threw her, and she hit her head on a log. I held her in my arms as she took her last breath."

The muscles in Abigail's chest tightened. "I'm so sorry. Caroline told me a little, but I really didn't know. I can imagine how worried you are whenever Caroline rides off, especially when she's alone, or with someone like me who has no idea how to protect her. I'm sorry I chose to take her on the field trip, and you can be assured it won't happen again."

Lucas nodded, then looked out away from the cabin. "I couldn't live if something happened to Caroline, too." His voice was but a whisper.

Did he even know he'd said the words out loud?

Abigail got up and placed a hand on his arm. "I've never experienced loss as you have, and no one can say they understand what you've gone through, but do believe me when I say, I want to understand. I'm so sorry you and Caroline must live without Sarah."

Lucas looked down at her hand still on his arm.

She pulled it back and stepped away.

He nodded again, stuck his hat on his head, and turned. "I'll see you at dinner." Before he walked down the steps, he looked at the door to the cabin for a long second, then hurried down into the yard.

Abigail clenched her hands. The man still suffered from

the loss of his wife. Had he been in the cabin since it had been fixed for her? Should she invite him in sometimes or would it be too hard for him?

Watching Lucas walk away, she placed her hands on the railings. He'd called her Abigail at the stream. Like a silly boy-crazy young girl, she'd allowed herself to think he wanted to get close, but now she had a feeling they could never be anything but friends. He was a man still in love with the past, and she was only the governess to his daughter.

Lucas walked up the porch of the house, then disappeared inside. Would she ever be able to wipe away the vision of the pain on his face as he talked about Sarah and her accident? He still loved Sarah deeply.

She pushed away from the railing. Lucas Fletcher would never be anything but her boss, but she hoped she could be his friend as well. Even though he was the best looking man she had ever seen, from here on out she had to look at him as nothing more than a friend and a boss.

She thought about the carriage ride with Pastor Smith. Would he come back to the ranch to see her? Could she ever look at him as anything but her pastor? She doubted it.

With a loud exhale of air, she turned to go inside.

Maybe she was meant to be a spinster.

CHAPTER ELEVEN

After class the next day, Abigail sat in her rocker again on her porch looking over one of her books she'd brought with her, but Mrs. Fletcher caught her attention as she walked toward her cabin.

"This is a nice surprise. Please come up and visit." Abigail stood to welcome the lady.

"Thank you, Miss Cook. I wanted to talk with you about the party. I know it's over a month away, but I like to get started early."

"Yes, please, come up. I'm excited to know more about it and how I can help."

"Are you available now? I had one of the men take down some decorations from the attic. It's not a lot, but we can work with them if you're not busy."

Abigail jumped up. "Let me take my book in, and I'll be ready."

As she followed Mrs. Fletcher to the house, she couldn't contain her excitement. She was never a big fan of having socials while she was in Boston, but there was something different about this event. Her mother's idea of a party involved formal attire, servants doing all the decorations, fancy food served by immaculately dressed servants, and music played by a small orchestra. She had attended the affairs but never enjoyed the evenings. This party would not be like her mother's.

"Can I ask what the attire will be?"

"Our neighbors don't have a lot of opportunities to dress up, so they come in their Sunday best, but nothing formal. I've noticed your wardrobe is a fine one. You can wear any of your dresses and you will be appropriate."

"I didn't bring a lot, of course. I was limited to just two trunks and I filled one of them with my teaching supplies. I do have a couple dresses still packed away. I will wear one of them."

"Splendid."

They talked about the meat that the men would barbeque and the dishes that Carmella and Bonita would help prepare. "I like to make pies. This time of year offers so many wonderful fruits to be used. Most of the women who come bring homemade breads and side dishes. Some will make desserts, too, but we never have too much. Even if the tables are still full when the party is over, everyone takes home enough for their family, and, of course, our workers here feast on the leftovers for days."

"Your party sounds wonderful."

"I'm sure you are used to having much more elaborate affairs in Boston. Ours are much simpler, more about being with our friends and having fun. They're a way to celebrate our neighbors and the end of all the cattle drives. Our winters are not horribly cold, but people tend to stay near their own homes. It's hard for friends to get together."

Abigail bit her tongue. She almost asked if the two gossiping ladies from church would be invited, but she didn't ask. If they came, she be as gracious as she could be to them.

She grasped Mrs. Fletcher's hands. "I will look forward to this party more than any of formal affairs back home. I had no interest in them because they were more about impressing important people rather than celebrating friendships—a complete waste of time."

"I'm glad you feel that way about our get-together."

For the rest of the afternoon, Abigail helped Mrs. Fletcher refresh decorations that had been stored away. Big brown ribbons had to be pressed and hung and then retied into huge bows that would hang on the entrance to the ranch. Smaller ones would embellish some of the tables.

"We'll take out a few pieces of pottery that have been in our family for generations. I like to fill them with spring flowers and greenery from the surrounding woods."

"Sounds perfect as long as we have permission to go into the woods. I don't want to bring on the wrath of your son or to face a lion."

"You do have a point. I'll make sure Lucas knows when we go, and I'm sure he'll have someone go with us for protection."

"If you need help with your dress, feel free to ask Bonita or Carmella to help you get the wrinkles out."

"Thank you, but I don't mind doing for myself."

Mrs. Fletcher looked directly into Abigail's eyes. "From what I've gathered, your family must've had servants to help with mundane duties around the house."

"Yes, ma'am, we did, but while I was away with my studies, I had to learn to take care of my things, and I enjoy doing it. I always felt silly asking someone on my family's staff to take care of my clothes. I find doing for myself is quite fulfilling."

Mrs. Fletcher smiled. "We have always had paid servants as well, but I, too, enjoy doing a lot of things in my house. Since I've gotten older, I have to rely on our hired help more and more, but I understand that comes with age."

"And I'm sure you deserve it, but you do know you are still young."

"Young at heart maybe." Mrs. Fletcher laughed.

Abigail stood. "I'd best get back to my cabin to get ready for dinner." She turned to leave, but turned back. "I'll change my lesson plans for the next few weeks and concentrate on music. Will it be okay to use the piano in the parlor?"

"Certainly. You can come into the house anytime and work with it."

"What do you think about working with Matthew as well? Maybe show him a few dance steps?"

Mrs. Fletcher laughed. "You can certainly try, but I wouldn't count on his cooperation."

Feeling good about her part in the celebration, Abigail headed back to her cabin. She couldn't decide if she was more excited about the party or about sitting at a piano once again. Since Caroline's lesson would be sooner than the party, she concentrated on that and hoped she had packed her music sheets in the trunk before she left Boston.

During her stagecoach trip, she longed to sit and play music. Even though she wasn't a great piano player, she loved losing herself in the music. Playing the piano was a solitary endeavor. Like books, the piano gave her time to forget the world around her. She hoped she could get Caroline to enjoy it as well.

The next day Abigail met Caroline for her lessons at the door. "Today, we have a surprise."

"Did you get Father to let us ride out again?"

Abigail laughed. "No, I doubt we'll be riding out again until they take care of the lion problem. I have something even better. Today we're going to start piano and dance lessons."

Caroline took a step away from Abigail. "No, I don't want to do that."

Surprised at the girl's outburst, Abigail took a moment to find the right words. "But, Caroline, every lady needs to learn to dance and to play the piano. She should be able to entertain when company comes into her home and be confident if a young man asks her to dance. Don't you want that?"

Caroline frowned. "I don't need to do that."

"Maybe not, but your father and your grandmother wants you to enjoy the piano again. I know you used to play a little with your mother."

Caroline crossed her arms in front of her chest. "She's gone."

"I know she is, but by playing you will help her memory live on for you and for your family."

Caroline turned and sat down in a rocker. "I hardly remember her anymore."

Abigail stooped down by her. "That's normal. It's God's way of helping us cope with loss." She placed her hand on Caroline's chest. "Your mother is with you every day right here. You won't remember everything she did for you and with you, but you will always have her love. Maybe the music we learn to play on the piano will bring back more memories, happy memories."

Caroline looked at Abigail. Tears filled her blue eyes and beaded on her long lashes. "I want her here. I don't want a memory."

Abigail pulled her into an embrace. "I know, sweetie. Life isn't always as we want it to be, but there is always a way to cope and to find happiness with what we have."

Caroline pulled away and swiped the tears away.

Abigail stood and hoped her student would cooperate. "Will you go into the house with me and sit at the piano?"

She nodded. "But I don't want to dance."

* * * *

"Whoa, boy."

Lucas stopped Charger near the corral and stared at the house. A soulful melody from the keys of the abandoned piano in the parlor floated across the front lawn of Fletcher Ranch. Memories of Sarah crushed his chest. No one had played that piano since Sarah's death. He had asked Abigail to help Caroline with music, but hearing the melody now shocked him.

He closed his eyes and let the tune wrap around his head

and swirl around his heart. The song that Abigail played had been Sarah's favorite. He could still see Sarah at the piano swaying to the music with her eyes closed and her long blond hair flowing down her back. Sometimes he joined her at the piano. He didn't play as well as she did, but he loved sharing what she loved. Those evenings were magical. Now someone else was sitting at her piano.

For so long no one in his family participated in their music evenings. Had he been wrong not to encourage the gatherings? Avoiding memories was his way of coping, but after all the years since Sarah had been gone, he needed to move on so his daughter would have a normal life.

What about him? Was he ready to move on?

He straightened his shoulders. Life moved forward whether he wanted it to or not. Abigail was doing exactly as he had instructed. He'd have to accept it.

"Come on, Charger. Let's get you inside. I'll bet that music will relax you."

Mason walked out of the barn as Lucas headed in. He took the reins as Lucas slid off Charger's back.

"Any signs of that mountain lion today?"

Lucas shook his head. "We found a few tracks up by the back range, but they weren't fresh."

"Maybe our lion went up into the hill country."

"Maybe, but I doubt it. He got a taste of our cattle. He's not giving up that easily."

"I hoped he'd be found before we left on the drive. What's our next step?"

Lucas rolled his head to loosen the tight shoulder muscles. "We'll keep doing what we're doing. Keep a few men on guard throughout the night. I don't know what else to do until we can locate him again."

"I'm glad Caroline and Miss Cook didn't get into trouble with that animal when they were out." Mason shook his head. "Scares me to death to know he's so close to the house."

"Me too."

"I'll get Charger settled. Will you be riding out again soon?"

"Probably, but it will be an hour or so. I have some office work to do." Lucas patted Charger's rump as he turned to the house. The music still came from the parlor. For a moment he considered getting back on Charger and riding out alone until Caroline's lesson was complete, but that would be the chicken way out. This morning presented as good a time as any to confront his feelings. Usually he faced problems head on. He could certainly face this one.

Without letting his mind bog down in emotions, he walked directly into the front door and turned into the parlor. What he saw nearly stopped his heart. Abigail and Caroline sat on the piano stool together. Abigail's hands were on the keys playing a simple tune. Caroline copied her motions. His daughter's blond hair flowed down her back just as Sarah's hair had done when she played.

He closed his eyes, took a deep breath, then walked into the room.

Abigail turned around. "Mr. Fletcher, we didn't know you had come in. Your mother gave us permission to work on a music lesson today. I hope you don't mind."

Lucas stepped toward the piano. "Of course not. In fact, I'm thrilled Caroline might one day follow in her mother's interest of music."

"Father, you know I'd rather be outside with the animals."

"I'm aware of that, but having multiple pastimes makes for an interesting person."

She hung her head. "I'm not so sure I can do this."

Lucas stepped closer to Caroline. "Don't you remember sitting here with your mother and running your fingers across the keys? You even learned a couple songs the two of you played together."

Caroline shook her head. "I don't remember."

Her words crushed his heart. He wanted her to remember Sarah, but he understood. His memories faded each day as well. He took a deep breath. "I remember the two of you playing. Even though you were little, you said one day you'd play in the concert halls in Paris."

She looked down at the piano keys. "Maybe I remember doing some of that."

Abigail sat quietly with her hands in her lap. Lucas looked at her. "Thank you for helping Caroline with music lessons. I used to love our evenings together in the parlor as Sarah played. I would enjoy having those evenings again."

"That will be our goal. Whether she believes it or not, Caroline has a natural talent. She'll be able to play quite soon."

"Again, I thank you. And, Caroline, I'm proud of you for trying."

She scrunched her nose. "I'd rather be riding Honey Cup."

He laughed. "Maybe Miss Cook will cut classes short today. You can do some riding, but you have to promise me you'll stay close to the house. That big cat is still out there somewhere."

"I promise."

Lucas nodded to them and left the room. Once in the hallway, he inhaled deeply. Seeing Caroline at the piano had taken his breath away, but then what did he expect? Every day his daughter looked more and more like Sarah. He'd have to get used to it. The party was in less than a month away. Could he and his mother convince her to wear the new dress she was making? She would never pick out that fabric and the color on her own, but he wanted so much for her to dress like a lady for the occasion.

He headed to his room, thinking about the cattle drive that would take place in a few days and party when the men returned. So much was left to do. He didn't remember parties in the past being so complicated. Sarah and his mother had always taken care of just about everything. He and Douglas and his father had been in charge of the outdoor areas and making sure there would be enough meat to go around. Everything else seemed to fall into place. He hadn't worried about the decorations—not that he thought any were needed. They seemed to appear magically on the day of the party. Sarah's knack for making the house and the yard look spectacular always amazed him. Now things were different. He hoped he hadn't made a big mistake by trying to duplicate something that had vanished from their lives.

Inside his room he walked straight to his armoire and stared at the few nice outfits stuck in the back. He'd ask Carmella to look over them so he could decide what he'd wear when he returned from the drive. Even though it was an outdoor barbeque and party, he would dress the part of the ranch owner and party host, just as his dad had done in the past.

He walked to his desk and pulled out papers, but instead of beginning his work, his thoughts turned to Abigail. Would she think about him while he was away with his cattle, or would she enjoy the time with her boss being away? As much as he didn't want to think about her as anything but his daughter's governess, he couldn't get her out of his head.

What would she wear to the party? He found himself taking note of her dresses each day. The fine fabrics and intricate designs on her clothing told him from the beginning that she was from a well-to-do family. She had not explained thoroughly why she'd left Boston and her family to travel to Independence. What she'd said about breaking her engagement didn't seem cause enough for her father to reject her. One day he hoped she'd open up.

Music from the first floor reached his ear. Abigail played beautifully. The music drew his thoughts to the party's entertainment. Would he dare dance with Abigail? Would Pastor Smith join the party and keep Abigail entertained? Of course the pastor would be invited and would probably corner him and question him about attending church services again. Maybe one day he'd surprise the man and show up in church with his family, but right now he couldn't do it. He wasn't a hypocrite. Blaming God for taking Sarah was wrong, but until he made peace in his heart with God, he couldn't sit in church as if everything was right.

Maybe the pastor would be too busy entertaining Abigail to have time to talk with him about religion. Other bachelors from the area would be invited. How many of them would take notice of her? He shook his head. All of them would notice her. Beautiful and refined, she'd be the belle of the ball. He chuckled. Maybe the belle of the barbeque. He wanted her to have a good time. The cold winter months would be here before anyone was ready and being stuck on the ranch might discourage her from staying. He needed her to help with Caroline, and if he admitted it he enjoyed having her here.

He looked down at the names of those who had been invited and who were still left to be contacted. He'd have to finalize the invitation list and get one of his men to ride out to their ranches before he left. As he looked at the list once more, Pastor Smith's name caught his eye. Personally, he liked the man, but how would he feel if the pastor spent all day with Abigail? He shouldn't care, but he did. Shaking his head to clear his head, he concentrated on last-minute plans for the drive.

After spending about an hour at his desk, he realized he needed to grab a light lunch and get back out to where the men worked on a broken pump. As he came down the staircase, Abigail stepped out of the parlor.

"How was my daughter's lesson?"

Abigail smiled. "Very good. She remembered some of what she learned from Sarah."

"Good. I'd like to see her get an interest in music."

"Mr. Fletcher, Lucas," she corrected herself, "I wondered how you'd feel if I worked with Matthew a little.

Your mother said Sarah helped him with his lessons when he was younger. I'd love to see how much he can do and start some lessons with him, if you give your permission."

Lucas rubbed a hand across his chin. "Yes, I guess that would be okay. He needs to have the basic skills to be able to function in the world, but he does have chores to do."

"Of course, I would never take him away from his responsibilities."

She looked down at the floor, then quickly back up. "You mother and I have been talking about the party. I'd like to help him with a couple of dance steps if he shows an interest."

"So you think he might dance at the party?"

"He's at the age to look at the girls who will be there, Caroline being one of them."

Lucas put both hands on his hips and frowned. "That's what I'm afraid of."

"There's nothing to be afraid of, Lucas. It's natural for boys and girls to notice each other. They are both beyond their childhood."

He didn't want to have his daughter dance with Matthew or with any other boy, but he couldn't ignore reality. "I know." He took a huge breath. "If you think the boy needs to learn to dance, fine. Show him a few steps. If he must dance with my daughter, I'd rather him not trip her and hurt both of them."

Abigail laughed. Her sweet smile reached her eyes.

"I'll try to get him to be able to stay on his feet."

Now, Lucas felt a chuckle bubble in his chest. "Thank you. I want them both to have a good time. She is one of the reasons I suggested this party."

"The fabric for the party dress you picked out is beautiful. She will be lovely in that color. You're a good father with a nice sense of style."

"Really?" Again he laughed. "I've never been told I have a sense of style, but I'll accept that as a compliment."

"And it certainly is."

"I assume you might also help Caroline with a few dance steps as well."

"I would love to."

Lucas nodded. "I'm heading to the kitchen for a light lunch. Have you eaten?"

"No, not yet."

"Join me. Where's Caroline?"

"She wanted to check on Honey Cup, but she said she'd come eat with me."

Lucas walked down the last couple steps. "Let's see what Carmella has for us."

CHAPTER TWELVE

Abigail followed Lucas into the kitchen then to the dining area, each with a small plate of meats and bread. Douglas had already finished his lunch.

Lucas sat next to his brother. "Where's Mother?"

Douglas picked up his plate. "I'm not sure. I'm finished so I'll go check on her." He left the room.

Abigail took a taste of the bread and meat.

Lucas took a bite as well then looked up as Caroline ran into the room. "Carmella has your plate fixed. I told her to hold it until you came in."

Caroline left for the kitchen and quickly returned.

Abigail waited for Caroline to sit. "How was Honey Cup?"

"Ready for a ride."

"We'll cut our class short this afternoon, but you do need to do a few more lessons."

Lucas chuckled. "You and Honey Cup are always ready to ride, but lessons come first."

Douglas shoved open the door to the dining room. "Lucas, Mother isn't feeling well. Come up with me." He turned. His steps pounded on the staircase.

Lucas jumped up and turned to Abigail on his way out the door. "Come with us."

Abigail rushed up the steps following Lucas and Douglas. After entering Mrs. Fletcher's bedroom, they found her fully dressed lying across the bed with her head on her pillow. Lucas went to the basin and wet a cloth.

Abigail looked at Douglas. "Do you know what happened?"

Even though Abigail's words were a whisper, Mrs. Fletcher opened her eyes. "I got a little weak and slid to the floor. Nothing unusual for an older woman. I'm okay."

"Mother, we need to make sure you're okay." Lucas frowned. "I don't want you to get up." He placed the wet cloth on his her forehead.

Abigail stepped by Lucas. "Does she have a fever?"

"She feels warm, but I'm not sure."

"Do you mind?" Abigail reached across Lucas. As she stretched, her arm brushed against his chest. Their gazes connected momentarily. With her heart racing, she forced herself to look at Mrs. Fletcher. "I don't think you have a fever, but I agree with your son that you need to rest."

"I'll get Carmella to bring your lunch up when you feel like eating." Douglas walked around by Lucas, said something low in his ear, then left the room.

"That would be nice." Mrs. Fletcher sat up, but both Abigail and Lucas reached for her at the same time.

"Mother, please don't get up right now. When Carmella brings in your lunch, I'll help you sit up and eat."

Mrs. Fletcher didn't argue. She closed her eyes.

"I'll be glad to stay with her this afternoon. I'm sure Caroline would love to have the afternoon free."

Lucas stood up and nodded for Abigail to follow him. In the hallway, he closed his mother's door. "Douglas and I are worried about Mother. He's sending one of the men to town to get our doctor. I appreciate your offer to help us. Why don't you go down to eat first and check on Caroline? Afterwards if you'll stay with her for a couple of hours, I'll finish what I have to do and come relieve you. I'm sorry to ask you to do this. It's not why you came here."

"Lucas, you didn't ask me to stay with your mother. I offered. I'll eat quickly and be back up."

"Thank you." He took her hand. "I really mean it."

Abigail was touched. A knot formed in her throat. She nodded and headed down the stairs, not knowing why she had gotten so choked up. Maybe it was because Mrs. Fletcher had been so kind, but also because Lucas looked so upset. She knew what he was thinking. How could he deal if something happened to his mother? Abigail could do nothing but nod and be available. Her heart broke for him, Douglas, and Caroline.

What would she do if something happened to her mother or her father while she was across the country? How would she even know? Did she do the right thing by leaving?

Later that afternoon, Abigail sat with Mrs. Fletcher once more when Lucas rode out to one of the pastures.

"You're still here?" Mrs. Fletcher opened her eyes and turned her head toward her. "I'm perfectly okay if you'd like to do something else."

"I'm fine. I've enjoyed the relaxation. I'm not bothering you by being here, am I?"

"Oh, no. My sons would be driving me crazy if I didn't have someone sitting by me. Men are not very good sitters." She pulled her arms out from under the covers. "Would you help me sit up?"

Abigail propped her up, got her a glass of water, then sat back down.

"I want all of you to know I'm okay. The doctor thinks I just need to build my blood. He's sending out some tonic." She took another sip of water and looked directly at Abigail. "I have a request of you. Lucas has a lot on his mind with the cattle drive, but I'd like your help in convincing my son to continue with the plans for the party. He wants to cancel everything, but I don't want him to do that. This party would give me something to look forward to. I want to do it." Mrs.

Fletcher took her hand. "Would you please convince Lucas to continue with it?"

"I don't know, Mrs. Fletcher. Are you sure you'll be up to a party?"

"We don't have that much more to do. The plans are in place. Carmella said her family could help. They could use the money and it would take the load off Carmella and Bonita. I can sit right here in the bed to finish Caroline's dress."

Abigail leaned back, not knowing what to say. She looked forward to the party as everyone did and really wanted it to happen, but not at the expense of Mrs. Fletcher's health.

"Miss Cook, look at me."

Abigail raised her gaze to Mrs. Fletcher. Even though she looked frail, her eyes sparkled.

"Can I tell something?"

"Certainly."

"And can I call you Abigail?"

Abigail's heart melted. "I'd love that."

Mrs. Fletcher smiled and took Abigail's hand and squeezed it. "I want to have this party, not just for me, but for Lucas. He needs this. We all need this. Since he came back from the war, he hasn't shown an interest in anything but his cattle and running the ranch." She pulled her hand back and clasped them in front of her chest. "I want to tell you something personal, but you can never tell Lucas I shared this." She sat up straight and took a huge breath. "He and Victor joined the war effort shortly after Sarah died. He was in a horrible state. According to Victor, Lucas threw himself into his work, took dangerous risks, and barely survived. Victor said he was wounded twice, but refused to be sent home. He had given up living and when he didn't die, he worked harder so he wouldn't think about what had happened to Sarah."

Abigail stood up and walked to the window. She stared

out the window thinking about what Mrs. Fletcher had told her. Her heart broke for Lucas. She turned back to Mrs. Fletcher. "I'm so sorry. I knew he must've gone through a difficult time, but now I understand more."

"There's more, Abigail. Victor came home without him. Lucas stayed to work for the government and came back only when he got word my husband died. Being gone helped him cope, but at the same he didn't have the opportunity to mourn. He was an empty shell when he came home. It has taken him this long to live again and to mourn her death. He had to face the reality of Sarah being gone once he got home."

Abigail sat and took Mrs. Fletcher's hand again. "I am so sorry. He seems like such a wonderful man. I hate him and the family must cope without Sarah."

"He is a wonderful man and a wonderful father. It's been over three years since Sarah's been gone, but it might as well have been last week. He's just getting over it, so please be patient with him and help him."

"I wish I knew how."

"Just be there for him. He'll come around. One day he might open up to you or to someone else and lighten his heart. I hoped he'd confide in Pastor Smith, but he hasn't. He keeps his emotions and his thoughts inside."

Abigail remembered the look on Lucas's face when Pastor Smith had come to the ranch and had taken her for a buggy ride.

Mrs. Fletcher dropped her head, swiped her hand across her eyes, then clapped. "Now, please tell me you'll try to convince him to have this party. It will make me happy, and I swear I'll let you and Carmella and her family do the work. I'll stay out of it."

"How does Douglas feel?"

"He agreed with Lucas that I needed to rest, but he thought we could still have the party if I behaved, as he put it."

Abigail wrung her hands. "I'm not sure Lucas would want to have me interfere with his family's affairs."

"Please, Abigail. You wouldn't be interfering. You'd be doing this family and our friends a huge favor if you could get Lucas to agree to the party." Mrs. Fletcher tilted her head to one side and pouted.

Abigail couldn't tell her no. "I'm not sure I have any influence on your son, but I'll see what I can do."

"You won't regret it, I promise."

"Let's hope I won't."

The next day Abigail worked with Caroline on the piano in the morning, then gave her lessons to do in her room. She had convinced Matthew, with Lucas's help, to come to her cabin after lunch to start a few lessons.

She answered the knock on the door with a smile on her face but with trepidation in her heart. Trying to get Matthew interested in anything but ranch work would not be easy.

"Come in, Matthew. I've been waiting for you."

Matthew held his hat in his hand. His pants had dust on them, but it appeared he'd washed his face. "I'm not sure why I'm here. I'm doing fine on the ranch."

"Yes, you are. Mr. Fletcher brags about your work, but he wants you to have the skills to be more than a ranch hand. If you ever decide to have your own place, you will need a few other basic skills. That's all we're helping you with." She stepped aside. "Come in."

He hesitated, then walked in. He looked around the cabin. "This looks different."

"I love the little cabin. It's exactly what I need, and I've enjoyed putting my own little touches on it."

"This was Mr. and Mrs. Fletcher's cabin. When I was little, Miss Sarah would bring Caroline and me in here and read or tell us stories while Mr. Lucas worked."

"I know this cabin was special to her and the time you and Caroline spent here with her is special to you. Those are wonderful memories you will always cherish. I'm honored

Mr. Fletcher allowed me to stay here."

He nodded, but looked down at the floor.

Abigail understood how Matthew must feel. He'd lost his parents, then lost Sarah, who had taken the place of his mother. She walked past him and picked up a pad. "I'd like to see what you know and go from there. Come sit by me."

He sat and took the pad she handed him. After an hour or so of following her instructions, Abigail knew where she should start with him.

"Matthew, I'm so pleased that you know your letters and numbers. Tomorrow I want to work on math."

"I don't need. . ."

She cut him off. "Yes, you do. If you ever want to do anything but work as a laborer you need to know how to do a little more math than you do now."

She stood up and hoped what she told him next wouldn't send him out the door. "Now, we are still planning to have a party at the ranch when the men return from the cattle drive. Mr. Fletcher wants me to help you with a couple other things."

"Like what?"

"He wants to make sure you know a couple of simple dance steps."

Matthew's eyes widened. "Oh, no, the other men will laugh at me if I get up and try to dance."

"Why would you say that? If you are confident that you can lead a young lady around a dance floor, no one will laugh at you. Several young girls and single women will attend. I can guarantee the other ranch hands will be up on the dance floor trying to impress the ladies. The only way they will laugh at you is if you hide and not try to keep up with them. Women expect a man to know how to dance."

Matthew frowned. He looked down at the floor.

"I happen to know that Caroline will be wearing a new dress her grandmother is working on, and she will expect you do ask her to dance."

"You think Mr. Fletcher will let me dance with her?"

"Why wouldn't he? You will be expected to dance with her and the other young ladies since you'll be part of the family hosting the event."

He swallowed and paled. "I don't know. He thinks I'm still a child. He won't let me go with the men on the drive."

"You're needed here. That's as big of a responsibility, especially now that Grandmother Fletcher isn't feeling well." She smiled. "Let's get started. We don't have music, but I'll show you a few steps and I'll hum a melody if you won't laugh at me."

For the first time Matthew smiled.

"Great. Let's start."

For almost an hour Abigail worked with Matthew. At first he didn't want to touch her hands, but by the end of the hour he relaxed and had picked up several steps.

"That was fun. Thank you, Matthew. We'll do this again a couple more times before the party, and I'll expect to have a dance with you at the party."

"Will you be my first dance so I won't feel so scared with the other girls?"

"It would be my pleasure." They walked out on the porch. "Let's plan to do this again tomorrow when you have your chores done."

She watched Matthew bounce down the stairs and across the lawn to the stables. As much as he didn't want to have dance lessons, he looked pleased with himself.

Inside, Abigail dug into her trunk and pulled out the two dresses she had been keeping for special occasions. Since this would be an outside affair, she chose the simpler of the two, a dark brown with embellishments only around the neckline. Both dresses were made of beautiful imported fabrics that her mother had insisted she have made for her honeymoon.

A ranch-style barbeque with dancing in a barn wasn't exactly a grand ball room in New York where Mr. Baker had planned to take her after the wedding, but Abigail looked forward to this event much more.

Would Lucas cancel the party because of his mother's health? She hoped not, but even more than that, she hoped Grandmother Fletcher would be well and would be able to attend.

If the party took place, would Lucas let down his guard and ask her dance?

And then there was Pastor Smith. Surely he would be invited. Would he ask her to dance as well?

Along with the excitement, a hint of confusion sat on her shoulders. She'd never been comfortable in a social situation. Sitting alone studying or working with her students were much more to her liking. Would she fit in with the ranch families? Would they look at her as an outsider and a disgraced woman who had traveled alone across country? The remarks from the two ladies at the church luncheon still made her insides tighten. Would they be at the party?

So many questions popped into her head, but she was determined to do her part and enjoy the day. She looked up to heaven. *Please, God, let me fit in.*

* * * *

Lucas closed the door to his mother's bedroom and leaned against it. How could she possibly want him to continue with the party when she was so weak? He shook his head. Her plan sounded reasonable having Carmella's family come down to help. Carmella and her husband and children, along with several other ranch hands and their families, all lived about a mile from the big house. Lucas's grandfather had given plots of land to them to build on and to raise small crops for themselves. For two generations the arrangement had worked out well for everyone. For the party, Carmella's family could stay with her and also in one of the empty houses near her.

He pushed away from the door and stomped down the stairs. He's the one who had originally wanted the party, but now he wished he had not mentioned it. He walked out on the front porch and stood at the railing staring at the sky. With hardly any clouds, the moon and millions of stars lit his ranch. He let the silence of the night surround him. He loved living here away from the noise of the town. Even as a young boy he never wanted to live anywhere else. His father did send him to school for several years in St. Louis, but he couldn't wait to return to the land he so loved.

With a big breath of fresh air, he headed for one of the rockers but stopped when he saw Abigail on her front porch. Without giving himself time to talk himself out of it, he walked down the steps and along the wooden walkway to the cabin.

"Would you like some company tonight?"

Abigail sat up in her chair. "Yes, please come up. I was so deep in thought enjoying this night I didn't hear you come up."

Lucas stepped up onto the porch and stood by the post.

"Please, have a seat if you'd like. I don't have anything to offer you but water. Would you like a cup?"

He sat in the rocker next to her. "I'm fine. I just left Mother's room and needed some fresh air. That woman is driving me crazy. Do you know she still wants to have the party?"

"She told me, and in her usual manner, she seems to have it all planned. Lucas, she really is looking forward to having it. What does the doctor say about her health?"

"He's not worried. He thinks it's mostly her age, but it might be she's not eating correctly. If you've ever noticed, she doesn't eat much at dinner."

"I've never noticed, but she is very thin."

She leaned her head on the rocker back and looked his way. Normally she wore her hair pinned up, but tonight it fell onto her shoulders and shone in the moonlight. He swallowed and looked away.

"Do you think you can pull the party together without

her help? I know Carmella can do her part, and, of course, I'll help."

He stared into the sky. "Getting the party together is not the problem. We can do it, but I'm worried about her."

"I understand, but having the party might give her an incentive to get her strength back."

"You might be right. Mother has always had a project of some sort going. Maybe it would help her." He chanced to look at Abigail. "If you help with the party, will you still be able to work with Caroline?"

"Of course I can. After her lessons yesterday I got Matthew in here and worked with him with his numbers and writing." She laughed softly.

Her laughter warmed his heart.

"I convinced him to let me show him a few dance steps."

"How'd he take that?"

"At first, not too excited, but then when he realized how easy it was, he saw how much fun it would be to dance with someone his age."

"I've got to have a real conversation with that boy. He used to spend a lot of time with us in the house. In fact, that's where he lived, but now he wants to be with the men in the bunkhouse. It's my fault he's pulled away from the family. He's a good boy, and I'm lucky he's here with me. I've got to make more time to spend with him."

"Your mother told me about how he came here. He's a lucky boy to have had your family take him in."

"He was part of the family, but I'm not so sure he still feels that way. He was the son I never had, but after. . ." He quit talking— embarrassed he'd made such a personal comment.

Abigail's glance told him she understood. "His age is a strange one. He'll come around and see how much he is still loved."

"I hope so. I love that kid. One day I want him to have

a part of this ranch." He looked out over the back field. "The moon is bright tonight. You can see across the ranch."

"It's so beautiful. I love sitting out here when it's a clear night."

"I do, too. The quiet nights bring me peace." Lucas inhaled deeply and realized he had very little these days to bring peace into his life, except for his family, of course. He looked at Abigail, who always seemed to have a smile on her face. He wished he knew her well enough to find out more about why she chose to cross the country. Maybe if he were lucky the two of them could spend more time together.

He surprised himself by letting that thought form, but if he were honest with himself he had to admit he really did want to do more with Abigail.

He stood up. "Thank you for letting me share your pleasant evening. I'll think about keeping the party. Maybe Mother needs something to motivate her. We haven't had a lot to be joyful about for the past few years. The men need something like this party when they get back from the drive. They're always tired and ready to have a little fun. I'd rather them have it here, than in the saloons in Independence."

"I agree. Everyone in the area would also like a diversion from work. I know I'm looking forward to it."

"I'm glad to hear you say that." He nodded. "I'll tell Carmella to ask her family to come down to help. If they can come, we'll have us a party when the drive is over." He felt his face break into a smile.

"I'll keep my fingers crossed that her family can come."

Lucas took his time walking back to the house, thinking about his few minutes with Abigail.

Would he dare allow himself to spend more time with her?

CHAPTER THIRTEEN

For the next few days, chaos ruled Fletcher Ranch. Lucas and Douglas rarely ate with the ladies in the evening, and in the mornings they were already out on the ranges. She knew very little about cattle drives except they were long and dangerous. She worked to keep life normal for Caroline, but she couldn't sit still.

"Caroline, you know you father will be okay, right?"

"I don't know that. Men get killed on cattle drives. Vigilantes sometimes attack the men on their way home and steal the money. Grandfather came home with a broken leg one time. I was little but I remember Grandmother running out to the wagon crying when they brought him home. I don't want anything to happen to Father."

Abigail stepped next to Caroline and put her arm around her shoulder. "I don't either, but we have to think good thoughts, not bad ones."

She wished she could believe her own words. The more she heard about the drives, the more she envisioned horrible things happening to the men she'd come to know and like.

The night before the drive took place, Lucas and Douglas came into the dining room for the first time in several days. Still wearing work clothes, they looked tired.

"Ladies, I hope you haven't given our chair away."

Douglas eased over to his mother for his usual sweet kiss on her head, then headed for his chair.

"I'm so glad you two joined us tonight."

Lucas followed Douglas and took a seat. "We wouldn't leave without having a meal with my favorite ladies. You'll have to excuse our clothes. We're not quite finished."

"We're glad you found the time to share a meal with us."

Douglas looked up. "Mother, I'll say grace tonight." With bowed head, he asked the blessing over the food and safe journey for the men." When he finished, he looked at his mother. "You know we've done everything in our power to keep the drive safe."

Mrs. Fletcher raised her head with tears in her eyes and nodded.

Lucas cleared his throat and took his daughter's hand. "Caroline, while we're gone you and Miss Cook will need to help your grandmother plan the party. The men are looking forward to a wonderful time when they return. Can you promise me you'll help?"

Caroline looked up and nodded. "I don't want you and Uncle Douglas to go."

Lucas got up and threw his arms around her. "We don't want to leave you either, but you know a cattle drive is part of being on a ranch. It has to be done. I promise we'll both be careful. All the men are looking forward to dancing and eating and having a great time at the party when we get back."

He pulled her in tightly, closed his eyes, and kissed the top of her head. He returned to his seat with glassy eyes. Grandmother kept the conversation light, but the remainder of the evening meal was solemn.

As Abigail walked toward her porch, she heard steps behind her. Turning, she found Lucas not far from her.

"Abigail, may I talk with you."

She stopped. "Certainly."

"Let's go sit." He took her arm and led her up the steps.

Abigail's heart thumped from the feel of his hand on her.

She sat, but Lucas stood by the railing. He fidgeted with his hat. "I wanted to tell you good-bye tonight. We'll start out before sunup, and I'm sure you won't be up."

"I'm flattered you'd even think about me with so much going on."

"You're hard not to think about, Abigail." He bit his lip and looked into her eyes.

Abigail's breath hitched. "Lucas, I'm doubly flattered now. Thank you."

"While I'm gone, I'll feel better about Mother and Caroline knowing you're here with them. Matthew will stay here as well. He's upset I'm not taking him, but I need him here. I promised him he'd go along next year. I'll also have about three other men here. The rest will ride out with Douglas and me."

"I don't guess you know how long you'll be gone."

"We're usually back in three weeks if the weather holds, and we don't have any trouble. We don't like to drive the cattle too fast. We only cover about twenty to twenty-five miles a day."

"You mentioned trouble. Trouble like vigilantes? Caroline mentioned them."

Lucas looked away. "It's possible, but Mason told me the men haven't had trouble with them in a few years."

"I'll pray it's that way this year." Abigail stood up. "I'll do my best to keep your mother and Caroline occupied and safe." She laughed. "Not that I could do anything if something happened. I do yell really loud."

Lucas laughed with her. "Yelling is a good think, but I guess I should've shown you how to shoot a gun. Maybe one of the men or Matthew could give you a few lessons." He looked at the bunkhouse. "I have to go. We still have a few issues to deal with." He didn't move.

Abigail took a huge breath and stepped toward him. He stepped toward her and put his arms around her shoulders and pulled her tightly. His movement took her off guard. She grabbed his shirt and held onto him as well. With her head against his chest, she could hear the thumping of his heart. The musty scent of cattle and dust on his clothes tickled her nose. She didn't ever want to pull out of his embrace, but it had to be.

Lucas stepped away. "I'll think about you on the drive."

"And I'll think about you. Be safe, Lucas."

He nodded and walked down the steps. At the bottom he turned, looked at her once more then hurried to the bunkhouse.

What had just happened? Had he actually held her in an embrace as if she meant something?

Holding onto the porch railing, she watched him disappear into the bunkhouse. Confusion sent her brain into turmoil. No man had ever held her the way he'd just done. Never had she placed her face against a man's chest. A feeling of peace—and something else she couldn't put her finger on—made her want to stay in his arms forever.

She let out a huge breath and turned to go inside her cabin. She had a lot to think about.

* * * *

Before sunup the next day, Lucas led Charger to the bunkhouse. He'd already gone upstairs and kissed his daughter and mother. Caroline didn't wake up, but his mother hugged him and made him promise not to take any chances. Now, in the darkness, he glanced at Abigail's cabin and wished he felt comfortable enough to knock on her door. But that would never happen, at least not now.

He'd already wasted a half-night's sleep thinking about holding her last evening. Never in his wildest dreams could he imagine wanting to hold anyone but Sarah. He wasn't sure what made him pull her into his arms. When he did, he didn't want to let her go. If he were honest with himself, he wanted to kiss her.

"Lucas, the men are ready. Douglas is with them in the north pasture." Mason came down the steps of the bunkhouse. "I wanted to make sure you didn't need me for anything up here before I headed out."

Lucas shook his head. He had a cattle drive to head. No way should he be dreaming of a female like he was some young kid. "Nope, all good." He gripped the reins and nodded to Mason. "Let's get going."

Mason jumped on his horse and galloped off. Lucas turned Charger, but from the corner of his eye, he saw Abigail standing in her doorway. She was only a silhouette against the light of a lone candle inside, but he saw her as angelic.

He raised his hand, not even sure she could make out his image in the morning darkness, but she surprised him by waving back. It was all he could do not to slide off Charger and give her one more hug and that kiss he so wanted last night. Instead, he tipped his hat and headed off across the inside pasture toward the north where his men would already have the cattle in bunches and moving.

This drive was his first since returning from his stay in the army. In the past the excitement of the drive kept his senses sharp. He loved being out on the range with the cattle and the men. This drive was different. He was different. He was leaving an ailing mother, a discontented daughter, and a beautiful governess who was making him rethink his life.

What would he return to when the drive was over?

* * * *

Abigail put her hands together as she watched Lucas disappear into the morning darkness. She closed her eyes and whispered a short prayer for him and his men to return safely. The unknown of what they'd face on the trail terrified her. He and his family had found their way into her heart, and she wasn't sure what she'd do if something happened to him or to Douglas.

She pushed away from the door. All of a sudden her cabin and her life seemed empty. Was it possible she was falling in love with Lucas? She shook her head. Surely not. The man still loved Sarah. She walked to the bed and sat. He might still be in love with his former wife, but last night he'd held her in his arms and made her feel special. Is that the way a man acted when he wanted to get to know someone better.

She dropped her head back and stared at the ceiling. *I'm so confused.* Never in her entire life had she felt toward a man as she felt at this moment. *Mama, I need you right now. I don't understand my life anymore.*

Lying across the bed, she curled up and imagined what it would be like to sit on a horse for days on end, to sleep on the hard ground at night, and to fight off heaven-knows-what on the trail. *Please, God, watch over Lucas and his men. Bring them home safely.* She closed her eyes and hoped to go back to sleep, but to no avail.

By six o'clock Abigail walked into the dining room.

Mrs. Fletcher greeted her with a smile. "Good morning, my dear. You're up early."

"I heard the men leave this morning. I couldn't go back to sleep." Abigail pulled out a chair and sat.

"I understand. I listened to Lucas ride off and my heart broke. Cattle drives are a necessary part of our life, but it never gets easier. Sarah and I used to sit on the porch at night and hold each other's hands when my husband and Lucas would be gone. It's not an easy time for the women of the area."

"So your husband and father did the drives as well?"

"Yes, my father started the ranch when I was a child, but I remember Mother crying when he'd leave to take the cattle. At the time it was a small scale ranch and the herds were not large, but dangers were still there."

Abigail wanted to ask about the dangers, but she didn't want to dredge up bad memories for Lucas's mother. "We will have to keep ourselves busy while they are gone."

"Yes, especially Caroline. She was upset last night. Please make sure she knows Lucas kissed her this morning. He said she was asleep when he went in to tell her goodbye."

"Certainly." Abigail looked at the lady whose dull eyes had black circles under them. "Are you getting your strength back?"

"I am, but today I plan to stay in my room and rest. I didn't sleep much last night worrying about the men."

"I know what you mean. I didn't sleep well either. When you're feeling up to it, we can devote out time to the party preparations. It will be fun and will help to pass the time."

"I agree. Caroline needs something to think about as well. I also have her dress to finish." She looked up and smiled. "The men will be back healthy and eager to have a party before we know it."

Abigail hoped so.

The remaining time in the dining room was quiet. She sensed Mrs. Fletcher was exhausted so before she left, Abigail stopped in the kitchen and asked Carmella to check on her during the day, then she headed to her cabin to get ready for Caroline's lessons. As she walked down the sidewalk, she looked at the bunkhouse and imagined Lucas still sitting on Charger.

She had a feeling the next few weeks would drag by.

* * * *

For the next two weeks, Abigail did everything in her power to keep Caroline busy and happy. She brought Matthew into the cabin toward the end of several lessons, hoping it would cheer Caroline, and for the most part it did. She could tell Matthew loved spending time with Caroline.

Several days Abigail worked up lessons around the landscape and took Matthew with them for safety. The boy kept his gun near and reveled in the chore of protecting the two ladies. She also included him in helping with the party preparations, as well as dance lessons. As long as she kept herself busy, her mind didn't settle on what was happening on the trail.

By the middle of the fourth week Abigail didn't mention the timeline to Caroline or to Mrs. Fletcher, but she knew everyone worried why the men were not home. Bad rain storms had come through the week before and Abigail prayed that the weather had slowed their progress and not some other threat.

Everyone seemed to have their eyes directed to the trails through the north pastures where the men would ride in.

Where are you, Lucas?

* * * *

Lucas sat in the dark with his back to a tree, his rifle in his hand. Two other men also sat up around the camp, ready to defend their exhausted companions. Douglas would take the next shift in an hour or so, and Lucas would be able to rest his eyes and body. In a day and a half they'd be riding back through his property, and he couldn't remember a time, he wanted it more than he did now. He'd heard rumors of two groups of vigilantes who had attacked cattle drives along the way. These men were smart. They didn't want to take their cattle as the old gangs used to do. They waited until the cattle drive was over and stole the money from the exhausted men.

No way would Lucas allow that to happen. He rubbed his shoulder and stretched his back. Sitting in the saddle for so long had taken a toll on him.

You're getting soft, Lucas Fletcher.

Chuckling, he got up and walked around the campsite, nodded to one of the other men on guard tonight, then headed out to the horses. Charger had his eyes open so Lucas walked over and rubbed his head. "We'll be home soon, boy. You'll be back in your safe, comfortable stall before you know it."

Charger leaned into Lucas's hand. "You like that, huh, boy?' After a few minutes, Lucas turned to head back to talk with the other guards, when Charger threw his head up and tugged at his rein. Several other horses stomped and tugged.

Instantly Lucas turned and aimed his rifle into the darkness. Quietly, he eased through the campsite to one of the other guards to warn him, woke Douglas and several of the other men, then turned to go back toward the horses. He heard his men come to life, grab their weapons and take cover. On alert, Lucas stopped before he got to the horses, sensing, rather than seeing anything in the darkness. He crouched down by a tree, ready to fire.

Within seconds, chaos erupted around him. At least six men charged into camp on horseback shooting. Lucas aimed his rifle, but before he had time to get off a shot, he was thrown back against a tree, his right side on fire.

Blackness took over.

FRAN MCNABB

CHAPTER FOURTEEN

After dinner toward the end of the fourth week, Abigail sat with Mrs. Fletcher on the big porch, neither of them talking. The men should've been home by now, and the women could do nothing but sit and wait.

"Is it always like this?" Abigail broke the silence.

"I'm afraid so unless the weather cooperates and the men get home early. They'll be home soon. I feel it."

"I certainly hope so. I'm having a hard time keeping Caroline occupied. She's worried as we are."

Mrs. Fletcher surprised Abigail by reaching over and taking her hand. "I want you to know how much I appreciate what you're doing for the family. I don't think I could've handled this drive alone."

Abigail squeezed her hand. "I have no doubt you would've been just fine." She was about to say more, but two riders raced through the north pasture and headed toward the house.

Both ladies stood up.

"This isn't good." Mrs. Fletcher grabbed her arm. "Something is wrong."

Abigail's breath caught in her throat. She couldn't answer. Together she and Mrs. Fletcher rushed down the steps and headed toward the riders.

One rider raced past them into the barn while the other one stopped and jumped off the horse. "Mrs. Fletcher, Mr. Lucas has been shot. He's okay, but Evans is going to town to get the doctor as soon as he changes horses."

Mrs. Fletcher grabbed Abigail and nearly slid to the ground. Abigail and the rider held her up.

"I'm sorry. I'm okay." Mrs. Fletcher straightened up. "Where is he?"

"We have him on the grub wagon. They're not far from here. We want you to get a bed ready for him."

Abigail took Mrs. Fletcher's arm. "Come on. Let's get his room ready."

"Grab some clean bandages." The man shouted as they turned.

"I knew something had happened." Mrs. Fletcher mumbled as they climbed the steps. "I could feel it in my heart."

"Our man said he was okay. Let's not jump to any conclusions."

Abigail stayed with her until they got to the bottom of the staircase. "If you're okay, you go up to his room. I'll get Carmella and make sure we come up with something for bandages."

Mrs. Fletcher nodded and climbed the steps.

Carmella was already digging through a pantry when Abigail stepped into the kitchen.

"I heard. Go up. I have bandages."

Abigail nodded and headed up the stairs but then turned and rushed out the door. Coming through the north pasture was the rest of the ranch hands with the wagon not too far behind. She grabbed the railing with shaking hands and watched as the men got closer. They were not in any hurry. Did something happen? Was Lucas still alive?

Finally, she rushed down the front porch steps and met the wagon as it pulled up to the house. Mason and Douglas jumped down.

Douglas ran up to Abigail. "The men will get him up the steps. Are you okay? How about Mother?"

"We're okay. Is Lucas?" Abigail stepped back to let several men get off horses and go to the back of the wagon. Her heart pounded. She wrung her hands.

"He's alive." Douglas touched her hand, then headed to the back of the wagon.

Douglas's words did not give her any comfort.

"Father!" Caroline ran down the steps.

Abigail grabbed her and held her. "Let the men get him inside. He's okay, but we can't get in the way. He needs to get upstairs."

Caroline clung to Abigail. Her body trembled as she sobbed.

The men pulled Lucas out of the wagon by his legs, then held him until his entire body was out. Together, six men carried him past Abigail and Caroline.

"Father. Father."

"He probably can't hear you. We'll go upstairs when they get him up."

Abigail fought to control her voice. She needed to scream or cry or do something besides hold onto Caroline. Lucas had his eyes closed. His skin was grey. The side of his shirt was saturated with blood. A bloody cloth was tied around his head. She had never seen anyone who'd been shot, but Lucas didn't look good.

Caroline sobbed uncontrollably.

Abigail had to be strong for her. She inhaled a huge breath and rubbed Caroline's back. "Let's head inside. One of the men went to town to get the doctor."

For the next six hours the door to Lucas's room stayed closed. Abigail and Caroline had pulled chairs in the hallway and sat waiting for any news. Douglas and Mrs. Fletcher sat with them on and off, but kept going in and out of Lucas's room.

Victor had ridden in as quickly as he'd heard the news. He came up the stairs and took Caroline and then Abigail into his arms. "How is he?"

"The doctor is working on him. He got the bullet out and he said the wound looked good. He cleaned his head where a bullet nicked him."

"That's good. I'm going in. They might throw me out, but I'm going to try." Victor threw open the door and disappeared inside.

Abigail stepped aside, put her arm around Caroline's shoulders, then sat back down to wait.

After a long thirty minutes, Victor came back out.

Caroline grabbed her uncle's hand. "Is he talking?"

"No, not yet. Sometimes when you get a head wound, it takes a while before you're able to say anything."

Abigail remembered Sarah died from a head wound. She prayed that Caroline wasn't thinking the same thing.

Victor looked at Abigail. "After the doctor leaves, he wants someone to stay with him at all times. When he wakes up, he doesn't want him to get out of bed, and you know Lucas, that's the first thing he'll want to do. It's hard to keep him down."

Victor tried to lighten the moment so Abigail forced a smile. "You're right there."

Victor turned to Caroline. "I have to get back to town. Why don't you come with me? My kids would love to have some company. You really can't do anything here right now."

"But what if he wakes up and wants to see me?"

"I promise I'll get you back tomorrow."

Caroline looked at Abigail. "Should I leave?"

"I think so. You don't need to sit here with all these adults waiting for him to wake up."

Caroline nodded. "Okay, but only if you swear you'll get me back tomorrow."

"Promise. Now go get you some clothes."

As soon as Caroline left, Abigail took Victor's hand. "How bad is it?"

"I won't lie. It's not real good, but the doctor doesn't think any infection has set in. He'll be okay if we can keep that from happening."

Abigail slumped against her chair.

"Mrs. Fletcher needs you now and when Lucas wakes up, he'll need you. Will you be okay? I can send Betty over if you think it's too much."

"Of course I'm okay. I'll do whatever they need from me."

The doctor walked out and nodded to them. "He has a good chance if the family can keep him down and keep the wounds cleaned. He can't lose any more blood."

His words energized Abigail. "We'll do it."

"And, Miss Cook, Mrs. Fletcher should get some rest. Don't let her sit by Lucas all day and night."

"I'll make sure she rests."

The doctor walked past them then turned back around and looked at Abigail. "We're all glad you're here."

That night was the longest Abigail had ever spent. Thankfully, Victor took Caroline to town. Douglas needed to get some rest, so Carmella, Mrs. Fletcher and Abigail took turns sitting by Lucas.

Throughout the night Lucas tossed from side to side and called out Sarah's name. Abigail did the only thing she could think of. She grabbed his hand each time and whispered, "I'm with you, Lucas." Each time he relaxed and went back to sleep. If it eased his mind to think Sarah was by his side, then that's what she had to do.

Before daylight Abigail sat quietly as she had for the last several hours. She took Lucas's hand and rubbed her finger over the top of his. "Lucas, if you hear me, you need to wake up. Everyone is worried about you. Your men all got back okay, and they said they saved the payroll. Victor took two vigilantes to town to lock up. No one else from the ranch was hurt."

She rubbed his hand again. "While you were gone, I missed you and worried about you. I'm so glad you're home, but you need to talk to us." She squeezed his hand and did the unthinkable. She leaned over Lucas and kissed him lightly on the cheek. "Please wake up."

She kept his hand in hers and was about to lean back when Lucas squeezed hers.

"Lucas? Lucas, are you awake? Can you hear me?"

Lucas grunted, moved his head from side to side, then eased open one eye.

"Oh, God, thank you. Lucas, you're home in your own bed." She fought back tears of joy.

"Abigail?" His voice was barely audible.

"Yes. It's me. Abigail. Your mom and Carmella and I have been with you since your men got you home."

He took a moment to look at her. "Thank you," he whispered and looked around the room. "My men?'

"Everyone is okay. They got you home yesterday afternoon."

He closed his eyes and a tiny smile creased his face.

"Everyone will be thrilled to hear you're awake, but I'm not going to get your mom. She needs her rest."

"Caroline?"

"She's with Victor. He was here, too. We thought she'd be better off with Victor's kids. She was very concerned about you, Lucas."

Lucas looked directly into her eyes. "I'm glad you're here."

"I wouldn't want to be anywhere else."

He closed his eyes. His soft, steady breathing told her he was asleep again.

Abigail leaned back in her chair, closed her eyes and prayed a silent thank you.

Carmella came in and relieved Abigail for a couple of hours, but she was back by his side before daylight. She sat in her chair with her head bobbing from fatigue.

"Abigail?"

Her eyes flew open. "Lucas, yes, I'm here." She reached out and took his hand.

He opened his eyes. "You've been here all night?"

"Carmella and I have taken turns. Would you like a sip of water?"

He nodded, then groaned.

She went to a side table, grabbed a cup, and poured a small amount of water. When she got to the bed, Lucas had his eyes closed again.

"Are you awake?"

He grunted.

"Is that a 'yes'?"

The right side of his mouth tilted up. "I think so."

Abigail pulled her chair up as close as she could get and slipped her hand under his head.

As she raised it, he grimaced, but opened his eyes.

She held the cup to his lips. He took a sip, then dropped his head back and closed his eyes once more.

"My head feels like Charger kicked me behind the ears."

"You were nicked by a bullet."

"Just nicked? It feels like the bullet ripped half my head off." He smiled.

Abigail smiled with him, got him to sip more of the water, then sat back down.

"Did the doctor get the bullet out of my side?"

"He did, but he had a hard time. Your men had already tried to get it, but, let's just say, they didn't succeed."

"I kind of remember being butchered." This time he chuckled low. "Did you tell me earlier Caroline is with Victor's family?"

"Good, the bullet didn't mess your memory. Yes, she is. We didn't want her sitting up all night waiting for you to wake."

"How's my mother?"

"She's worried sick, of course, but she's getting stronger every day and is excited about the party."

"You didn't know you were going to get into nursing when you accepted this job, did you? First mother. Now me."

"I haven't done any nursing. I have done a lot of sitting by beds though, but I don't mind doing that for people I care about."

Lucas smiled, then closed his eyes once more.

When Abigail realized he was asleep, she relaxed against her chair for the first time since Lucas had been brought home.

Is this what it's like to love someone?
* * * *

Two days after Lucas had been carried home in a wagon, he insisted the ladies leave his room so he could get some work done.

He sat at his desk trying to ignore the pain in his side. Thankfully, his head felt much better, but his side would take time. Concentrating on the books helped get his mind off his body and off of Abigail. Waking up and finding her at his side warmed his heart, but sometimes during the night he felt as if Sarah had been with him. Had he dreamed that he heard her voice? It had felt so real.

Shaking his head, he returned to the books. Douglas had come in earlier, helped him out of bed, then helped him organize the expenses from the drive. Mason brought in the money still in the saddlebags. Lucas couldn't ask for a better ranch supervisor and planned to reward him generously, as well as all the hands. Without them he would've died on the trail.

How had things gone so wrong, so fast? One moment he was checking on Charger, and the next thing he remembered was one of his men digging in his side for the bullet. Everything ran together in his mind until he woke up with Abigail by his side.

A knock on the door pulled his mind back to the present. "Come in."

His mother walked in with a tray of cake and tea.

"Mother, you didn't have to do that. I ate lunch not too long ago."

"Dr. Walton said to get you to eat. You have to get your strength back." She put the tray down on his desk. "Are you okay sitting or would you like to get back in bed?"

"I'd like to lie down, but let me eat a little cake first. It's just what the doctor ordered."

Mrs. Fletcher served him, then pulled up a chair and placed a hand on his arm. "I've been so worried about you. You look so much better today. Are you still hurting as bad as you were?"

"I'm doing a lot better, but I don't have any energy."

"That's from losing so much blood. You'll get that energy back soon."

He took a bite of cake and a sip of tea. "You look like you have something on your mind."

"I do. I know you have a lot on your mind as well and a lot to get finished since the drive, but I wondered what you thought about still having the party, maybe not next week as we planned, but when you're up to it."

Lucas took her hand. "Of course, and if I can count on the men to help with the work, I see no reason why we can't have it next week. By then I'll be up and around."

"Oh, son, that makes me so happy."

"The men deserve a little fun after all they went through on that drive. Did you finish Caroline's dress?"

"Almost. I don't sew as fast as I used to." She smiled big. "I'm so glad you found that fabric. She won't admit it, but underneath all that grumbling she loves the dress. She's going to be beautiful."

"I can't wait to see her in it. Thanks, Mother." He took a last bite. "Would you give me a hand to get to the bed?"

Mrs. Fletcher stood close, but he got up on his own. "Look at me. I learned a new trick."

"Like I said, you'll be back to your old self in no time." After helping him lie down, she turned to leave. "I have a lot of work to finish if we'll still have the party. I'm so glad you agreed to it."

Lucas watched his mother leave. How could he be so weak? He wanted to sleep, but his mind flitted from thinking about what had happened on the cattle drive to his daughter dressing up for the party. She was growing up so fast. Seeing her in something feminine would've made Sarah happy. He took a deep breath.

Could he enjoy a party and not think about Sarah all night? He hoped so because he wanted to have a good time. Surely his body would allow him to join in the festivities. His thoughts turned to Abigail. He couldn't wait to see her in a social situation. What would she think about their down-to-earth get-together? Would she think the party pathetic compared with her big city events? He hoped not because he wanted her to enjoy herself.

CHAPTER FIFTEEN

At sunup on the morning of the party, Fletcher Ranch bustled with activity. Abigail walked into the barn carrying tablecloths that Carmella's family had pressed and headed straight to the tables to be used for food. Out of the corner of her eye she caught a glimpse of Lucas sitting in a chair talking with several men.

As she laid the tablecloths on one table, Lucas eased up out of his seat and walked up to her. "You fit right into this chaos this morning."

"And good morning to you, Mr. Fletcher."

"Aah, I'm back to being Mr. Fletcher." He laughed.

"You have the look of the man in charge of all this chaos so I don't want to get on your bad side, so Mr. Fletcher it is."

"That, Miss Cook, is not the way to stay on my good side. It's Lucas to you." His smile nearly did her in.

Abigail drew in a big breath. "How are you feeling?"

"I'm making it. I might go lie down for a little while before guests start coming in."

"I hope you feel up to having a good time today. Please let me know if I can do anything to help you get through the day."

"Thanks, Abigail, but I'll be fine. I'm really looking forward to seeing some of my old friends." He looked at the activity in the barn. "We're pretty much on track."

"We seem to be, but, of course, I have no idea what all has to be done. Did I see the men starting the pits this early?"

"They'd better be. We have about five hours of barbequing to get all the meat done by lunchtime. Our guests will start coming in early and they'll need an early meal. The big meal will be at dinner tonight, but the party starts early. It's an all-day affair. I just hope it's not too much work on all of you." He frowned and rubbed his side. "Doesn't look like I'll be much help."

"The men and your family needed this. No one will complain about the work. Your mother is already up. She ate the biggest breakfast I've ever seen her eat so I know she's excited."

"I'm happy she's feeling up to having a good day. You do know this party started out as her birthday celebration. Even though she won't turn fifty-five until next week, we will present her with a cake and make her the lady of the hour, not that she isn't already."

"It's wonderful you're doing this. Fifty-five isn't old as she calls herself. She's lively and usually energetic. I hope whatever is making her feel weak will soon pass."

"I have no doubt it will." Lucas looked at the door of the barn and nodded to one of his workers. "He waved him in. I look forward to spending a wonderful day. The men will set up the band outside to entertain the early guests. Later, they'll move into here. I hope you'll save me a dance."

"Of course I'll save you a dance. I'd be honored." Abigail's heart beat with joy.

Lucas smiled, hesitated, then turned toward his man.

Abigail worked on the table but kept on eye on Lucas. He looked better than she'd seen him since he'd been carried into the house. She hoped he would find time to lie down before the guests arrived.

This is going to be a great day.

Abigail and one of Carmella's nieces helped with the

decorations in the barn. Bonita had the food under control in the kitchen and the men had already taken off the first round of meat from the grill. The day activities had begun. She knew everything was ready for the onslaught of people from the surrounding areas. She only hoped she was also ready. Remembering the drama of her mother getting ready for her society functions, pre-social jitters gripped her. She hated those days.

Grow up, Abigail. You're not a kid anymore. Mother's not standing over me making sure I do everything socially right.

With a shake of her head, she plastered a smile on her face.

When the helpers had things under control in the barn and the kitchen, Abigail checked on Lucas. He asked to be walked to his bed for a short rest, then she went to her cabin to get ready. Later, she joined Mrs. Fletcher, who sat in her rocker on the front porch ready to greet visitors. Abigail took a seat by her. Just as Lucas said, the first wagonload of guests pulled through the gates of the ranch about ten o'clock.

"That's the Lopez family. They live quite a way from here. They must have left their home before sunrise."

Her dress of royal blue put color on her face. She looked like the lady of the hour with her hair swept up away from her face held back with a small pink flower. Her sparkling eyes and huge smile showed her excitement about the day.

"I'm glad Lucas got word to them." Mrs. Fletcher grabbed her hand. "Thank you so much for helping us put on this party."

"I had fun. I thoroughly enjoyed myself."

"And I have to say you look beautiful today. That dress is spectacular. I've never seen fabric like that before."

"My mother had this dress made for my honeymoon. As usual, I disappointed her by calling off the wedding. Mother thought I should settle down and get married and have children as most young women do by my age." She bit her lip. "I'm sorry. I shouldn't have said all that. This is your day. You don't need to hear about my disastrous social life in Boston."

"Oh, dear, having to conform to the ideas of our parents is tortuous sometimes. Ask Lucas about that. When he announced he wanted to marry Sarah, his father pitched a fit. He wanted Lucas to marry someone with his Scot-Irish heritage, not her German. His father didn't want any part of the marriage, but Lucas insisted his love for her and married her anyway, even though both of them were not even twenty years old. Thankfully, my husband came around because he, too, came to love Sarah. Pleasing your parents isn't always easy."

"Thank you for telling me that." She turned as the Lopez wagon pulled up in front of the porch. Two ranch hands ran up to help the children and women get out and to take care of the horses.

Within minutes, the Lopez family surrounded Mrs. Fletcher. She introduced Abigail, but after the introduction, Abigail stepped back to allow Mrs. Fletcher to visit. She went inside to see if Carmella needed any help in the kitchen. She was much more comfortable doing that. Before going into the kitchen she glanced up the staircase and hoped Lucas was still resting.

By two o'clock families and ranch hands filled the areas in front and on the side of the house. Abigail found a seat under a tree to watch the festivities. Several men carrying guitars set chairs outside. As soon as they started playing, the first dancers found space to dance while others still sat around outside nibbling on different small dishes from the grill and the kitchen.

Abigail loved watching the simple festivities. No one put on airs. No one seemed to be trying to impress anyone. She relaxed for the first time today.

"Enjoying yourself?"

Abigail turned to find Lucas standing next to her.

Dressed in dark brown slacks, shiny brown boots, and a white shirt, he took her breath away. Just looking at him, no one would know he'd been near death just over a week ago.

"Yes, this is wonderful. Your family seems to have quite a lot of friends."

"When you live in the same spot for several generations, you get to know everyone in the area. Some of these families have been here as long as my family has. I hope you get to meet most of them." He glanced at the couples dancing, but stuck his hands in his pocket. "I need to check on my mother. Do you need anything before I go?"

"No, but thank you for asking. And, Lucas, please don't do too much."

He turned and winked at her.

Abigail's breath caught in her throat.

As soon as he walked away, Pastor Smith stepped next to her. "Miss Abigail, you look stunning today."

"Why, thank you, Pastor."

"What happened to calling me Alfred?"

Abigail clasped her hands in her lap. "Alfred, of course. I guess I still see you as the man behind the pulpit."

"Since I am the man behind the pulpit, I guess that's a compliment, but I'd really like you to see me as something more."

"Pastor. Alfred," she corrected herself, "I'm so new to the area, I would love to have you as a friend."

He sucked in a long breath, then smiled and nodded. "Being friends would be a great beginning." He looked at the band. "Later on when we move inside I'd like to have a dance with you. I'm not known for my great dance steps so the barn floor would make it easier for me to try to lead."

"I would love to have a dance with you. I'm enjoying the music already."

A young lady and someone who appeared as her mother walked up to the Pastor Smith.

"Pastor, this is my daughter MaryAnn. I'm not sure

you've met her."

Abigail sat back and watched Alfred talk to the two ladies, the younger one with long black hair and a perfect figure. Alfred held her hand as he introduced himself. The lady blushed. Just as Mrs. Fletcher said, ladies in town saw the preacher as quite the eligible bachelor. Again, she felt honored he had paid attention to her, but could she see him as anything but a friend?

After visiting with the pastor and with several other families, Abigail walked toward Caroline speaking to a group of older ladies. She wore the blue dress made by her grandmother and had her hair brushed and hanging down around her shoulders.

"You look beautiful, Caroline. I know your father is so proud of you."

She looked down at her dress and rubbed her hand down the fabric. "It really is a beautiful dress, isn't it?" She looked at Abigail. "Yours is amazing, too. Who would've thought a brown dress could be so beautiful?"

"I thank you for the compliment. I can't take credit for it. My mother had it designed." She stopped, not wanting to talk about a wedding that didn't take place. "Now, come introduce me to some of these people."

By early evening everyone started going into the barn where tables of food had been filled. Carmella and her family stood behind the tables making sure everyone had what they needed. Abigail got in line and filled her plate with chicken and vegetables and a few potatoes. She wanted to save room for the gorgeous desserts. As she sat, Lucas pulled out a chair next to her.

"Do you mind if I sit here?"

"I'll be glad to share my table since I've met all these people, but can't remember anyone's name. It will be nice to talk to someone and not have to try to have my brain reeling."

Lucas laughed. He turned the chair around and sat with

his back to the table. His elbow rubbed against hers as he got comfortable. He looked at her, then back out into the crowd.

She picked up her fork. "You don't have a plate. Aren't you going to eat?"

"I will later. I've sampled meats all morning." He looked toward a group of ladies sitting with his mother. "Mother seems to be having a wonderful time. She wouldn't even go up for a little rest this afternoon. She has more energy today than I've seen her in months."

"I agree. She's looks happy." Abigail took a bite. "And your daughter is beautiful."

Lucas smiled. "Her beauty shocked me when she came down the stairs. She looks so grown up." He looked down at the floor. "She looks like Sarah tonight."

Abigail touched his arm. "Lucas, I know that must be hard on you, but I hope you can enjoy her happiness tonight. She seems to be floating."

"I want her to have a great time. That's the primary reason I did this. I still can't believe my little girl is growing up so fast."

"She'll always be your little girl."

Lucas turned and looked directly into her eyes. "Is that the way your father sees you?"

His question took her by surprise. "At one time, yes, but as I got older, he didn't approve of my independence. When I left to continue my education, we drifted apart. I didn't conform to what he thought his little girl ought to be doing."

"But he didn't hold that against you, did he?"

"I'm afraid he did. When I agreed to marry Mr. Baker, he accepted me again, but that ended with the broken engagement."

Lucas sat up straight and took her hand. "I'm so sorry. That must still hurt."

Abigail nodded. The touch of his hand on hers sent warmth throughout her body as if she had known him all of her life. Did he understand her? "I don't know if he'll ever accept me again, especially since I came out here alone. Maybe one day if I ever see him I can do something to show him and my mother I love them."

Lucas squeezed her hand, then let it go. "I hope you can mend the break with him, but I hope you're not thinking about leaving us too soon. A visit to the East one day could be arranged, but I'd—we'd be devastated if you didn't return to us."

"Oh, no, it has never occurred to me to leave. I love it here. You and your family have made me feel accepted. This area feels more like home to me than Boston ever did. I hope I can stay on for a while."

"We hope so as well." He stood up, his hand automatically going to his side.

"Are you okay?"

He nodded. "Yes, I forget I can't jump up." He straightened up and smiled. "Remember, you promised me a dance later."

"If you're up to it, I look forward to it."

She watched him walk away. He stopped to talk with just about everyone he passed. She rubbed her finger on the hand he'd held and closed her eyes. He offered her comfort, nothing more, but the warmth of his touch wrapped around her like a warm blanket. How she would love to have him wrap his arms around her again. She snapped her head up and bit her lip. *Don't go there, Abigail.* Lucas Fletcher is still in love with his wife. She had no place in his heart or in his arms.

By the time most of the guests finished eating, Lucas and Douglas stepped up on a small platform to begin the evening festivities. After he welcomed everyone, Douglas escorted their mother up. They wished her a happy birthday, presented her with a cake and gifts, and then had the band play a beautiful slow dance number.

Watching Lucas handle his role as host, Abigail was impressed, but when he carefully led his mother out to dance, her heart swelled. Mrs. Fletcher beamed and smiled at her guests, but when she looked at her son, her love for him shone. Tears flooded Abigail's eyes, and she looked around, she realized she was not alone. Everyone seemed to be as touched as she was.

About halfway through the dance, Douglas cut in. As he twirled his mother around, Lucas walked over and escorted Caroline to dancefloor. Both father and daughter moved to the music as if they had been dancing together for years. A smile shone on Lucas's face, but it did not reach his eyes. After hearing him say that Caroline looked like Sarah, Abigail knew Lucas's heart broke as he danced with his daughter. Everyone else smiled and clapped at the father-daughter couple, but Abigail fought back tears knowing what must be going through his mind. She closed her eyes and prayed that he could move on with his life.

When he and Douglas walked their ladies to the table, the band started with a faster number. The dance floor filled. Abigail moved to another table near the wall to allow couples to dance, but before she sat, Alfred came up and offered his hand.

"A dance, Miss Abigail?"

"Certainly." With so many people watching, she wasn't sure she wanted to have the first dance with him, but she certainly wasn't going to decline an offer from the town's pastor and her friend.

She followed him to the center of the barn floor and turned into his arms. Thankfully, he held her at a proper distance. The gossips of Independence didn't need any more fodder than they already had. The two ladies from the church luncheon were on the front of the sideline watching her every move.

Blowing out a breath, she relaxed and followed Alfred. "You said you didn't dance well, but I find you're quite the dancer for a pastor."

"Hmmm. I'm not sure what I'm supposed to make of

that comment, but I'll accept it as a compliment."

"It certainly is a compliment."

He swung her around and as she turned she caught Lucas's gaze. He stood by his mother, but he watched her and Alfred.

Alfred must've felt him staring as well. "Miss Abigail, I am so glad you said you'd be my friend. I hoped for more, but I am happy to have you as a friend." He cleared his throat. "I'm going to take a chance and say something—and I hope you don't think I'm overstepping—but our host has feelings for you."

"What? You have that all wrong. Mr. Fletcher still loves his former wife. He's not ready to look at another woman."

"You mean the way he's looking at you right now?"

She turned her head and sure enough, Lucas still watched her dance with the pastor. Her breath caught in her throat.

"You don't have to answer that." He held her at arm's length as they swayed to the music. "As a pastor I talk with people about their problems and their emotions. I'm pretty good at recognizing when someone cares for someone else. Lucas Fletcher might not know it, but he has feelings for you. It might take a little time for him to realize he can open up his heart and love again. It's hard for a widowed spouse to start over without feeling he's turning away from his first love."

Abigail blinked. "I don't know what to say."

"No need to say anything. I hope it happens for the two of you, but if it doesn't, remember your friend behind the pulpit."

She smiled. "I could never forget you, Alfred."

They finished the dance, and he escorted her back to her table. Abigail sat.

"Do you mind if I sit with you for a few minutes?"

"I'd love to have the company." Alfred sat across the table from her, and he chatted about some of the families at the party. She watched as Lucas escorted his sister-in-law out to the dance floor. He placed his arm around her waist and danced the slow song. With his head bent down, they seemed to be talking. She would've loved to hear what he said, but, of course, that was impossible. She turned her attention to Alfred's comments about different people at the party. Abigail listened, but she couldn't pull her mind away from that one couple on the floor and about what Alfred had said earlier about Lucas.

Could it be possible Lucas had feelings for her?

CHAPTER SIXTEEN

After dancing with his sister-in-law, Lucas grabbed something to drink and a piece of cake and headed out the barn to get some fresh air. Men hung in groups next to the buggies and leaned on corral railings. Their talking and laughing floated to Lucas, but he only waved in their direction and went into the other barn straight to Charger's stall.

"Hey, boy. I'll bet you're having a hard time understanding all this noise, aren't you? It's been quite a while since we had a party on the ranch." He rubbed Charger's head, but something else clouded his mind. Betty's presence always dredged up memories of Sarah—not that he needed anything else to remind him of her. Tonight as he danced with her, something was different. They danced and talked about her children and Victor, and when the subject turned to Sarah, he was able to talk without the usual heartache.

"You're moving on, aren't you?" Betty asked. *"It's time, you know. Sarah would want you to live again. Victor and I want you to live again."*

Her question and comments stunned him. Was he? Was he ready to move on? He would never forget Sarah, but he knew he had to change. Caroline and his mother deserved better.

He patted Charger once more. "I promise things will go back to normal tomorrow. Bear with us, boy."

Lucas stopped outside the barn and talked with some of the men, then headed back into the party. He took his job as host seriously. He mingled with the guests, speaking with every person who had given up a day of work to come to Fletcher Ranch to celebrate his mother's birthday, the end of the cattle drives, and each other. He danced with a few ladies, but his side told him he needed to take it easier. Before he took a seat, he saw Abigail standing by the food table. He wanted to dance with her all night. He'd promised her a dance and would fulfil that promise unless his side told him otherwise.

As he made his way through the crowd, he spotted Caroline dancing with a young man he didn't recognize. The boy looked much older and held her awfully close. Lucas gritted his teeth. He'd been worried that the ranch hands and Matthew had kept her on the dancefloor most of the night, but seeing her with this stranger upset him.

He grabbed a cup of water and waited for the dance to be over. Immediately, he stepped by his daughter and stuck out his hand to the young man. "I'm Lucas Fletcher, Caroline's father. I haven't seen you around. Are you from town?"

The boy fidgeted, but stuck out his hand and shook Lucas's. "Yes, sir. I came from St. Louis with my father who's working on a ranch across the river. He knows a man in Independence, and I'm staying with him for a few months to pick up some schooling. I'm not sure why he thinks I need all that stuff. I'd rather be helping him with cattle and horses."

"I agree with your father. You need as much education as you can get to manage in this changing world. If I were you, I'd stay in school." He looked at Caroline. "When the music quits, could you make sure your grandmother gets into the house okay. I have all these other people to help."

Caroline frowned, but said she would.

He looked at the boy. "I didn't catch you name."

"Ronald."

His curt tone rubbed Lucas wrong. He waited to see if the boy finished his answer. Finally, he threw his shoulders back. "Last name?"

Ronald let out a big breath. "Ronald Harrington."

"Okay, Ronald Harrington. I'm glad you joined us tonight, but my daughter has responsibilities now that the party is almost over. You have a safe ride back into town."

Caroline huffed. "Father."

"Caroline, remember you are the hostess here. You should help me thank all these people for coming."

Caroline glared at him. Lucas nodded and walked away. He made sure he could see his daughter and the Harrington boy, who walked with Caroline to the food table, then he and Caroline headed toward the front door. Irritation nipped at his chest. How did that boy even know about the party? Lucas knew everyone else here. Who had invited him?

He stood with his hands on his hips as he daughter and the uninvited kid disappeared out the front door. He gritted his teeth and headed outside, but before he got there two single ladies found him and showered him with attention. After glancing at the barn door, he talked with them, but told them he couldn't dance until he rested a bit. He politely led them back to their tables.

He knew the women in town saw him and Douglas as an eligible bachelors, just as Pastor Smith was, but he never returned any of their attention. Was something wrong with him? He shook his head, but remembered Betty's words. He might be ready to move on, but why would he want to get involved with one of the women from town he had no interest in just to have a female in his life? He would enjoy spending more time with Abigail, but Pastor Smith seemed to have her attention.

He let out a big breath as one of his mother's older friends took his arm. He smiled and led her to the middle of the floor. "We'll dance if you'll be gentle with me."

She laughed out loud and clung to Lucas. They talked a little, but his mind kept floating back to his circumstance. Maybe he was changing. Seeing Abigail dance with the pastor and several other men had bothered him. Was he jealous? He didn't think so, but then why would he care with whom Abigail danced?

"You're in deep thought." Lucas's partner looked up at him and smiled. "Thinking you'd rather be dancing with one of those young women instead of someone old like me?"

"Absolutely not. The ladies in my mother's generation absolutely know how to dance. I love having you as a partner."

"Your mother and father taught you to say the right thing to make an old lady happy." She laughed, stepped away, spun around, then ended back into his arms.

Lucas laughed. "I love a lady to take the lead."

The song ended and the two of them bowed to several people who clapped.

"Dancing with you is always lovely. Thank you, Lucas." She kissed him on the cheek. "Now, go find one of those young ladies who have been ogling you all day."

He didn't have to search far. One of the widows with whom he'd already danced, looped her arm through his. "I'd love one more dance, Lucas."

"Camille, I'd love to, but it will have to be slow and short." He escorted her to the other couples dancing, and as he turned, he realized Pastor Smith had Abigail on the floor right next to them. Lucas nodded and swirled Camille around, but he made sure he ended up facing Abigail and the pastor. She smiled. Pastor Smith nodded.

When the song ended, Lucas escorted Camille to her table. Out of the corner of his eye he saw Abigail walking

Pastor Smith to the door. He breathed a sigh of relief.

When the party neared its end and a few people already said their goodbyes, he found Abigail helping Carmella's niece pick up serving dishes. His side burned but he wasn't about to end the party without a dance with the only woman he wanted to have in his arms tonight. He stepped close. The smile she flashed made his heart flutter.

He found his voice. "The band will play only a couple more songs. Remember, you promised me a dance."

She put down her dishes and reached for his hand. "I certainly did."

Having her delicate hand in his nearly did him in, especially when she faced him and stepped into his arms. With her face resting just below his chin, her breath warmed his skin. He swallowed and made himself concentrate on the music as he took the first step. She moved with him effortlessly and as gracefully as a butterfly.

"You're an excellent dancer." She smiled. "And you've had a lot of practice tonight. You were quite the host, Lucas. You made a lot of ladies smile tonight in spite of your aches and pains."

"I felt pretty good most of the night"

"Ouch, does that mean you're hurting now. We don't have to dance."

"Absolutely not. I've been waiting all night to dance with you."

"You're making me blush."

Lucas smiled and held her close. Abigail had a way of making him happy. Her chestnut hair, brushed back on one side and held by the same jeweled clasp she wore the first day he saw her in Independence, shone from the lantern flames. He had the urge to run his hand through her hair, but instead concentrated on the music.

"And how was your night, Miss Abigail? I saw you out here on the dancefloor quite a lot."

"I enjoyed my entire day. I've met quite a few new

people from the area. Everyone made me feel as if I had lived here all my life."

He wanted to ask about Pastor Smith but instead pulled her a little tighter. She melted against him. He swallowed and together they swayed to the music. The song ended, but he held onto her hand. "Looks as though they plan to play one more."

"If you're asking, I would love to dance another one with you."

His heart skipped. "I'm definitely asking."

The song started and he pulled her into his arms, took a long breath, and closed his eyes as Sarah's image popped into his mind. She loved music and dancing. Abigail danced as well as she did. He opened his eyes and waited for the deep hurt to hit him. It didn't. For the last three years, he couldn't think about Sarah without feeling depressed. Tonight, having Abigail in his arms made him happy.

He looked down at her and she smiled. "Did you meet the young boy who danced with Caroline?"

"Yes, he seemed okay, but we didn't speak long. I've never seen him on the ranch."

"That's because he's never been. He's not from this area. His dad is working on some ranch near here. The boy is staying in town for a few months of schooling."

"I think that's a good thing, don't you?"

Lucas shook his head. "I'm not sure. He could be a really good kid, but I'm not even sure how he knew we were having a party. I can't wait to talk with Caroline. I don't like her hanging with someone I don't know."

"I agree, and if you want me to talk with her about the dangers that exist in this world with strangers, I certainly will, but only if you want me to. I don't want to step on toes."

"I would love for you to talk with her." He pulled her back closer and enjoyed the dance.

Abigail had been like a breath of fresh air coming onto the ranch. Would he dare allow himself to get closer? Of course not. Pastor Smith had not said anything, but it seemed clear he wanted to court her. By the time the song ended, he had decided not to stand in her way if she wanted to spend time with the pastor. Even though he enjoyed dancing with her, he didn't know if he could go through with the idea of being with someone else and didn't want to give her a false impression.

"Thank you, Mr. Lucas. I'm glad you saved the last dance for me." She looked down then back up. "I should go finish my job with the dishes."

Lucas touched her arm. "You know you don't have to do that. We're paying Carmella's family to help. They might be offended if they didn't do the work themselves. Her family is proud."

"I didn't know. I would never do anything to hurt someone's feelings. I simply wanted to be helpful."

Lucas looked around. "You can do me a favor and help me escort these people to their wagons tonight, then we'll see if anyone needs help in the house. Only a couple of families are staying."

"I can do that."

* * * *

Later that night Abigail stretched across her bed. Compared to the parties and balls in Boston, this party had ended early. Still, exhaustion took over her body. She'd been up since daylight and had not stopped. She invited Caroline to spend the night, but surprisingly the girl said she'd sleep in the parlor of the big house. Her declining hurt a little, but Abigail was too tired to argue.

She looked at her journal. Did she have the energy to write in it? Knowing she couldn't go to sleep without expression her emotions about her evening, she sat up and opened the book.

Today and tonight were exceptional. I enjoyed the Fletcher party so much more than the formal parties, dinners, and balls in Boston. I danced most of the night, but ended the night with Lucas.

She stopped writing and closed her eyes remembering being held in his arms. The total joy she'd felt when he pulled her close compared to nothing she'd ever felt in her life. She let the warmth of that moment wash over her.

Shaking her head, she concentrated on the journal.

Pastor Alfred Smith showered me with attention, but in the end he told me he would step aside because he thought Lucas had feelings for me. Could that be possible? I don't think he's ready to look at another woman, but as he held me on the dancefloor, I got a different feeling.

What am I going to do about him and the way I feel when I'm near him?

For all the years in Boston and then at school, she'd never wanted to get close to any of the young men who showed her attention. She'd never felt the excitement the other girls talked about when they were with the guys vying for their attention. Is this what they meant? Was she falling for someone who still loved his former wife?

She closed her journal and pulled the light blanket up. Moonlight shone through the curtains. Several men hung around the bunkhouse and their light talk floated through the night. Was Lucas with them or had he gone to his room?

With her eyes closed she envisioned walking through the moonlit night in his arms, having him pull her close as he did on the dancefloor tonight, and then kissing her as he walked her to her door. She swallowed and opened her eyes knowing that thoughts like that could lead to heartache. Trying to get Lucas out of her thoughts, she turned on her side and hugged the pillow. What would it feel like to have the love of a man like Lucas Fletcher?

CHATER SEVENTEEN

Fletcher Ranch settled into its normal routine after the last of the party guests left the next day. Abigail walked to the big house to see if Mrs. Fletcher needed her help, but she insisted she was okay. Mrs. Fletcher still had a spring in her step, but when the last wagon pulled out, she told Abigail she'd be in her room if anyone needed her. Abigail returned to her cabin until lunch when she headed back to the house in hopes of finding leftovers from the party.

Lucas came down the stairs as she walked into the front door. He seemed to be holding on to the railing tightly. She hoped he had not done too much yesterday.

"Good morning, Abigail. I hope you had enough rest last night."

"I did, but I look forward to a relaxing Sunday afternoon and a lunch of leftovers from the party. I'm glad to see you up and about. I assumed after the day you had you'd be in bed all day."

"I thought about it, but I'm starving. We gave Carmella and the rest of the staff the day off. I'm sure they're exhausted, but I'm told there is a little food left from last night. Everyone took something home and the ranch hands took out huge plates for today's meal. Carmella said she kept enough for the family." At the bottom of the staircase, he held onto the post. "Let's go see what we can find."

Abigail didn't mention the fact that he appeared to be in pain. She followed him into the dimly lit kitchen. Usually, Carmella and Bonita kept the room bustling, but with no one here, it sat quiet and immaculate.

"They must've worked into the wee hours of the morning to get this so clean after all the cooking yesterday."

"I'm sure they did. Carmella's family is the best thing that has ever happened to the Fletchers." He looked around, found some containers stored away in the pie safe cupboard. "Let's fix a plate and go sit on the porch to eat. It's a gorgeous day."

She nodded, grabbed a plate and helped herself to a couple slices of meat and a potato dish she'd tasted last night and loved. On the porch she sat in one of the big rockers and put her plate on a small table. Lucas did the same, sharing her table.

"What are your plans for today?" He took a big bite of meat and bread.

"Nothing too strenuous." She laughed.

"How would you like to take a ride with me?"

Abigail took a small bite of potatoes, looked down at the table, then nodded. "Are you sure your body is up to a ride?"

"Riding will do me some good." He looked directly at her. "You're not expecting company today, are you?"

She tilted her head, not sure what he meant. "After last night, I'm sure no one is planning to come out, especially to see me."

"I thought Pastor Smith might come out to take you for a ride again. You and he danced a lot last night."

"I danced with quite a few men last night, including you."

Lucas smiled. "Yes, you did, and I loved my time on the

dancefloor with you." He put down his fork. "It's none of my business what you do with your time when you're not working with Caroline. You are free to see anyone you want, and we will accommodate you as much as possible to give you time to do it."

Pastor Smith's words came back about Lucas's feelings toward her. The way he spoke now, nothing made sense—but then he had just asked her to take a ride with. Even though confusion came down hard on her, she smiled.

"Lucas, I'm not expecting anyone to come today or any day in the near future. If Pastor Smith comes out to take me for a ride, it will only be as friends."

"Are you sure it would be as only friends? You looked more than friends last night and the Sunday he came by for your buggy ride." Lucas picked up his fork and raised an eyebrow. "He's welcome here anytime, though, no matter how you see him."

"Pastor Smith is a gentleman and an interesting man to talk with. If he comes out again, I'd love for you to join us."

He chuckled. "We'll see, but don't count on it."

Abigail wasn't sure what his answer meant, but she liked the fact that he'd noticed Pastor Smith had paid her attention. She changed the subject. "What time would you like to ride?"

Lucas had a few things to do on the ranch before he could go, but he said he'd meet her in the barn in about an hour.

Abigail went back to her cabin, looked over her lessons for tomorrow, then started a letter to her parents. She had not gotten an answer from any of her earlier letters, but she kept writing. One day they might forgive her for leaving home. Every night she prayed for their forgiveness as well as forgiveness for her own actions. Her leaving had caused them distress and heartache and their standing in the community. She never understood why their status in society meant so much to them, but it did. Maybe their society friends had already forgotten the situation with her and Mr. Baker, or maybe they would forever hold it against the family?

She put her pen down. Thoughts about her life in Boston swept over her. She loved her parents and wanted them to love her, but she feared they would never understand her. In their eyes their daughter did not fit in with their idea of respectable.

At least here on Fletcher Ranch the family accepted her for what she was—a governess with a lot to offer a young lady. After hearing the two ladies at the church luncheon speak about her, she knew everyone in Independence didn't feel that way about her, but she could live with that. Fletcher Ranch had become her safe haven. In fact, she'd made a conscious effort at the party to talk with the two ladies. She knew their smiles were not genuine, but that didn't bother her. She'd work hard to show them and the rest of Independence who she really was.

Shortly before heading out to the barn to meet Lucas, a knock surprised her. She opened the door to find Lucas standing with a piece of clothing in his hand.

"Lucas, am I late?"

"No, not at all." He cleared his throat. "I noticed you didn't have riding clothes the last time we went. I don't want to offend you by offering this to you." He held out a skirt. "This riding skirt belonged to Sarah. It might fit you if you want to try."

Emotion overwhelmed Abigail. Letting someone wear what belonged to Sarah had to be hard for Lucas. She didn't take the gesture lightly.

She touched his hand holding the skirt. "I'm touched you would share what belonged to Sarah. If it fits, I'll wear the skirt today if it won't make it difficult for you."

"I want you to wear it. You'll be more comfortable with this skirt. It's made like pants." He handed it to her.

She ran her hand over the fabric. "It's beautiful and so

well made. I hope it fits. If it doesn't, do you mind if I mend it."

"You do whatever it takes. It belongs to you now."

Abigail took his hand. "Thank you, Lucas. This means a lot to me."

He nodded. "I'll be in the barn when you're ready." He turned and left Abigail standing on her porch.

Abigail couldn't believe what he'd done. Maybe he realized it was time to move on. She closed her eyes and held the skirt close, knowing how difficult it must've been for him to pass this onto her.

* * * *

In the barn, Douglas stepped away from Charger. "Okay, brother, you're all saddled, but I'm not sure you ought to be riding."

"I want to give it a try. I haven't been on a horse since we were on the drive."

"May I remind you about the bullet you took?"

Lucas laughed. "No one has to remind me. My side tells me about that hole in my side all day long. I appreciate you lifting the saddle for me. I'd hate to start bleeding on my ride."

Douglas stepped next to his brother. "Blood doesn't really impress a young lady." He laughed, then got serious. "I'm glad to see you wanting to spend time with Abigail. It's time to move on."

He and his brother had always been close, but they never talked about their emotions. Lucas let down his guard. "I'm glad I'm taking a step in that direction. I think I'd like to get to know her a little better." He stopped. "But, don't read too much into it. This is all new to me."

Douglas patted Lucas on the back. "Just enjoy yourself. Abigail is a sweet person. When you get back, don't lift the saddle. Let someone help you." He turned and headed to the door.

Lucas rubbed Charger's head, then turned as Abigail

walked into the barn. When he realized she wore Sarah's skirt, he waited for the usual depression to kick in. It didn't. Instead, he felt relief he was able to offer her the skirt.

"You look like a seasoned rider. I'm glad the skirt fit. It looks nice on you."

"I love it. Thank you so much. I'll cherish it."

Lucas's throat clogged with emotion, but he plastered a smile on his face. "Come on. Sugar and Charger are ready to get out of here."

He let her get into the saddle by herself. Abigail sat up straight and smiled at him. "I did it."

"And I'm proud of you."

She looked down at him. "Have you been on Charger since you were wounded?"

"No, but I think I'll be okay. We'll know in a minute." He winked at her, hoping he wouldn't hurt himself.

Slowly he threw his leg over Charger, but before rushing out, he sat a moment to let the pain in his side ease.

"Are you okay? We don't have to do this, Lucas."

"I really want to." He blew out a breath, then settled into the saddle. "You ready?"

"I am, if you are."

He pressed his knees to Charger's side and took the lead out of the barn. Sugar and Abigail followed close behind. As they rode out the gate, Abigail caught up and rode at his side.

She had come a long way since the first time he'd helped her into the saddle. Of course, remembering how she'd fell into his arms as she'd gotten off the horse, he pulled in a big breath. Today, she had gotten on Sugar just as she'd followed him on the dancefloor last night—with grace and beauty. He glanced at her, and the smile she gave him melted his heart.

He led her to the stream where they had gone on their last ride, not saying too much as they rode through the trails. His gaze roamed from side to side into the thick brush. No signs of the lion had been found in the last week, but he wasn't taking any chances. His sidearm and rifle were both loaded and ready to be used if necessary.

At the stream, he slid off Charger and stepped to Sugar's side. "Let me help you."

She looked down and smiled. "Thanks." She slid into his arms.

Lucas held her with both hands on her waist, realized he had not let her go, then quickly stepped back. He cleared his throat. "You're getting pretty good with your riding."

"I'm proud of myself, that's for sure. I didn't think I could do this, but your daughter is a pretty good teacher."

Lucas took the reins of both horses and wrapped them around a bush, then grabbed a satchel from Charger's back. Just as their last outing, he spread a blanket near the stream, He helped Abigail sit, then went back to Charger where he pulled out the rifle and returned to the blanket.

Abigail's hand went to her chest. "Do you think we might need that?"

"I hope not. I'm just being overly cautious. My men haven't seen any signs of the lion in over a week. We're thinking he might've gone back up into the mountains." He sat next to Abigail and placed the rifle and his sidearm on the edge of the blanket. He looked directly into her eyes. "I'm glad you came out today. We both needed a rest after this past week. Yesterday was pretty hectic."

Abigail looked at the two guns, then pulled her gaze back to Lucas. "I'd say, but all the work was worth it. Your mother enjoyed herself, and Caroline had fun too. She looked lovely."

"Speaking of Caroline, I hope she forgets about that boy from town last night. I worry about her. She's led a pretty sheltered life."

"Caroline is a smart girl. She'll make good choices, but the boy did look a little worldly."

"That's what I'm afraid of. She's a smart girl, but I'm not sure she's ready for someone like him. If you can work it into your lessons, I'd love for you to say something about choices." He reached into the saddlebag and pulled out a small tin. "I grabbed us dessert before I left the house." Inside the tin sat two pieces of pound cake.

"How did you know I wanted a piece of that last night but never had a chance to get any?" She took the tin and served each of them a piece on a cloth napkin while Lucas poured them a cup of water.

Afterwards, Lucas lay back on the blanket with his arm under his head. Nostalgia wrapped around him. "When I was a child, my mother would bring me out here and we'd lie here and see what animals we could make out of the clouds. You ought to try it." He left out the part that Sarah also loved to lie on the blanket with him.

Abigail lay back and placed her arm under her head just as he had done. He pointed out a couple of cloud formations, then he closed his eyes. The sun warmed his face. He inhaled and let exhaustion take him.

He opened his eyes, not sure where he was or what time it was. He blinked. The clear sky and the ripple of the stream reminded him he was at the stream. He couldn't believe he'd let down his guard and fallen asleep. He looked to his side. Abigail still lay on the blanket with her eyes closed. Her quiet, even breathing told him she had fallen asleep, too. He sat up and rubbed his side, his movement waking her. "I'm sorry. You were sleeping so sound. I didn't want to wake you."

She sat up and rubbed her eyes. With her hair mussed from lying down, she looked so cute, he wanted to run his hand through it, and, yes, kiss her. That thought shocked him.

"I can't believe I fell asleep, too. That lion could've come up and dragged us both off."

Lucas laughed. "We would've heard the horses. They would've sensed him. Still, falling asleep did leave us vulnerable. I had no intention of doing that." He looked at the sky. "We'd better go. I'm not sure what time it is, but we don't want to be out after dark."

"You don't have to convince me."

Lucas stood up, then held out his hand to help her. She smiled and took it. When she got to her feet, she wobbled. He grabbed her and pulled her close. With her face inches from him, he leaned down and kissed her softly on the lips.

She looked up into his eyes, then kissed him back.

He nearly lost control. The soft feel of her lips was everything he'd anticipated. He kissed her harder for a second, then stepped away still holding her hand.

Abigail blinked.

"I'm sorry, Abigail. I had no intention of doing that, but I couldn't help myself. You looked so beautiful. I hope I didn't offend you."

Her smile was huge. "Offend me? Lucas, I loved that you kissed me."

He swallowed and raised his hands to cup her face. "I haven't kissed anyone since. . ."

"I know. I'm glad you chose me, even if it was just a spur of moment gesture. We don't have to read too much into it. Not now. You have a lot to work through, and if you need to know, so do I. Maybe with God's help, we can be there for each other as we move on."

He held her tightly. "Thank you for coming into my life." He allowed himself to enjoy her soft warmth for a moment more, then he stepped back, but before he let go of her hands, he gave them a quick squeeze.

Then she surprised him. She placed her hands on each side of his face and kissed him softly on the lips. "And I thank you for taking me in and sharing your life here."

For a long moment he stared into her eyes, then stepped back. "We should leave." He picked up his firearms and headed to Charger.

He had kissed the beautiful lady who had come into his life unexpectedly. Now what? How could he manage to work

on the ranch with her there?
    Had he made a fool of himself?

CHAPTER EIGHTEEN

Abigail lay in bed that night reliving all that had happened in the last two days. Her mind spun. She rubbed her finger across her lips where Lucas had kissed her. She could still feel the tingle on her lips and the shiver that ran through her body. Never in her entire life had she felt this way. Mr. Baker and his few kisses on her cheek were nice, but kissing Lucas showed her what a kiss between a man and a woman should feel like.

The flicker of the candlelight on the ceiling reminded her of the flicker of hope that might be growing in Lucas. Could he open up to allow love into his heart once again? Now that she'd gotten to know him a little better, she saw his many sides. His admirable, strict business side had kept Fletcher Ranch profitable and running as it had for three generations. That side of him made her cautious, but respectful, when she'd first arrived. Over the past few weeks, she'd seen another side of him: The love for his daughter and mother, his respect for the land and the animals on the ranch and in the wild, and the care he showed for the men on his ranch. Today, she realized the tough boss of the ranch could let down his guard.

He'd kissed her and held her as no one else had ever

done. What did it mean? Would he show that side again, or would he become the businessman once more in her presence?

Why was life so confusing? When she made the difficult decision to shun social norms to get her education and to teach children, she knew the consequences. It wasn't easy, but dealing with these emotions she felt toward Lucas topped anything she ever faced.

She closed her eyes. *God, I know you have a plan for me. Help me open my eyes and heart to understand what it is.*

She opened her journal, then stared at the blank page. How could she write her feelings down when she didn't understand them? She picked up her pen, dipped it in the ink well, then wrote: *Lucas kissed me at the stream today.* One simple sentence said it all. Maybe one day she could write what that kiss meant, but not now. Too much needed to be thought about.

She blew out the candle and let the memories of the day wash over her.

Feeling refreshed on Monday morning, she opened the door to find Caroline standing outside on the porch with red eyes and nose.

"Sweetie, what's wrong? Have you been crying?"

"I don't want to talk about it." She pushed her way into the cabin.

Stunned, Abigail stood for a moment. *Is this sweet Caroline?*

Caroline plopped down in her chair near the small desk by the window. She stared out the window, not saying anything.

Before anything else could be done today, Abigail had to find out what had happened. Abigail pulled up her own chair next to Caroline's. She leaned back. "I'm waiting."

Caroline looked at her and frowned. "For what?"

"For you to tell me what happened because we won't

get through our lessons today with that attitude you brought into our classroom."

"This isn't a classroom. It's your cabin. It's my mom and dad's cabin." Tears flooded her eyes.

Abigail put her arm around Caroline's shoulders. "Oh, darling, I know this was your parent's special place. I feel honored that I've been allowed to use it and to make it into our classroom and it *is* a classroom. We can sit outside under a tree and that would be our classroom. Anywhere learning takes place can be a classroom."

She waited for Caroline to respond. She didn't.

"Now that we have that settled, tell me why you're upset. What happened?"

"My father is so old fashioned. He thinks he's still living thirty years ago. He doesn't realize this is 1849, not some year in his boring childhood."

The girl's answer surprised Abigail. She sat up straight. "What did he do to bring this on?"

"He hates Ronald and he doesn't even know him."

"Ronald? Oh, the boy at the party." Now she understood. "I see. You like him and he won't let you see him again."

"Can you believe that? Ronald is so smart. He's been all over. He knows about stuff that I've never heard of. Father could learn something from him."

"I'm not so sure about that, Caroline. Your father is an amazing man. He's been around the country and in Mexico. He has seen and been places that Ronald hasn't. Experience in life makes for an interesting person."

"So why am I inside learning from a book instead of experiencing life? I can learn so much more if I spend time with Ronald."

"How old is Ronald?"

Caroline put her head down.

"Caroline? He's a lot older than you, isn't he?"

"He's seventeen. That's not that much older than I am.

I'm almost fourteen."

Abigail chose her words carefully. "When you're young, three or four years can be an eternity. By the time you are seventeen, you won't be anything like you are now. You'll have learned so much. Everything you learn builds on what you've already experienced. That's why you're learning from books now. You'll have a wonderful base to add to. I'm not sure Ronald has that base."

"You don't know him either."

"No, I don't. Why don't you tell me about him?"

"He's lived everywhere. His father goes from town to town and finds jobs and he takes Ronald with him. He knows about so much and so many places. That's experience like you said."

"That does make him interesting, but he can't keep traveling around without finishing his education. He'll never amount to anything without it."

"You're just like my father. You're jumping to conclusions." Caroline snapped her head toward the window and crossed her arms.

"I'm simply telling you what adults have found out from living." Abigail remembered how she'd felt when her father told her she couldn't go off to school. She was much older than Caroline, but the feelings were the same. She chose her words carefully. "What did your father tell you?"

Caroline spun around in her chair. "He told me if I let him come back to the ranch or if I tried to see him, he'd take Honey Cup away from me. That's ridiculous."

Abigail didn't have children of her own. Was Lucas being too harsh or did he understand the boundaries Caroline needed?

"Caroline, your father is trying to protect you."

"I don't need protecting."

"Yes, you do. I know you're impressed with someone older, but you have to be careful."

"Can you talk to him? I want to see Ronald again."

Getting between Lucas and his daughter didn't sit well with Abigail, but she didn't want to lose Caroline either.

"I'll talk with him, but I don't guarantee he'll change his mind. He's your father, and you have to go along with what he asks you to do."

"You didn't."

"What?"

"I heard you talking. Your father didn't want you to go off to college or to come out here."

"I'm twenty-nine. What I did is not the same as your situation."

Caroline started to answer, but Abigail cut her off.

"We have lessons to do. The best I can do is talk to your father. Now, let's start with math this morning."

By the time she'd gone through the lessons for the day, Abigail had reached her limits. Caroline pushed back on everything Abigail wanted her to do. As the girl walked out the door, Abigail sighed. *Now comes the hard part.* She groaned. Why had she promised she'd speak with Lucas?

She searched for Lucas before dinner but with no luck so she went into the dining room. Mrs. Fletcher and Douglas were already seated. A sixth place sat empty next to Caroline's place. Before Abigail could ask about it, Caroline came into the room, followed by Lucas with a frown on his face. Caroline slouched in her chair and refused to look at him.

Douglas leaned over to Abigail. "This ought to be fun."

Abigail smiled at his remark but knew it would be anything but fun.

Mrs. Fletcher bowed her head to ask a blessing, but Lucas stopped her and looked toward the hallway. The front door opened and shut and Matthew walked into the room. Dressed in a nice pair of slacks that he'd worn at the party and a clean shirt, the fifteen-year-old stood at the door with his hat in his hand.

Lucas nodded with a smile. "Come in, Matthew. It's

been too long since you've joined us for dinner."

Mrs. Fletcher smiled as well. "Yes, you are always welcome here."

Matthew looked from Lucas to Caroline then back to Lucas.

"What did I tell you?" Douglas raised an eyebrow.

Lucas stood and faced Matthew. "Have a seat, please. Mother was just about to ask a blessing." When the boy sat, Lucas did the same.

Caroline put her head down and didn't say a word to Lucas or to Matthew. Abigail didn't know what had transpired, but she had a feeling it concerned Ronald.

Mrs. Fletcher asked a blessing over the food and over her family, the shortest blessing given at the Fletcher table since Abigail had been there, but it hit the point.

As Carmella and Bonita brought in the food, Lucas started a conversation with Matthew. He talked about the ranch and the animals and about the party. Matthew answered in succinct phrases. The boy couldn't hide his discomfort.

Abigail's heart went out to Matthew. She assumed Lucas wanted to get Caroline's mind off Ronald by introducing Matthew to the table, but the effort failed. By the time dinner was over, Caroline excused herself and left the dining room, never having said a direct word to Matthew.

Lucas inhaled a huge breath and looked up at the ceiling. "Matthew, I'm so glad you joined us tonight. You need to do this often. We love having you as part of the family."

"Yes, sir, but I'm afraid Caroline doesn't feel that way."

"Caroline is going through a difficult time right now. It has nothing to do with you." Lucas went to the sideboard and poured a glass of wine. "Please do join us again soon."

"Yes, sir. May I be excused?" Matthew got up before Lucas answered and headed toward the hallway.

As the front door closed, Mrs. Fletcher looked at her

son. "What in heaven's name were you thinking? You know that young man is welcome in our home anytime, but why tonight?"

"I thought Caroline would be happy to have someone else to talk with besides us." He tilted his head. "Obviously, it didn't work."

"You used that boy and put him in a bad situation." Mrs. Fletcher tossed her linen napkin on the table and shoved her chair back. "You should apologize to him."

"I will, Mother."

"And soon." Mrs. Fletcher marched out of the room.

Lucas looked at Douglas. "Don't say a word."

"Not me, big brother." He stood up. "I'd love to hear the rest of this night's conversation." He looked at Abigail. "But, I have some work to finish." He nodded to her, then to his brother, and left.

Lucas downed his glass of wine, then looked at Abigail. "Go ahead and say it. I know you want to throw in your two cents."

Abigail raised her two hands palms up. "I'm not sure what to say about inviting Matthew in on a night when you knew Caroline was already upset. It might have been a little too early after your discussion this morning."

"So, she told you about our disagreement."

"She did. She came to class upset. In fact, she'd been crying."

"And?"

"And what?" Abigail held back her words, wanting so badly to tell him what he'd done wrong, but it was not her place. Finally, she put her napkin in her plate and looked directly at Lucas. "Caroline *is* your daughter, and ultimately you have the final say. I realize you are protecting her by keeping her away from an older boy, but I have a feeling you . . ."

"I, what, Abigail?"

She bit her lip, knowing her next statement would

infuriate him. She picked her words carefully. "Sometimes when we tell someone they can't do something, it backfires. I'm afraid Caroline is determined to see that boy again whether you tell her she can or not."

"So you don't agree with the way I handled the situation. How would you have handled her?"

"I don't know, but I'm afraid if she doesn't see him again with your permission, she'll find a way."

"He's too old for her."

"Maybe she needs to figure that out for herself." Abigail stood up. "Lucas, I don't have children. I can only tell you when I've learned in my teaching courses."

"You're right. You don't have children. You have no idea what I'm going through with her."

His words and his tone shocked her. "I'm sorry I voiced my opinion. Good evening, Lucas." Abigail spun around, hoping Lucas would call her back and they could talk civilly. It didn't happen. She left the house and headed to the cabin, but before she got there, she saw Matthew walk into the barn. She turned and headed that way.

As she stepped in, Matthew had his arm around Charger's neck whispering.

"Mind if I join you?"

The boy nodded.

"Matthew, I was glad to see you in the Fletcher house for dinner. Lucas has told me he wishes you'd feel comfortable being part of the family again."

"I won't go back in there."

"Don't say that. They love you."

"Caroline hates me and I don't know why." He pushed away from the stall and picked up a bucket.

"Tonight was not a good night to ask you to join the family. Mr. Fletcher hoped your presence would cheer Caroline up, but it didn't work. She's mad at her father and you got stuck in the middle. This has nothing to do with you."

"Is it that kid that came to the party? Is that why everything is upside down?"

She liked his description. "Mr. Fletcher doesn't want her to see him again and she's mad."

Matthew spun around. "I'm glad. That kid is a jerk. He thinks he's better than all of us on the ranch."

"Did something happen at the party?"

"He made bad comments about the ranch. I wanted to defend us, but decided it would lead to a fight so I turned my back and left him. I didn't want to cause trouble at Mrs. Fletcher's party."

"That was very considerate and very grown-up of you." Abigail walked closer. "I don't think you ought to mention I told you anything about why Caroline and her father are having problems. I simply wanted you to know you were not the reason Caroline acted as she did at the dinner table."

"Yes, ma'am. I won't."

Abigail went back to her cabin alone, but she had a feeling life on the ranch would not be peaceful for the next few days. Possibly life here would never be the same. Maybe she ought to think about leaving Fletcher Ranch. Would she dare think about going back to Boston? Rejoining her family's superficial society life tore through everything she believed in. This ranch had become her home, but Lucas had made it clear he wasn't happy with her.

Now that she'd opened her heart to Lucas, how would she face the future without him?

CHAPTER NINETEEN

The next day Lucas berated himself for his actions at dinner. He sat in the saddle on Charger on a ridge as he stared at his pastures in front of him. He'd ridden out alone at sunrise, hardly remembering riding through the trails. Now he sat, more confused than when he'd left the house this morning.

Is this what it was like to be a father, a father without a wife to help with the problems? Since he'd been back from the war, life on the ranch had been peaceful, or so he thought. Maybe everyone had tip-toed around him. Had there been problems with his daughter and he had not recognized them? Had he been so wrapped up in his own depressing life that he had lost touch with his family?

Even Abigail, someone not in his family, knew it was wrong to invite Matthew to dinner. How could he have been so stupid? He'd have to take time with Matthew to make it up to him. And, then there was Abigail. He'd lashed out at her. Now he wouldn't blame her if she packed her bags left. He had to do something to let her know how he felt.

He sat up straighter. How did he feel about Abigail? How could he possibly let her know his feelings when he had no idea what to do with the emotions that swirled around his chest?

"Come on, Charger. I can't hide out here all day. I have things to do to end this mess." He turned Charger and headed home, still determined that Caroline's innocence did not match Ronald's age and experience, but understanding that he probably could've handled the situation better. He'd find a solution.

He rode up to a group of his men working on a fence line. He called one over and gave him some instructions. He felt better as he rode away. Maybe he could fix the situation with Caroline, but he wasn't sure what he'd do about Abigail. After kissing her on Sunday, she'd been on his mind constantly. Had that been a mistake? Maybe he should've shown more control.

He shook his head as rode toward the house. He didn't regret kissing Abigail—or at least he didn't think he did. By kissing her, he'd opened himself up for more heartache, but by kissing her he proved to himself and her he could move on. Abigail was a special lady, someone who had helped him live again. He hoped he hadn't messed up the possibilities with her before they even started.

Lucas skipped lunch and worked with his men in the pastures until sundown. He led Charger into the barn, and to his surprise Matthew stood by Honey Cup filling her water trough. He hadn't expected to talk with the boy this soon, but he couldn't let the opportunity pass. He hoped he could find the right words to make up for his bad decision.

"Matthew, I'm glad you're in here. I wanted to talk with you." Lucas slid out of the saddle and led Charger to his stall where he lifted the heavy saddle, grimacing at the stick in his side.

Matthew turned from his chore but didn't move to Charger's stall. Any other time the boy would've rushed over to help. Lucas understood. He swallowed. Matthew wasn't going to make this easy on him. His actions had hurt the boy, and now he had to make it right.

Carefully he threw the saddle over the railing hoping

he hadn't messed up the healing gash in his side and prayed he could make Matthew understand. He'd always looked at him as the son he never had, but since Sarah's death and his absence with the war, the boy had put space between the two of them. Lucas understood.

Lucas blew out a big breath. "Matthew, I'm glad you joined us for dinner last night, but I'm sorry things got tense. I've missed having you at our evening meals, but last night's invitation should've been put off." He stopped, hoping Matthew would let him know how he felt. Nothing. His face showed no emotion at all. Lucas cleared his throat. "The problem last night started earlier in the day between Caroline and me. It had nothing to do with you. I hoped your presence would make her feel better, but her anger at me didn't let you in. When things calm down with my daughter and me, I want you to start joining us again at our evening meals. I miss having you with us."

Matthew still stared at him.

"Say something, Matthew. If you're mad at me, tell me."

"I didn't feel right being at the family table. Everything has changed."

Lucas took big steps toward the boy but stopped inches from him. "I know things have changed. I'm sorry I've been distant with you since I got back. I've been distant with everyone. It's not your fault. I had to find myself. I lost my will to live when I lost Sarah. I didn't know how to handle it."

"I lost her, too. She became my mother when I moved here."

Matthew's words crashed down on him. "I know. Sarah felt as if you were our son. We both did. We loved you like our own. I'm sorry I lost all those years with you. It took me a long time to start living again. Can you forgive me?" He stopped. "And for trying to use you last night. I had no right."

"I forgive you." Tears flooded the boy's eyes.

Lucas threw his arms around the boy's shoulder and pulled him close. He held him tight. Matthew's body shook. Lucas's heart broke knowing how he'd hurt the boy. "I'm so sorry," he whispered.

When Lucas felt both he and Matthew were in control, he stepped away. Matthew's eyes were red. His lips still quivered. "You know I'm proud of you, and I want you to be part of our family again."

"Thank you for saying that, but I don't feel like your family anymore. I don't even know you since you've returned."

"That's my fault. Will you let me work on it? I was gone a long time, and I changed, but somewhere in me is still the man you used to know."

Matthew looked down at the barn floor. "I want to be part of your family again, but I'm comfortable in the bunkhouse with the men. I like them."

"I understand." Matthew's words hurt, but Lucas didn't give up. "I'd really like you to join us for the dinner meal as often as you want. My mother and Caroline think of you as family."

"Mrs. Fletcher is like my grandmother, but I don't see Caroline as my sister." His words were sharp.

Lucas remembered the boy staring at Caroline as a young man would with someone he wanted to date. Realization hit. "I see. If Caroline isn't your sister, which she isn't, then you can court her. Is that what you want?"

Matthew swirled his foot through the sand on the floor of the barn. "Maybe."

The turn in the conversation surprised Lucas. He chose his words carefully. He didn't want to ruin this situation, too. "Caroline is not quite fourteen. She's too young to see any man, but you have my permission to talk with her and to ride with her. She's growing up quickly before my eyes. I trust you Matthew, but please give me and Caroline a little time. Right now she sees that Ronald kid as someone exciting.

He's older and worldly. I don't see him that way, but she won't listen to me. She's got to make that decision herself."

Matthew looked away. "I don't like him."

"I understand." He remembered Abigail's words. "I don't either, but as I said, Caroline might do something bad if I tell her she can't see him." He shook his head. "Matthew, I'm new at all this father stuff, even with my own daughter, but I'm trying. I made the decision to invite Ronald to the ranch."

"What?"

"Hear me out, please. I want Caroline to see what kind of boy this Ronald is. My plan might backfire on me, but I have to do something."

"When's he coming?"

"I don't know. Today I sent someone to town for the sheriff to check him and his father out. If they're okay, then I'll invite the boy. I'll let you know if that happens. When he gets here, we can all keep an eye on them. Would you help me with this?"

"I will, but I'm not going to be chummy-chummy with him. He's a jerk."

"I understand, but let's see what happens. I might have to throw him off the ranch again, but I hope Caroline will see Ronald for what he is. And then again, he might turn out to be a decent guy."

"I doubt it."

Matthew's words were low, but Lucas heard him. "Thanks for understanding."

Matthew simply nodded.

After finishing with Charger, Lucas pressed his hand to his side, again, hoping he hadn't set the healing back. He headed to the house feeling good about his relationship with Matthew, but not so much with his plan to bring Ronald back to the ranch.

Now he had to deal with Abigail. He hoped she would be as accepting of his apology.

* * * *

Abigail ate a big lunch so she wouldn't have to join the family at the dinner hour. Instead, she walked outside into the evening air. For June the evening air had lost its chill, but was not yet warm. She pulled a wrap around her shoulders and headed to the barn. Being with the animals would be more comfortable than sitting at the same table as Lucas. Her insides still ached from their confrontation last night. No way would she repeat it tonight or sit in uncomfortable silence.

Inside, she inhaled the scent of hay and animals. The comforting smell relaxed her now, something totally different from her reactions to the barn smells when she'd first arrived.

"Hi, Sugar. Are you having a good day? I hope yours is better than mine." Her time with Caroline had gone okay, but the girl's attitude worried Abigail. Much too quiet and overly cooperative, Caroline's mind seemed to be on something besides her studies. A few days ago Lucas had asked her to talk with his daughter, but now he'd made it clear her opinion did not matter.

Sugar ambled over to the railing and nudged Abigail's hand.

"You're a sweetie, aren't you?" She rubbed the horse's head and leaned her head against it. "If I were confident enough, I'd take you out for a ride, but I'm afraid that would end up in a disaster. We don't need to add to the family's problems."

For the next thirty minutes, she stayed by Sugar, found her a treat, then moved to Honey Cup and gave her a treat. Charger stood at the railing and neighed, waiting for his treat. His strength and massive body frightened her, but she didn't want to ignore the animal. She found another treat and walked to his stall.

"Are you going to let me give this to you? You're not going to bite me, are you?"

"He won't bite you." Lucas stood at the door of the barn.

Abigail spun around. "I didn't hear you." She turned back to Charger and held up the treat. He nibbled it from the palm of her hand. She felt Lucas walk up behind her.

"I missed you at dinner. Caroline didn't show up either. She told her grandmother she wasn't hunger."

"I wasn't hungry either." She didn't turn around.

Lucas put his hands on her shoulder and turned her.

She closed her eyes and stood still. The feel of his big hands on her took her breath away.

"Abigail, look at me."

She opened her eyes. His strained expression broke her heart. Deep stress lines around his eyes and dark circles under them told her he had not had a good day or a good night.

"I'm so sorry I spoke to you the way I did last night. You were only giving me your professional opinion. I overreacted." He stopped talking.

She knew he waited for her to respond, but she wasn't sure what to say. Yes, he expressed his sorrow now, but did he really mean what he'd said last night?

"Abigail, please say something. Please tell me you forgive me."

"I do forgive you for voicing what you felt, but I'm scared you really meant those words. I realize I don't have a child of my own, but I've worked with many students. I feel I understand them, not like you of course, but I do understand what makes them do what they do."

He started to speak but she held up her hand.

"Please let me finish. I'm afraid you feel I don't have what it takes to be a parent or understand parenthood."

"Stop, Abigail. Yes, I said those words and maybe I did feel that way. No one can understand what a parent feels until that person has a child of his or her own. That doesn't mean I know more about parenthood than you. In fact, I don't know much at all." He took his hands from her shoulders and a step back. "Parenting never came easy for me. Sarah made my job easy, but in reality she did most of the parenting. I simply gave her support and Caroline love. I stayed busy on the ranch, too busy to get too involved with raising my daughter. After Sarah died, I went away to war for too long. I don't even know if Caroline remembered me when I came back home."

Listening to Lucas open up pulled at Abigail's heart, but she let him finish.

"Mother and Father raised Caroline during my absence, and Mother continued alone after Father died. I stayed away a long time, too long. I chose to remain in the service to my country after the war ended. Victor came home. I stayed. Now I know that was wrong. I didn't know my daughter, and she didn't know me. You probably know more about her than I do."

Abigail touched his arm. "That's not true, Lucas. A father understands his children. That love and strength comes from within and from God. You know you are not alone in your struggles. If you'd open your heart to Him, it might help."

Lucas shook his head. "God abandoned me a long time ago."

"No, God doesn't abandon anyone. We abandon him."

He let out a ragged breath. His chest heaved. "Would you help me with Caroline?"

"If you really want me to, I will."

"I do. Let me tell you what I've done. Maybe I should've talked it over with you first, but I'm used to giving orders and making decisions on my own. Running the ranch and being an officer in the military makes a person that way."

Abigail looked into his eyes that seemed to beg her to help.

"What you said last night made sense after I had time to think about it. By giving Caroline an ultimatum she might rebel. So, I sent a message to Victor asking him to check out Ronald and his dad. I'm sure they're okay, but that has to be the first step. If they check out, I'll send an invitation for Ronald to come to the ranch on Saturday. He and Caroline can do something around here together. I want her to see what kind of boy he is. Do you think I've done the right thing?"

"That's a start in the right direction. Caroline is smart enough to see his true self."

Lucas's shoulders sagged. Had he gotten a weight off his shoulders? Had her opinion of what he'd done meant so much?

"So, are we okay?" He took her hands.

She smiled and nodded. "Give me a little time."

Lucas smiled for the first time since he'd entered the barn. "I can do that. I'm trying, Abigail. I really am. I'm trying to be the man I used to be."

"You'll find that man, Lucas, but it will take time as well."

Lucas squeezed her hand, kissed her lightly on her cheek, then walked out of the barn.

Abigail went back to Sugar. "What do you think, Miss Sugar? You think he'll change? What about me? Have I changed?"

She snuggled her head against Sugar's neck. Last night she'd even considered moving off the ranch. What about now? Was this her home, or did she belong back in Boston?

CHAPTER TWENTY

After yesterday's emotional ups and downs, Abigail chose a lighter lesson plan for the day. She hoped music lessons in the morning and a ride in the afternoon might help Caroline's mood. Glancing at her pocket watch, Abigail frowned. Caroline was fifteen minutes late, not something she'd ever done before.

Abigail went out on the porch, hoping to see Caroline coming out the house. She wasn't. She sat in her rocker and waited telling herself Caroline had simply overslept. After a while, she glanced at her watch again. Thirty minutes had passed. Worry now set in. She left the cabin porch and headed inside the house straight to the dining area. Her hopes fell when it stood empty.

Abigail's chest tightened. She stuck her head in the kitchen. "Carmella, have you seen Caroline?"

"Not this morning."

"I'd like to see if she's still in her room. Would you direct me?"

After getting directions from Carmella, Abigail ran up the staircase and headed to a room in the middle of the long hallway. She knocked. No one answered. She squeezed her eyes. *I have to know she's okay.* Abigail opened the door to a room that definitely belonged to a girl. White and light greens were everywhere, but Abigail couldn't take the time to enjoy the decorating. Caroline was not in the room.

Abigail swallowed. Her heart raced. *Where was Caroline?*

Two doors down from Caroline's, Abigail knocked on Mrs. Fletcher's door.

"Come in."

Abigail prayed Caroline would be with her grandmother or at least had told her where she'd be.

Mrs. Fletcher sat alone in a chair by the window with the Bible in her lap. "Why, Miss Cook, what do I owe the pleasure this morning?"

"I'm looking for Caroline. She's not in her room and she didn't come to class."

Mrs. Fletcher stood up, her hand on her heart. "Oh, no, I didn't check on her today. She's been getting up by herself. Lucas and I wanted to teach her responsibility. I should've checked on her."

Abigail touched her arm. "It's not your fault. I'm sure she's okay. She might be in the barn with Honey Cup. I didn't check there." She turned to go.

"Please, let me know if you find her. She was so upset yesterday I'm afraid what she might do." Her eyes watered.

Abigail took Mrs. Fletcher's hand and squeezed. "We'll find her. I'm sure everything is okay." Abigail turned and wished she believed her own words.

She hurried to the barn, but stopped just inside. Honey Cup's stall stood empty.

Abigail ran outside and found one of the ranch hands. "Do you know where Mr. Fletcher is?"

"He said he'd be in the south pastures checking out a sighting of that mountain lion."

Abigail's heart raced. "Would you help me get Sugar ready to ride?" She ran back into the barn with the ranch hand. As the man worked, Abigail questioned him about the area and the trail. Since the south trail led to Independence, she assumed Caroline might've gone in that direction to find Ronald in town. She hoped she could find Lucas in the vicinity.

Making sure the ranch hand understood the situation and what to do if Lucas came back to the house, she headed out. Riding alone terrified her, but knowing Caroline might be facing a hungry lion scared her more. She prayed for the strength to find Lucas quickly because if she faced the animal alone, she had no idea what she'd do.

Riding safely across the open fields closest to the house gave her encouragement. She could do this if she kept her mind focused on what could happen to Caroline and not on the dangers she could encounter. She had only been on the trail heading to town a couple of towns, but she knew she could find her way.

By the time the trail left the open area of the ranch and crossed a wooded area, her courage slipped away. Slowing Sugar, she eyed the wooded areas hoping she'd see crushed down shrub where Honey Cup might have gone. Everything looked normal. Finally, she reached the end of the wooded area. The open range appeared in front of her, and in the distance she saw a group of men. *Please let Lucas be there.* She turned Sugar toward the group.

As she neared, several men stepped away from the fence line with their guns aimed at her, but lowered them when she got closer.

Lucas ran toward Abigail. "What's wrong?"

"It's Caroline. We can't find her. Honey Cup is gone too."

Lucas paled and froze, but immediately pulled himself together and helped Abigail off Sugar. "When? When did you realize she was missing?"

"When she didn't show up for her lessons. Lucas, I'm scared she headed to town to find Ronald."

"That would be my guess." He spun around and gave instructions to his men, then he turned back to Abigail. "You should get back to the house for your safety. We found signs of the cat in the pasture. I don't want you out here."

"No, Lucas, I want to stay with you. Please."

He nodded. "I can't believe my daughter would do this." He spoke low as he ran toward Charger.

Abigail got back on her horse and waited to follow him. Even knowing she wouldn't be much help, she couldn't go back to the house while Caroline was out in the woods.

Lucas eased Charger next to Sugar. "My men will spread out in different directions. You and I will take the direct trail to town. Caroline knows the way. She wouldn't wander off track." He looked directly into his eyes. "Thank you for being here." With those words he kneed Charger and headed down the trail.

Abigail followed close behind. *God, please help Lucas find his daughter. Let her be safe. Please, let her be safe.*

Her mind flitted from prayers for Caroline and Lucas to imagining a lion charging them on the trail. Her insides clenched. Her breath came in short spurts. She could only imagine what Lucas felt.

* * * *

Lucas pushed Charger across the open pastures, slowing down periodically to look at the dirt for tracks off to the sides of the trails and to check on Abigail. When had Caroline left the house? He knew Honey Cup was in her stall when he saddled Charger this morning before daylight. It had to be later than that. He'd been awakened by one of his men when they sighted fresh tracks.

Did Caroline ride away before daylight as well? His chest heaved as he fought to breathe normally. Why had she done this? Why put herself in danger like this? *Does she hate me that much?*

Abigail rode up alongside of him. He realized he'd let Charger slow down. He looked at her and his heart melted.

Wind whipped through her long chestnut hair spreading it across her back. She looked directly into his eyes as she eased up by him.

He slowed Charger. "Are you okay?"

"I'm fine. Are you?"

He shook his head. "I won't be okay until we find Caroline. I can't imagine her being out here alone."

"Did the men see the lion?"

He nodded. "One of the night scouts saw it dragging a small animal into the wooded area. He fired a shot, but missed. That's why I was out here so early. The cat hasn't done any harm to the cattle, but we think it's hungry. Since this one is being so aggressive, it might be a female with a kitten to feed." Just saying the words made his stomach muscles clench. "I want to get to Independence as fast as I can. Can you keep up?"

She nodded.

He kneed Charger and took off, heading toward town. For several minutes nothing unusual showed itself. Off to their right, he saw his men spreading out. With so many looking for her, Caroline would be found.

"Lucas." Abigail's voice pulled his attention to his left.

He slowed Charger.

"Look." Abigail pointed to her left. "Is that Honey Cup?"

Lucas saw the horse, too. She grazed near a low patch of shrub, looking calm. He nodded and pushed Charger in that direction. *Please, please, please be there, Caroline.*

Sweat rolled down his back and his face as he raced toward Honey Cup. He threw himself off Charger before the horse came to a complete stop. Honey Cup spooked and went into the brush.

"It's okay, Honey Cup. It's me. Don't be afraid." The horse raised her head and stomped her feet but backed away as Lucas neared. "Don't run off. We're here to help you."

Honey Cup stopped. He grabbed her reins and held

them as he examined the horse. He ran his hand down her side and down her legs. On her rear right leg a long gash still oozed blood.

His breath hitched. The muscles in his chest squeezed the air. Something had spooked this animal. Was it the lion? A snake? A person? Were vigilantes on his land? Had Honey Cup thrown Caroline and, if so, where?

He looked around. Caroline was nowhere to be seen. He threw his head back and squeezed his eyes, then fell to his knees. *God, I know you don't know me anymore, but you know Caroline. Please let her be okay. Please let me find her.*

He prayed silently. His eyes burned from unshed tears. A hand touched his arm. He looked up into Abigail's eyes.

"We're going to find her, Lucas. God will help us."

He placed his hand over hers and held on tightly.

Abigail knelt by him, still holding his hand, and prayed silently.

When his body stopped shaking and his breath eased, he looked at Abigail, her eyes closed.

She opened them. "Lucas, you're doing the right thing. We're so limited in what we can do, but God can guide us."

"Why would he listen to me now? I abandoned him when Sarah died."

"Because he loves you and wants you back." She stood up and held out her hand. "Let's go find your daughter."

Lucas nodded and got up slowly. Even afraid of what he might find, he had to continue the search. What would he do if something happened to Caroline? How could he go on living?

"I feel so helpless. Caroline could be dying right now."

Abigail cut him off. "Don't think like that. Honey Cup threw her, and she's probably sitting under a tree waiting for someone to find her. Let it be us."

Lucas pulled himself together. He had to find Caroline. The image of a mountain lion swirled around his brain until his thoughts scattered. The animal could be near here. Then the vision of vigilantes charging into camp on the cattle drive with their guns blazing nearly paralyzed him.

He pulled strength from deep within. "You're right. We need to go." He examined the gash on Honey Cup's leg. "The gash is too bad for her to go with us. We'll let her roam. If she's tethered to something, she's at the mercy of another animal. I'll send one of my men to get her." He couldn't bring himself to say the word "lion."

Abigail got back in Sugar's saddle. "Which way?"

Lucas stooped low to the ground looking for tracks. "These look like Honey Cup's. Let's head in this direction." He ran to Charger, jumped into the saddle, and headed off, with Abigail close behind.

If you hear me, God. Watch over my daughter. Please. I need her. He headed Charger out, then looked up to heaven. *Yes, God, I need you, too. I promise to be a better person. Just let me find my daughter.*

* * * *

Abigail followed alongside Lucas, trying to show strength for him, but keeping her fears intact got harder and harder with each minute. How would they ever find Caroline out here? If Honey Cup threw her while running through the brush, she and Lucas could wander through here for days and not locate her.

She didn't say that out loud. Surely, Lucas had thought the same thing. He didn't need to be reminded.

As she rode closer, he looked her way and smiled. She knew the effort that the smile took had to be enormous. She smiled back.

He nodded, then turned back to survey the area. He stopped and got off Charger to examine the ground closer. "These are still her tracks. I can't believe she ran so far." He looked up in the direction of the tracks. "Let's keep following them." He shouted Caroline's name over and over.

For the next few minutes they rode calling out to

Caroline. Abigail watched his hands clutch the reins until his knuckles turned white. She prayed constantly to find Caroline.

Unexpectedly, Lucas stopped. "Did you hear that?"

Abigail shook her head.

"There it is again." His eyes darted from one side of the trail to the other. When the sound caught his ears again, he pointed Charger into a grove of trees.

Abigail followed, daring to let her hopes fly high.

Lucas forced Charger to go faster. She followed through thick brush that tore at her skirt and legs. She worked to keep up, but Lucas darted ahead of her. Abigail followed Charger's trail, but Sugar refused to go into the brush. Finally, she saw Lucas on the ground up ahead.

"Hurry, Sugar. Hurry." Sugar threw her head up. "That's okay, girl." Abigail jumped to the ground, tethered Sugar, then ran through the brush to Lucas.

He knelt on the ground holding Caroline close to his body. He rocked back and forth and talked quietly.

Abigail couldn't hold back the tears any longer. They flooded her eyes and ran down her face.

Lucas finally looked at Abigail. Tears ran down his cheeks as well. "She's alive."

Abigail fell to the ground alongside of him and put her arms around both Lucas and his daughter. Caroline's eyes were closed. Dried blood plastered her face and throughout her hair. Abigail looked at her arms, covered in deep scratches and dried blood. She looked down at her legs. Her skirt had blood stains so Abigail lifted the hem of her skirt. A deep gash ran down the length of one of her legs. Even her shoes were soaked in blood.

"We have to get her out of here." Lucas lifted her. "I need your help to get her on Charger. I'll ride with her to hold her up. Can you help?"

"I'll do my best. Tell me what to do." He spoke to Caroline. "Baby, I'm going to lift you and put you on

Charger. If you can hear me, try to help so we don't hurt you. Miss Cook is here with us."

For Lucas's sake, Abigail held back the sobs that threatened to break through her body. Just seeing Caroline in distress scared her. She couldn't imagine how she got here in this thick area of brush.

Lucas got on his feet, squatted, then lifted Caroline. She whimpered when he pulled her close. "I'm sorry, but we have to get you out of here."

Lucas positioned Abigail on one side of Charger. He stood on the other and lifted his daughter. After a lot of work, he got her body in the saddle, but she slumped forward. Abigail reached over Charger's neck and held her while Lucas got on behind her.

"Where's Sugar?"

Abigail pointed. "She wouldn't go any farther. I have her tethered just over there. Don't worry about me. I'll find my way home."

He shook his head. "We're okay now. I'll wait for you. I don't want you out here alone."

Abigail trudged through the brush until she got to Sugar. "Good girl. Let's get you home, too. Let's go, girl."

She followed Lucas to a clearing and then to a recognizable trail.

He pulled his sidearm out of its holster. "Don't be frightened. I have to let the other men know we found her." With one arm holding Caroline tightly, he aimed the gun behind him and fired. Caroline screamed. Lucas immediately cuddled her next to his body and whispered in her ears.

The scene in front of her took her breath away. The love Lucas had for his daughter pulled at Abigail's heart. She could only imagine what love that strong would feel like. One day would she experience the love for a child as she saw with Lucas?

Throughout her life she'd seen other people start

families and have normal lives. They made it seem so simple. Where had she gone wrong?

CHAPTER TWENTY-ONE

Lucas walked out of Caroline's room and leaned against the wall in the hallway. He closed his eyes and inhaled a huge breath. He and Abigail had gotten his daughter home safely, but she'd never regained consciousness. He'd gotten her into her bed, and now his mother, Carmella, and Abigail cleaned the dried blood and dirt that covered her body. One of his ranch hands raced into town for the doctor once again.

He opened his eyes and looked around. His home was one of the finest built in the valley, beautifully decorated, and as comfortable as any family could hope for, but none of that mattered if he didn't have his daughter. Day by day he went through life without Sarah, but no way could he continue to live without Caroline.

Abigail stepped out of the room and closed the door. She put her hand on his arm. He faced her and pulled her into his body and held her as tightly as he could. She'd stayed by his side throughout the ordeal. He rubbed her back and let her warmth seep into his cold, empty body.

"Thank you for staying with me today." Reluctantly, he held her away. "You have no idea what it means to me to have you here."

"I wanted to be with you. I wouldn't have had it any

other way." She swallowed. "She's resting."

"I'm still terrified she lost too much blood. As I held her on Charger, I could barely hear her breathe."

Abigail reached up and kissed him softly on his cheek. "She's young and healthy. Let's think good thoughts and thank God for letting us find her."

He nodded and held her tight.

By early afternoon Dr. Watson's buggy pulled into the ranch entrance. Lucas had been sitting next to Caroline's bed with his mother. He got up and went to the window. "He's here. Thank goodness he was in town." For the first time today, his heart felt lighter. Caroline had not opened her eyes or responded to anyone. Lucas found himself praying over and over again for a miracle. He had prayed for the same kind of miracle with Sarah, but it never happened. Would God be so cruel as to let him lose both his wife and his daughter in the same way?

After Sarah died, he'd turned his anger and hurt to God. Now, after all these years, he begged the same merciful God to help his daughter. Would he dare listen to a man who had turned against Him for so long? Was it He who had led them to Caroline's location?

He'd never know, but he had to keep hope in his heart.

Lucas opened Caroline's door before Dr. Watson knocked. Lucas grabbed the doctor's hand. "Thank you so much for coming out. She's in bad shape. We don't know what else to do."

Dr. Watson squeezed Lucas's hand. "Why don't you go downstairs and get a cup of coffee. I'll probably be with her a while. I'll find you after I finish her examination."

Lucas looked from Dr. Watson to his mother. He wanted to be with his daughter, but he understood. He nodded.

"I'll take care of Caroline, Lucas. Have some faith."

Lucas walked down the stairs thinking about his words. Did he have faith?

He found Abigail sitting in the kitchen with a cup of coffee. She jumped up when she saw him. "I heard the doctor come in. Come sit. Let me get you some coffee."

Abigail fixed him a cup. He took it but couldn't take a sip. His mind and his heart were in Caroline's room.

Abigail touched his hand. He looked down and covered hers with his other one. "Dr. Watson will know what to do."

"I know. I wish I had realized she was gone earlier."

"You had a lion to hunt. Don't blame yourself."

He squeezed her hand and tasted the hot coffee. "Why would she leave the house alone and go against everything she'd been told? Does she hate me that much?"

"She doesn't hate you at all. She's just confused. Caroline is thirteen years old. She has no idea what her role in this world is and where she fits in. Believe it or not, what she did is not uncommon."

"Disobeying a father is foreign to me. Our family has always been close. This is where she belongs, not going off to Independence trying to find that boy. Maybe I should've told her I was working on a plan to let Ronald come out to the ranch."

"You can tell her when she wakes up. One day when she is older, she'll look back on what she's done and realize the love she has here. We all go through things we don't understand when we're young." She smiled. "And sometimes even when we're older."

Lucas placed his cup down. "I get the feeling you're talking from experience." What had happened to make her leave a comfortable home in Boston?

Abigail fidgeted. She looked into her cup. "Maybe."

"I'd love for you to share with me. Sometimes I feel I'm the only one who's done stupid, selfish things in their lives."

"I can't imagine you've ever done anything that wasn't right. Look at you. You're running an empire on Fletcher Ranch. You take care of your mother and your daughter, and you take care of all these people working for you. No, you can't tell me you've ever done something that wasn't right."

"I left my daughter. I left my family."

"You went off to fight a war."

"And I'm glad I did, but I didn't have to go. Other men in the valley stayed with their families. I left because I was weak. I couldn't handle not having Sarah here so I left and dragged Victor with me."

Abigail didn't say anything. She simply squeezed his hand.

"Even after the war, when Victor came home, I stayed away. I couldn't see beyond my selfishness. In the process, I lost my daughter."

"She knows you and she loves you, Lucas. As I said, she'd thirteen. Had you never left or if Sarah were still here, she would probably have still spread her wings. Young girls and young men need to find their own way."

"Is that what you did?"

Abigail nodded. "Yes, I spread my wings and flew away from my family when I left to get my teaching credentials. When I came home, I wanted to be part of the family again, but something was missing. I blamed it on my father, but now I'm not so sure. Maybe it was me all along."

"I would think he'd be proud of you for getting an education and teaching."

"In my heart I hoped he was, but my actions widened the gap between us. Only when I agreed to marry Mr. Baker did he start to come around."

"But he got upset when you broke the engagement."

"More than upset." Abigail got up from her chair and walked to a window.

Would she open up or keep her secret inside? All of a sudden sharing her secret was important. Lucas got up and placed both his hands on her shoulders. "What happened, Abigail?"

"Breaking the engagement infuriated Father, but over time had I stayed in Boston he might have gotten over that.

What transpired next severed our relationship." Abigail quit talking.

Lucas gently turned her to face him. "Tell me what happened."

She looked up. "I guess a prosperous businessman like Mr. Baker couldn't handle being humiliated by his wife-to-be. He retaliated." She grimaced and looked down at the floor once more. "He started a rumor. He said he'd heard I'd been promiscuous during my studies, and he would never have a woman like that as his wife or the mother of his children. He told everyone he broke the engagement."

"What? What decent man would do that?" Anger swept across Lucas's chest. "I can't imagine anyone being so cruel. I can see why you'd want to start over someplace else."

"There's more."

Lucas stepped back. "What more could there be?"

"My father believed Mr. Baker. He threw me out of the house. Mother believed me, but she has no influence on him. He called me a disgrace to the family. He disowned me."

Lucas pulled her into an embrace. Abigail clung to him. He held her closer knowing that the entire time she'd crossed the country and while she'd been here, she'd carried that hurt inside. Now she'd opened up and his heart went out to her. He rubbed her back and kissed the top of her head. "I'm so sorry. I wish I could say something to make you feel better."

Finally, she pulled away and looked up into his eyes. "You don't have to say anything. There is nothing anyone can say to take away the hurt. I keep coming up with reasons my own father would do such a thing. He's a prestigious man in Boston. He was devastated as well. He didn't want me to go away to get an education. Nothing I did pleased him so when Mr. Baker made up the story, it fit into what he believed I had done."

Lucas pulled her close. "No father ought to turn his back on one of his children. Surely by now he has changed his mind."

"I'm not so sure. I've written letters every week, but they haven't written me back."

"Sometimes letters take weeks to reach their destination. Don't give up hope. Sometimes letters don't arrive at all."

"I'm not so sure I have any hope left."

"Don't say that. You are his flesh and blood. He'll love you again one day."

Abigail smiled. "Here I am in your kitchen with your daughter upstairs injured and you're comforting me. I'm so sorry. I'm as selfish as I said."

Lucas smiled and kissed her lightly on the lips. "No, Abigail, you're not selfish. I asked you to tell me your past, and for those few minutes I forgot my own pain. You did me a favor."

Abigail raised her face and kissed him on the lips then stepped away. "I know Caroline will be okay. She has to be."

"I don't know what I'll do if she isn't. I can't fathom life without my family."

"I'm not family, Lucas, but I'm here."

Her words lifted his spirits. He pulled her into his arms and kissed her hard, but immediately stepped away. "Thank you. Right now I need you more than you can ever know."

The kitchen door opened. "I figured I'd find you in here." Dr. Watson walked in and sat at the table.

Lucas took two big steps and pulled out a chair, but instead of sitting he held the back with his hands. "Is she okay?"

"She will be. It looks as if she took a bad fall off the horse, and, I can't be sure, but she might have even been dragged a little."

Lucas squeezed his eyes. His body felt numb.

Abigail put her arm around his shoulders. He looked at her, needing her strength.

"She took a bad hit to her head. It might take a couple days to come out of it, or she might wake up in a few minutes. These things are tricky."

"What about her leg?" Abigail asked.

"I put stitches on the gash and a splint on the leg. She might have a fracture. It's not a bad break, but she will need to stay off of it. Other than that, we simply have to give her body and her mind time to heal." He touched Lucas's hand. "She's going to come out of this, Lucas. I just know she is."

Lucas swallowed. "Thank you for coming out. What do we do for her?"

"I've given instructions to your mother. The bandages need to be changed in a day or two. I've left some with her. Mostly you need to get her to swallow water or chicken broth. When she comes to, she'll need to stay off her leg. Other than that, there is nothing else we can do. I wish there was more, but. . ."

Lucas squeezed his hand. Dr. Watson had come to the house when Sarah died and helped him get over his own wounds. He'd been with the family for as long as Lucas could remember. "Thank you, Doc. I appreciate you coming out."

"Don't hesitate to send someone if you think she needs something else. And, Lucas, you need to take care of yourself. Remember, I patched you up just a couple weeks ago. You're not completely healed. In fact, I'd like to take a look at your side."

Lucas shook his head. "I'm keeping it clean. It's healing, but thank you."

"Sit by your daughter. She might know you're there."

Lucas understood what he didn't say. Nothing else could be done for his daughter. He nodded.

When Dr. Watson left, Abigail squeezed his arm. "Let's go sit with her."

His throat clogged. No words came, but he nodded, looked at her, and attempted a smile. *How had this angel come into his life?*

* * * *

Two days after Lucas and Abigail found Caroline, Lucas climbed the staircase with a heavy heart. His daughter had not awakened since she'd been home, and his greatest fears choked the breath from him. He opened the door to her room.

Carmella looked up from her chair by her bedside. "Caroline is the same. Come take my seat."

Lucas walked to Caroline's bedside. "Thank you, Carmella. I don't know what my family would do without you and your family."

He sat down on the side of her bed and held Caroline's hand. "Caroline, this is Thursday. We'd love to get to town this weekend, go to church with your cousins, and have a nice covered dish dinner. Wouldn't you like to do that? You need to wake up and get your strength back, or we won't be able to do that."

He bent his head and prayed. He'd surprised himself by praying hard and often since he had found his daughter. The more he prayed the easier it became.

He started to pull his hand away and sit in the chair where he'd stayed for long periods of time when Caroline squeezed it. Lucas sat up straight. His hope zoomed. "Caroline, can you hear me? Open your eyes, darling. Let me know you're okay."

Nothing.

"Honey, you can do this. Open your eyes."

A tap at the door drew his attention. Abigail peeked in. "Is it okay for me to come in?"

Lucas smiled. "Please, I need you." He watched her tiptoe toward the bed.

When she stopped by him she placed her hand on his arm. "Looks as if she has more color in her face."

Lucas nodded. "She does. I swear she squeezed my hand just now, but then I haven't been able to get another sign from her."

"She'll start giving us more and more signs. I feel it in

my heart."

Lucas looked up. "Let me get you a chair. I'd love for you to sit with me."

"I can get it." She pulled a small bench from Caroline's dresser and placed it next to Lucas's and sat. "How are you doing?"

"I'm not sure. One minute I'm okay, but then I look at her, and I can hardly catch my breath. I feel so helpless."

"I know. I want to do something, too. I feel lost. I find myself praying all day long."

Lucas turned and took her hand. "I am, too. I hate it took something like this for me to be able to talk with God again. I've wanted to, but I never could."

Abigail's sweet smile warmed his heart.

"Carmella made a huge pot of vegetable soup and a delicious smelling loaf of bread. I know you haven't been eating, but I'd like for you to join me in the dining room later. Would you do that?"

Lucas didn't want to leave Caroline, but he did need to eat. "I'll do that if someone can sit with Caroline."

"You know they will."

Abigail sat by him and neither of them spoke. His thoughts scattered, one moment thinking how he could've handled the Ronald situation differently with Caroline to wondering what had spooked Honey Cup to throw Caroline off. Then he'd think about Abigail and his mind would settle. Was that a sign that he had feelings for her?

He looked at her. Today she had her hair pulled up and pinned in the back. Had she pulled it back in a hurry to get to the house? He smiled. He leaned toward her and pushed a few strands behind her eyes. "You're beautiful, Abigail."

She opened her mouth, but he put a finger on her lips.

"Don't say anything. You are beautiful even though I have a feeling you don't think so. You've been a blessing helping with my daughter. How can I ever repay you?"

"I don't want anything but to have Caroline back to

normal. We all need her."

Her words relaxed him. He looked at Caroline, took a big breath, then held it. Caroline moved her arms and her head, then opened her eyes. "Father?"

CHAPTER TWENTY-TWO

A week after Caroline opened her eyes and spoke with Abigail and Lucas, everyone at the ranch relaxed, celebrated quietly, then returned to their normal routine.

This morning Abigail worked on lessons for Caroline. She still walked with a cane, but she'd come to the cabin for the last few days to continue her studies. As she stacked papers on Caroline's desk a knock called her to the door.

Lucas stood on her porch. "May I come in?"

"Certainly. This is a surprise. I thought I'd find Caroline standing out here."

"Nope. Just me. Are you disappointed?"

"Never. Please come in."

Lucas had not stepped inside the cabin since Abigail had come to the ranch. Was he aware he'd asked to come into his and Sarah's space?

She stepped aside.

With his hat held against his chest, Lucas walked in, stopped and looked around. "It looks different."

"I've made it into a classroom for Caroline, and, of course, my own space." She raised her gaze. "Does that upset you?"

He surprised her by flashing a huge smile. "No, not at

all. This is wonderful. As I said one day, everyone has tiptoed around me since I've been home. No one mentioned this cabin being Sarah's and my private space. For a while I didn't want you or anyone else in here, but that has passed. I'm glad you're here and that you've made it your home."

"That makes me feel good to hear you say that."

He looked at the floor. "Can we sit? It's a gorgeous day. Let's go on the porch."

Understanding he probably felt more comfortable outside, she led the way and took a seat in her usual rocker.

He sat in the other one then looked at her. "Caroline is strong enough to ride into town on Sunday for church services."

"I agree."

"She and I have been talking, and she acts as if she understands how I feel." He put his head down. "I apologized for being gone so long during the war. I'm not sure how I could've been so selfish. The girl needed me. I wasn't here for her."

"But you are now."

"I'm trying to make up for lost time, but I know it will take a while." He looked out over the ranch, then back to her. "Have you heard the news about the lion?"

Abigail stopped rocking and waited. "No."

"Mason was in town yesterday. He ran into a ranch hand from one of the places adjacent to here. He said they found a big cat with a cub heading north. They didn't want to kill it because of the cub, but they pushed it farther north. We think it won't be giving us problems for a while."

"That's wonderful. I'm glad no one shot it while she was on your ranch."

"Me, too. No one on the ranch would take a mother away from her cub." He looked out over the front portion of his land. "I hate she put our cattle at risk. And Caroline. I keep thinking about what she told us. When that lion spooked Honey Cup, Caroline could've been hurt a lot worse. It pounced down from a tree and attacked the horse but could've just as well attacked Caroline. Makes me sick just thinking about it."

"But it didn't. She survived and will completely recover."

Lucas rubbed his chin.

Abigail waited. She could tell Lucas had more on his mind.

"I'm going to town with the family this Sunday." He looked directly into her eyes. "Pastor Smith will be happy. I want to go to service with all of you."

Abigail took his hand. "I'm happy, too. Worshipping together helps a family become closer."

"You know you've become part of this family, don't you?"

"I feel the same way toward all of you."

Lucas dropped her hand and stood up. He grabbed the railing with both his hands and looked out. "I think of you as more than just a member of the family. Abigail, you've worked you way into my heart." He turned. "I didn't think I could ever let anyone else in, but I have. I still love Sarah. I always will, but I have room for you as well. I love you and I hope you feel the same way."

Abigail's eyes filled with tears. She stood and took his hands. "I do love you, Lucas. I've never felt this way before. My heart is all yours, but I'm willing to share your heart with Sarah and with Caroline."

"Am I hearing you right, Abigail? Do you want to become a real part of this family? Are you willing to marry me?"

"Willing?" She laughed. "Yes, I'm willing to marry you, Mr. Fletcher. If that's a proposal, I accept."

With a huge smile, he pulled her close and kissed her, then stepped away and held her at arm's length. "I want to have a wedding before the cold weather sets in. We can announce it at church service on Sunday and you and Mother and Caroline can come up with a date, but there's one thing we have to do first."

Abigail's heart raced, but she cleared her head to listen.

"We have to make sure your family knows. I would love for them to be here or at least to give us their blessing."

Abigail nodded and swiped away tears that ran down her face.

"I would love for Mother and Father to come here. I want them to meet you and your mother and Caroline, but I don't know if they will make the journey."

"If they don't, you and I will travel to Boston after the wedding. You and your father must become a family again."

"Lucas, you'd do that for me?"

"I'd do that for us. Your family will be my family. I want them to see you've found someone who truly loves you."

Abigail reached up and threw her arms around his neck, then kissed him hard.

"With kisses like that, I want to marry you now."

Abigail laughed then snuggled against his neck. "You've made me so happy. Fletcher Ranch will really be my home, won't it?"

"It already is. I want you to be part of our home. I know it's not modern like the big city you were used to. Sometimes we have to face dangers like the vigilantes or that mountain lion, but most of the time our lives are normal. Do you think you could find it in your heart to make this your home?"

"It is my home, Lucas. As long as you are here with me, it doesn't matter where we live." She kissed him again, then stepped back. "What about Caroline? She misses her mother so much. Will she accept me as your wife?"

"Caroline is thrilled. I spoke with her last night after dinner. She's excited. I asked her not to say anything until I had time to talk with you, but I wasn't sure she'd wait. I'm surprised she didn't rush over here to wake you."

"She didn't, but that would've been fun to see her

excitement. Not as romantic as you asking me though."

"So you think I'm a romantic?"

"It's not something I've seen a lot of, but we have a lot of time for you to show me that side of you."

"That's a job I look forward to." He kissed her. "Let's go tell my mother and Caroline the good news that you've accepted."

Abigail stopped and grabbed his hand. "Lucas, this means I'm going to have a daughter of my own."

"Yes, a daughter, a mother, and a husband who love you just the way you are, and one day maybe we can add to this family with a brother or a sister for Caroline."

"This is the best day of my life. Thank you."

"Let's go to the house, your future home."

With a squeeze of his hand, Abigail walked side by side up to the big house, but in her heart she knew it wasn't the house that mattered. It was Lucas who was the home she didn't know she needed or wanted.

The unexpected was wonderful.

Life was wonderful.

THE END

ABOUT THE AUTHOR

 Fran McNabb grew up along the beaches and waterways of the Gulf Coast and has used this setting in many of her novels. She and her husband of fifty years live on a bayou harbor and love to spend time fishing and boating with their sons and families. Visit her at www.FranMcNabb.com, Twitter @FranMcNabb, Facebook Fran L McNabb.

Follow me on Amazon

Other books by Fran McNabb
Paradise Lane
Return to Paradise
Paradise Found
Gulf Coast Romances

www.ingramcontent.com/pod-product-compliance
Lightning Source LLC
LaVergne TN
LVHW011948060526
838201LV00061B/4248